MIGHTY TROY OF SALEM

BOOK ONE

THE OATS MISSION

CONRAD L. NEUDORF

Neudorf, Conrad L.
Mighty Troy of Salem: The Oats Mission
Edited by Darlene Oakley

ISBN 978-1-7780834-1-9

Book Design by Bob Canlas
Front Cover Illustration by James Lillich
Back Cover and Chapter Scene Illustrations by Ray Friesen
Character Illustrations: James Lillich – Mighty Troy, King Kappa, King Goar, Rodney, Chuba, Prince Saph, and Prince Lami
Lily-Rose Grondin – Arnie, the Patrol Cat
Bob Canlas – Methuselah

CONTENTS

ACKNOWLEDGEMENTS

I am so grateful to my wife Debbie who read my manuscript over many times, harmonizing inconsistencies and helping to develop more interesting characters.

There are so many friends who assisted in completing this story. Many thanks to Ava and Elijah, for interacting with the book and providing me with valuable suggestions and critique.

Many interesting ideas came from story time with my grandchildren. Their insights and inspiration gave life to the characters in this book.

DEDICATION

I dedicate this book to my grandchildren, Olivia, Evalyn, Elijah and Joseph. I would read to them a few chapters before they went to bed and the fantasy came into being.

I see the godly character of Troy in each one of you. You have taught me to always look at the things you can do rather than the things you cannot do. Remember, it is only through Christ that your weakness can become your greatest strength.

MIGHTY TROY OF SALEM: THE OATS MISSION

ONCE UPON A TIME, there lived a tiny, extraordinary, one-eyed mouse named Troy who began a revolution of love. He lived inside an orange grain elevator in the town of Salem, Saskatchewan along with his eight brothers, five sisters, Grandpapa Methuselah, the Rafter Rats, the Orange Bats, and Arnie the patrol cat.

The adventure of Mighty Troy is narrated by a giant named Mr. Wolfe, the elevator agent who bumped into the fearless mouse and his brothers one cold winter morning as they were attempting to steal his oats.

It is nearing the end of a cold winter and the elevator creatures are running low on food. Troy's mama and papa send their special pups on two dangerous missions. Troy's five sisters are to inform the two clans that food is on its way. The does use all their skills from the Royal Academy of Mouse Survival to overcome their mortal enemies.

After Troy's Papa Jesse presents him with the powerful Gold Sword of Justice and the Levi Shield of Faith, he leads his eight brothers on a dangerous mission to steal a bag of oats from the giant's cupboard. To accomplish their quest, they both must battle the Rafter Rats, outwit the Orange Bats, trip traps, and depend on the Great Creator to save their lives.

Goar's sons Lami and Saph hatch a flawless plan to steal the oats from the "cheese lovers" during the Great Rejoicing. Prepare for a surprise conclusion and look for the continuing adventures of Mighty Troy in the sequel, *The Sacred Scroll*.

Mighty Troy of Salem will reveal the special plan our Great Creator has for each person and will teach us to focus on what we can do, not what we can't do. Readers will discover that the secret to overcoming their disabilities is to understand how one's perceived weakness can become one's greatest strength.

NOTE FROM THE AUTHOR

THE INSPIRATION FOR THIS STORY CAME TO ME IN A vivid dream one magical night in December. A small, brave mouse jumped onto my shoulder from a stack of raw oats and introduced himself as Mighty Troy of Salem.

You will notice that I have woven various Biblical events throughout the book and the character of Troy is a type of David, King of Israel.

The inspiration for the story's location came from a real orange wheat elevator in the village of Osler, Saskatchewan, Canada. The structure had been a childhood landmark for most of my life until a tornado damaged the orange elevator beyond repair in 1996.

PROLOGUE

EMPIRICAL SCIENCE IS THE EVIDENCE OF THE

SENSES OR EVIDENCE BASED ON ONE'S REPEATED

EXPERIENCE. YET, I'M GOING TO LET YOU IN ON

A LITTLE SECRET. THERE ARE MANY THINGS IN

THIS WORLD YOU CANNOT SEE, TOUCH OR FEEL

THAT ARE JUST AS REAL AS THOSE YOU CAN.

THE GIANT

"FEE-FI-FO-FUM, I SMELL THE BLOOD OF A CHEESE lover!" Well, come on! That's what giants are supposed to say, right? Actually it was a little mouse that had the upper hand in this tale, and believe me, this is a tale you don't want to miss. It all began one cold winter day.

I'm not sure how long I had been out, but when I came to, everything began to spin. My head pounded and my ears rang like a church bell. A large bump had begun to form on my forehead and I moaned in pain.

"What is walking on my chest?" I muttered as I slowly lifted my head off the floor.

"Hey, don't move, you bad ol' giant!" Yelled a tiny mouse, his sword pointing at my throat.

The image was a blur but I'm sure it was a mouse peering down at me and yet I knew this wasn't just your average mouse. He had an old rag tied around his head, which covered one eye. He wore a frayed shoelace wrapped around his shoulder. His sword was a gold chrome nail and his shield a brass button attached to his left arm. I chuckled to myself as I noticed the word "Levi" inscribed on the front of the shield.

As he came into focus, this brave little mouse tucked the Levi shield behind his back, and placed a hand on his hip.

"My name is Troy! I don't know who you are, giant, but you'd better leave me and my brothers alone or I'll run you through with my papa's sword!"

I lay there for a moment not believing my eyes or ears.

I must be dreaming, I thought. Soon I'll wake up and tell my pals at the Salem coffee shop I had this crazy dream where a one-eyed mouse threatened to take my life. Yet, this wasn't even the strangest part of the dream; I could actually understand the little rodent. I blinked my eyes and tried to get up, but as soon as I moved, a searing pain blazed through my head.

"Ahhh," I moaned, holding on to my aching head.

Troy poked his sword at me. "Be quiet, you ol' giant. Stay down or the oats we took will be the least of your problems." This brave little mouse turned to his brothers and motioned them to come and check me out. "C'mon, bucks, you wanted to see a real giant? Well, here he is and he actually seems quite harmless if you ask me."

CHAPTER 1

MR. WOLFE

NEVER JUDGE SOMEONE FOR WHAT
THEY CANNOT DO, BUT FOR WHAT THEY
CAN DO. IT IS IN OUR WEAKNESS THAT WE
FIND THE GREATEST STRENGTH. EVIL HIDES
ITSELF IN THE ILLUSION OF POWER AND
CONTROL BECAUSE IT IS WEAK. PERFECT
LOVE DRIVES OUT FEAR AND ALWAYS
TRIUMPHS OVER EVIL.

BEFORE I CONTINUE THIS STRANGE, UNBELIEVABLE tale, I'd like to introduce myself. I am Mr. Wolfe and I live in the sacred town of Salem, Saskatchewan, where I have worked in the orange elevator all my life, as did my father and his father before him.

The following adventures are from the life and times of an extraordinary mouse named Troy Durum, later known as "Mighty Troy of Salem". These events I am about to share were told to me by Troy. I came to know him over the many years working as an agent at the elevator.

He taught me that just because you're born with a few disabilities doesn't mean you can't be used in a powerful way. As Troy shared with me his many adventures, I was inspired by his unfailing love and faith in our Creator. I learned to never look at someone for what they cannot do, but for what they can do. He showed me that perfect love can truly triumph over evil and that even a heart of stone can be softened.

The day the "miracle" happened, Troy and I began a very special relationship—but I'm getting ahead of myself.

It all unfolded on a cold Monday morning, March 15, 1957. This particular day began as every other one had since I began working at the orange elevator. I would wake up at 5 a.m., have my breakfast of bacon and eggs, and wash it down with a large cup of joe.

I made two ham sandwiches which I neatly placed inside my favourite lunch pail with a picture of Roy Rogers and Trigger on the front. I opened the fridge, took out a red apple and placed

it carefully next to my sandwich. I closed the lid, latched it, and put it down beside my beaded mukluks.

Reaching into my black wool pants I pulled out an old pocket watch. I gave it a good windup for the day and noticed it was already 5:30 a.m. I slipped into my mukluks, opened the closet and put on my down-filled parka. I grabbed my moose hide gloves off the shelf and lifted a large set of dangling keys off an old rusty nail in the porch. As I opened the front door a blast of winter air hit my face.

It was nearing the end of winter in Salem and even though the elevator was closed I had lots of work ahead preparing for the coming wheat and oat season. I stepped off the front porch and the snow crunched beneath my feet. The steam of my breath was visible as it hit the frozen air of winter. The moon cast its glow on the fluffy snow, which sparkled like diamonds as I walked along the path leading to the elevator, one kilometre through Mr. Potter's field.

When I finally arrived at the orange elevator, my face was already numb from the freezing wind. Stopping briefly before entering the door to my office, I looked up and marvelled at the height of this structure. It stretched into the prairie sky at over 100 feet.

The keys jangled in my hands as I turned the lock to the left, stepped through the doorway and entered the cold room. I flicked on the light and saw a blur of movement in every direction as the local elevator mice scurried for cover.

"Man, do we have a plague of mice around here this winter," I complained, placing two large pieces of wood in the potbelly stove to start a warm fire. After about twenty

minutes or so, the room was toasty and the stove hot enough to brew another cup of joe.

In the back room beside the office was a large bag of oats. I loved to take a couple of handfuls each morning and place them in a small pot. I'd add some water and let them cook on the stove beside the coffee.

I switched on the old transistor radio and went to the back room to get the oats for today's hot porridge. Elvis Presley was rocking his 1956 hit "Hound Dog" in the background as I reached for the bag of oats. It was usually lying on the top shelf, but today it was missing! I looked down and noticed an empty bag lying on the floor. There were only a few oat kernels visible and scattered around the room.

"Mice!" I yelled as I noticed the evidence of droppings on the wood floor. "What am I going to do about those pesky mice?" I searched the room for the little thieves.

At that moment, I had no idea what amazing adventures were about to unfold before me. In fact, my life would never be the same...

Once upon a time there was
a special little mouse named Troy...

When she was done, Dr. Agrarian asked Evette if he could take one of the male pups out to show Jesse, who was anxiously waiting outside.

CHAPTER 2

HUMBLE BEGINNINGS

IT IS OFTEN SAID THAT THE RISE TO

GREATNESS IS BIRTHED FROM HUMBLE

BEGINNINGS AND WORTHY LEADERS FIND

THEIR STRENGTH AND COURAGE FROM

TRIALS OF FIRE.

AFTER MY INITIAL TUMULTUOUS MEETING WITH Troy and his brothers, he came to visit me often. In our second meeting, he shared with me about his family and extraordinary birth.

Troy was born on November 7th, 1956, at 2 a.m. on a cold and stormy Sunday morning. When he eventually entered this world, Troy was warmly nestled inside a bag of soft wheat kernels together with thirteen brothers and sisters on the second floor of the orange elevator. The wind was blowing so hard that night the whole building creaked and groaned. Troy's Papa Jesse often reminded everyone that his special son came into this world during one of the worst winter blizzards ever recorded.

Jesse and Evette Durum were a young lively couple looking forward to their new family. Dr. Agrarian was the Durum family physician and took care of at least five other mouse families in the grain elevator. He was, needless to say, very, very busy.

The new couple had a large home behind the back wall of the elevator. They lived near the grain gleaner, which was close to a constant supply of food for the couple's mega family.

Evette was in her 19th day when she gave birth to her beautiful, hairless, pink babies. As Jesse patiently waited for his family to arrive, he stood guard outside. He held his gold sword in both hands just in case Arnie, the local elevator cat, came snooping around or one of the Orange Bats honed in on his pups. And their mortal enemies the Rafter Rats on level five were always on the hunt for young "cheese lovers." The cold wind blew through the open room and he couldn't stop shivering.

Once all 13 babies arrived, Evette began feeding the hungry brood. When she was done, Dr. Agrarian asked Evette if he could take one of the male pups out to show Jesse, who was anxiously waiting outside. It had already been 15 minutes since she had her last pup, so Doc was quite positive the delivery was complete.

He walked outside holding a male pup and stood beside Jesse.

"You have 13 wonderful, healthy pups, Jesse. I thought you would like to see one."

"Thanks, Doc, who do we have here?" The proud papa tucked the gold sword in his belt and carefully took the little mouse in his arms.

Doc made sure the pup was covered up from the cold, "I think this is a male pup, Jesse. The name will be up to you folks of course."

Jesse had the biggest smile as he rocked his precious pup back and forth. Then, with tears in his eyes, he looked up. "Praise be to the Creator for blessing me with 13 healthy pups." He turned and placed his free arm around his friend. "By the way, Doc, thanks for being here for us. How's my precious Evette doin'? She must be extremely tired after delivering all of my special little mouskins."

"Your wife is doing just fine, Jesse," answered Doc. "In fact, she's busy feeding them right now, so you can see them in a few minutes."

No one could be certain of their gender until a few days later but Jesse had to ask. "Were you able to guess how many bucks and does I had, Doc?"

"Well, my boy," Doc answered with a big smile, "It appears you have eight healthy bucks and five lovely does who are all very hungry. Speaking of which, I should get this little one back to his mama." The doctor carefully took the helpless pup from his papa and walked towards the doorway.

KAPPA'S ATTACK

KAPPA, KING OF THE ORANGE BATS, HAD BEEN WATCHing the two bucks with keen interest, especially when one of them brought out a tiny, tasty morsel. He squinted his red eyes as drool dripped from his mouth. A smile formed on his wrinkled face.

"This should be a quick and easy hunt tonight," the king muttered to himself as he swooped down towards the helpless pup lying in the doctor's arms.

Jesse heard the flapping of leather wings, followed by the shrill whistle of the bat's echolocation.

"Doc, quickly get the pup inside! I hear trouble."

Kappa adjusted his route as Doc Agrarian turned towards the doorway. The bat king was about to snatch the little pup's blanket and all, when he felt a sharp stab on his left wing.

"Ahhh," the king screamed in pain as Jesse's sword of justice hit its mark with a searing burn. The blow pushed the bat off its course and his talon grabbed hold of an empty blanket.

Kappa was furious and decided to fly back around to attack Jesse instead.

"So you want a piece of me do you, cheese lover?" His deep voice growled.

By now Doc and the pup were both safely inside, so Jesse said a quick prayer. He held the sword in both hands and pointed it towards the large bat flying at him. "You'll never get one of my precious pups, you orange devil." He swung the sword smoothly in a classic figure eight. It hummed loudly and seemed to anticipate every evasive move the bat made.

Kappa tried to dodge the large blade but it seemed to know his next move. It struck with deadly precision. The blow was quite painful this time as it came down on the side of his neck. The burning sensation became unbearable and so Kappa evaded Jesse just as the sword took another swipe, barely missing his tail.

As he flew home in pain on level 7 he asked himself, "What is this powerful new weapon the cheese lovers have? I must have it for myself."

BIRTH OF TROY

JESSE TUCKED THE GOLD SWORD OF JUSTICE BACK INTO his belt and ran inside to see his new family.

"Honey, are you okay?" He turned the corner and was happy to see Evette's smiling face surrounded by their pups digging and prodding for a better feeding position.

"I should ask you if you're alright, my hero." She held her paw out to welcome her husband. "Doc Agrarian told me you battled a rather large bat who was after one of our pups. He saw you strike it down with the golden sword of justice single-handedly."

Jesse smiled, held her paw and bent down to kiss her on the forehead. "I'm just glad you and the pups are okay, Evette."

Just then Evette jumped up disturbing the pups still feeding.

"What's wrong, my love?" asked Jesse with concern.

"I felt something move in my tummy, Jesse. I think there might be another pup." Again she felt pain, but this time it was like four tiny paws kicking inside.

Evette instantly knew there was another pup on its way, and this one would be special.

Sure enough, this mouskin came out fighting and kicking on that stormy winter night. He was feisty and full of life, in spite of being the runt of the litter. In fact, he measured only one inch from head to tail, and skinny as a rail. This late pup took one look at his mama and wouldn't stop smiling and giggling. It was as if he held onto a great secret that no one else knew.

As soon as Dr. Agrarian delivered the pup he noticed

not only was he extra small but he had a grave disability. Evette also noticed something was off because she always gave each pup a good look-over after they arrived, just to be sure they had all their parts. Not only was he a tiny little pup but there was a large hole where his eye was supposed to be.

"Well, he'll have to learn to get by as best he can," responded the Doc with concern. "You and Jesse will have to watch him all the time. If you're not careful I'm afraid he may not last beyond a few months."

At that moment the young pup gazed into mama's eyes and gave her the biggest, warmest smile she'd ever seen. Evette snuggled him against her cheek and cried with joy. She rocked her tiny buck back and forth singing lullabies until he fell sound asleep.

At midnight, she awoke to a still small voice whispering in her ear, "My daughter, do not cry or fear, for I have chosen him. He is the one I love. This pup will be a creature after my own heart. I, the Great Creator of the universe, will use this special pup to bring healing to all the creatures in the Orange Elevator. He will bring good news to the rats, the bats, the cats and all my precious ones. Just as I care for the sparrows of the field and the ants in the ground, so I will care for you and your kind.

"From today forward he shall be called 'Troy' because he will be a mighty foot soldier for the Logos. He will fight injustice and defeat the forces of evil. I will give Troy my power and he will be wise and strong. I will use him to rule a kingdom and to save his kind. You may see a mouse with disabilities, but I see a mouse with possibilities. You may see a mouse born in weakness, but I see a mouse born with the power of my love." The voice stopped and all was silent.

Evette rose up, smiled to herself and placed little Troy with the rest of his siblings. She treasured all she had heard deep in her heart.

In the coming weeks Jesse and Evette watched their 14 new pups grow strong and healthy. Even tiny Troy seemed to fight and dig just as hard as his brothers and sisters for his daily milk from Mama. The fact that he was small and had one eye caused him no difficulties at this stage in life, because all he had to do was eat, sleep, play—and poop.

CHAPTER 3

BLESSING OF SOCRATES

TO BE BLESSED BY THE CREATOR DOES

NOT MEAN WE HAVE RECEIVED MATERIAL

OR EVEN PHYSICAL REWARDS. TO BE TRULY

BLESSED IS TO LOVE AND BE LOVED BY THE

ONE IN WHOM WE FOLLOW. ONLY THEN

CAN WE BLESS OTHERS IN THE SAME WAY

WE WERE BLESSED.

WITH EACH PASSING DAY, THE CREATOR WAS WITH Troy Durum as he grew in wisdom and strength. It became quite obvious to everyone that this small pup had not only some special needs but also some amazing gifts. Troy would face many difficulties in life and so Mama made sure his siblings treated him with love and respect.

Jesse often thought about Troy's disabilities and cried. He worried his son would encounter bullies and be taken advantage of, so he decided to find outside help. He knew Evette had many connections.

"Evette, do you know of anyone that could give us some advice on how to help Troy deal with what he may face in the future?"

"Well, why don't you seek the advice of our Elders, Jesse?" Evette said almost immediately. "That's what they are there for."

Jesse loved the idea and requested a meeting as soon as possible. The next day, four Elders from each clan met in the Durum home. After Jesse and Evette told them of their dilemma, the Elders suggested they contact the Old Seer Socrates who lived on Potter's farm just outside of Salem. The Elders believed Troy needed wisdom from the Great Creator and the old owl had a close connection with Him.

It was agreed that Jesse should send a message to Socrates via the elevator's own Pigeon Postal Service.

POSTMASTER PIGGLY

JESSE MADE HIS WAY TO THE MAIN FLOOR OF THE ELEvator to find postmaster Piggly. "Master Piggly," as they called him, loved to eat and so, needless to say, was quite round. His red, pointy nose seemed to glow when he was excited and some say he pokes it where it doesn't belong. Master Piggly's voice was rather raspy and high pitched. His eyes were bright red and his fur snowy white. When he spoke his double chin bounced up and down and his unusual black moustache wiggled back and forth.

"Well, well, well," exclaimed Master Piggly, "what brings you down here on this cold winter morning, Jesse Durum? How's that feisty little girlfriend of yours doin'? What was her name again? Oh yes, Evette, Evette Spelt."

"That would be Evette Durum now, Master Piggly," corrected Jesse. "We were married a year ago, remember?"

"Oh yes, of course I remember now. You and your new wife recently had 14 new babies, didn't ya? Are they all doin' well, Jesse? I heard that the one named Troy was born with some dangerous abnormalities and may not survive the winter?"

"Well, you heard wrong, Master Piggly. They're all doing just fine and baby Troy has turned out to be the strongest of the bunch. In fact, I believe the Creator has blessed him with some very special gifts."

"Well, whatever the case, Jesse, Betty and I do wish you all the best and we're prayin' for you every day you know. She says it won't be easy raising a child with only one eye. The guys at the barbershop are sayin' that you'll have to watch him like a hawk or he won't live very long. Yes, indeed, he'll be easy pickin's for the Rafter Rats on level five. Then there's the Orange Bats, Jesse... well, they could sneak up on his blind side and snatch him up at any given moment. Let me tell you, it wouldn't be pretty."

Socrates lived in a large oak tree on Potter's farm

By now Jesse was as mad as a hornet, but he bit his tongue until Master Piggly stopped talking for a moment to breathe, just long enough for Jesse to give him the message he wanted delivered to Socrates.

"I want this message delivered to the Old Seer at Potter's farm as soon as possible, Master Piggly. How long will it take before we get a reply?" asked Jesse with a feigned smile.

"I would say you should hear back in a couple of days, Jesse. Oh, is this regarding your poor little Troy, if I may be so bold?" inquired Master Piggly.

"No, you may not," answered Jesse with a tone that ended the conversation abruptly. He left the letter of invitation with the nosey postmaster and headed back home to his family, but with a greater worry for his son than ever.

SOCRATES THE SEER

SOCRATES LIVED IN A LARGE OAK TREE ON POTTER'S farm, two kilometres from the Orange Elevator outside the town of Salem. The old owl had a bright orange beak and white feathers. He had black circles around his large, blue eyes. As far as he knew, he was the only owl in the world with blue eyes. When flying, he loved to wear a pair of goggles and an old leather aviator hat, the edges of which flapped in the wind. He enjoyed pretending to be an old World War II fighter pilot sent on dangerous missions behind enemy lines.

The Old Seer was startled by the flap of wings and a loud thump outside his door.

"I wonder who that could be at this hour in the morning? Must be another pigeon delivering a message from the Orange Elevator. That makes the fifth message this week. I wonder who this is from?"

He opened the front door and retrieved the scroll from the bird's leg. The seer quickly untied the letter and began reading it to himself as he closed the door and went back inside.

To Socrates, Wise Seer of Salem:
My name is Jesse Durum. I live with my wife, Evette, and our 14 pups on the second floor of the Orange Elevator in Salem. I have a son named Troy who is only a few weeks old. When he came into this world, he was quite different from the other pups. Troy is small in stature and yet tall in spirit. He has only one eye, however, we have noticed that he is able to hear much better than his siblings. He seems healthy, strong, and alert, but my wife and I worry that he will be bullied and teased until his confidence is broken. I also fear because of his one eye he may not be able to survive very long against the number of predators living within the Orange Elevator.
Please, Mr. Socrates, sir, would you be so kind as to come to our home at your earliest convenience to bless Troy? We would be greatly honoured if you could be-stow some words of wisdom so he can be the best he can, under the circumstances.

Thank you for your consideration.
Humbly Yours,
Jesse and Evette Durum

The Old Seer sighed and put the letter down on the table. He made himself a cup of joe, opened the pantry door and took a gingerbread cookie from his special cookie jar. He sat down on his big, brown thinking chair. Every now and then he would sip from his cup, take a bite from his delicious cookie and then think some more. What could he say that would help little Troy?

"Maybe I should ask the Creator what He wants me to do." He bowed his head. "Our Great Creator of all things, I humbly ask for Your guidance in providing a word of blessing for the Jesse Durum family and their troubled little pup, Troy."

Suddenly a blinding light surrounded him. He instinctively lowered his head and placed his hands over his eyes. Shaking uncontrollably, he risked a peek through his fingers and there standing before him was a magnificent Watcher of the Lord. He was wearing what looked like grey armour around his chest and down his legs. His face was so brilliant that Socrates couldn't decide if the Watcher was smiling or not and yet he knew that the Watcher meant him no harm. The large creature was an Archangel from the army of the Great Creator. He was leaning on his golden sword of fire, which he held in his right hand and his giant wings touched the ceiling.

He spoke in a soft and gentle tone so as not to frighten the owl. "Socrates, Seer of Salem, follower of Yahweh, be not afraid for I have come to give you great news regarding Troy, son of Jesse. The Creator wants you to open the Book of Truth to 1 Samuel 16 and begin reading. Then you will know what to do."

Socrates went to the bookshelf, pulled out the Great Book of Truth and carefully opened it. He put on his big round glasses and began to read: "The Lord said to Samuel... 'fill your horn with oil and be on your way; I am sending you to Jesse of Bethlehem. I have chosen one of his sons to be king... Invite Jesse to the sacrifice, and I will show you what to do. You are to anoint for me the one I indicate.'"

The old Seer stopped for a moment, squinted at the winged messenger and continued to read: "...When they arrived, (at Jesse's house) Samuel saw Eliab (one of Jesse's large handsome sons) and thought, 'Surely the Lord's anointed stands here before the Lord.' But the Lord said to Samuel, 'Do not consider his appearance or his height, for I have rejected him. The Lord does not look at the things people look at. People look at the outward appearance, but the Lord looks at the heart.'"

"This is it!" exclaimed Socrates. "This is what the Creator wants me to do, isn't it? He has anointed Troy to be king over all the clans, hasn't He?" Socrates looked up at the Watcher for confirmation. "Is this what I am supposed to do? Anoint Troy as a future king?"

The Watcher nodded and then spoke in a louder tone, "Socrates, Seer of Salem, the Creator has chosen you to bless Troy son of Jesse and to reveal the glory of Logos by turning his disabilities into his greatest strength.

"The Creator will give this special little mouse the gift of leadership. He will turn his fears into the courage of a thousand warriors. He will dispense justice with mercy. He will rise to become a great leader among the clans and will someday rule over all the creatures in the Orange Elevator.

Socrates, you are to tell Jesse son of Methuselah that from now on his son shall be called `Mighty Troy of Salem!' Thus saith the Great Creator and Sustainer of all things." When the Watcher had finished talking he pointed to the Book of Truth and told Socrates to continue reading.

Socrates began to read where the prophet Samuel had

asked to see the last son of Jesse: (So Jesse) "...sent for him (David the young shepherd boy) and had him brought in. He was glowing with health and had a fine appearance and handsome features. Then the Lord said, 'Rise and anoint him; this is the one.' So Samuel took the horn of oil and anointed him in the presence of his brothers, and from that day on the Spirit of the Lord came powerfully upon David."

Socrates slowly raised his head and noticed the mighty Watcher had vanished.

"By Jove, I know what I am to do," he exclaimed, placing the Holy Book of Truth back in its place on the bookshelf.

The Seer walked to his roll-top desk, removed a key from the top of the fridge, blew off the dust and slowly placed it inside the old lock. The door opened with a loud click. He reached inside and pulled out a silver flask filled with anointing oil. He placed it carefully in his satchel, which was tied to his waist then prepared himself for the flight to the Orange Elevator by donning his leather aviator hat and goggles. Then he opened the front door and stepped onto a branch. After saying a silent prayer, he jumped off the ledge, spread his wings and soared gracefully into the icy blue sky.

HOME OF JESSE DURUM

E VETTE HEARD A KNOCK AT THE FRONT DOOR AND went to see who was there.

"Good evening, madam," responded Socrates with a distinct British accent and a bow. "I have come at your request to see Master Troy of Salem." The Seer handed Evette a package wrapped in brown paper and tied with a butcher's string. "I thought your family would enjoy some aged cheddar from my favourite deli."

"Oh my, you didn't have to bring a gift, sir." Evette smiled with gratitude and beckoned their guest to come in out of the cold. She nodded her head toward the living room where Jesse was reading the newspaper and waved her paw. "Jesse come quickly! The Seer has arrived!"

He jumped up from his chair and went to greet Socrates.

"It is a great honour to have you visit our humble home, sir," he said. "Thank you so much for your quick response."

"You are very welcome, Sir Jesse and Lady Evette. I am grateful that you have invited me into your lovely home." Socrates looked around the small room, "I love what you have done with the place, Evette. It is so charming," he said with a wave of his wing.

"Thank you for your kind words, sir," Evette responded, as a blush coloured the pink skin beneath the white fur of her cheeks. "If you would like to sit down I can serve you a cup of tea and some cheese from your deli."

"That sounds lovely, my dear, thank you," responded Socrates as he sat in Jesse's special chair.

"Now that you're comfortable," Jesse said, "please excuse me for a moment. I'll go fetch Troy."

"Of course, my boy. Of course."

Jesse entered the room and found Troy in his crib playing with a little mouse doll he received from his mysterious Grandpapa.

"Come on, Troy," whispered Jesse, as he picked up his special little pup and placed him on his shoulder next to his cheek, "we have a special guest downstairs who wants to meet you."

Troy placed an arm around his papa's neck, gave him a hug and spoke a word for the first time—over and over again. "Papa, Papa, Papa." Never had a word sounded so sweet as it did on that magical day of Troy's blessing.

As the two of them went downstairs and entered the living room, Socrates placed his tea on the table and stood to greet them.

"Well, well, well, who do we have here?" He reached out to Troy but the little pup pulled back, wanting nothing to do with this scary old owl. "That's perfectly alright, little buck," comforted Socrates, "you are very special, do you know that? The Great Creator told me to anoint you with oil. He sent a large Watcher who told me you are to be called, 'Mighty Troy of Salem'. He announced you would someday be the first king to rule all the creatures in the Orange Elevator. The Watcher also foretold that the Creator's glory would be magnified through your life, Mighty Troy of Salem."

Evette gasped. "But, sir, may I ask how he is to become great when it is obvious he has so many disabilities to overcome?"

The Seer winked at Evette. "Ah, my dear, the Creator loves to take those we see as weak and make them strong. He reveals His power by overcoming any disabilities or disadvantages and turning them into our greatest strengths. In the Book of Truth, He chose an insignificant shepherd boy to be king over all his people. Why? Because he had a heart for Logos. This boy named David had an extraordinary love for people mixed with a courageous spirit. Jesse,

Evette, I believe the Creator desires to use Troy as a mighty warrior of love and justice. In the near future, everyone will look at what this mouse can do and totally forget what he can't do. The Creator has anointed this particular fellow for a special purpose."

Socrates reached into his satchel and pulled out the silver flask of oil. "So, let's begin, shall we?" he stated with authority. "This flask was handed down to me from my grandfather, Plato, who created it especially for the task of anointing." He peered into the eyes of Troy's parents. "Do you believe the Creator has chosen your pup for a special purpose?"

"Yes, we do now, sir," acknowledged Evette looking to Jesse for approval. "We've been praying the Creator would use him in some way and yet we never expected this."

Jesse stared at the floor. "I would agree with my wife, sir, and yet I never dreamt he would be a king."

Socrates shared with Troy's parents what had happened that morning.

"I asked the Creator what He wished me to say to you and specifically to Master Troy. I never imagined Logos would send me a Watcher. He was so brilliant I was not able look upon him without being blinded. He commanded me to read from 1 Samuel. Do you happen to have a copy of the Book of Truth, Jesse?"

Evette went to a shelf and pulled out a well-used leather book. The cover looked faded and thread bare. She placed it into Socrates' open hands. He seemed eager to receive it.

He bowed to Evette with respect, opened it and proceeded to read. "The Lord said to Samuel, 'Fill your horn with oil and be on your way; I am sending you to Jesse of Bethlehem. I have chosen one of his sons to be king.' Invite Jesse to the sacrifice, and I will show you what to do. You are to anoint for me the one I indicate.' I believe this passage is referring to Troy." He reached into his satchel and pulled out the silver flask, which had a carving of an ornate tree of life on it.

Socrates carefully poured a few precious drops of oil on the tip of his wing and proceeded to anoint Troy. He drew the shape of a cross with the oil on Troy's forehead and then said a special blessing: "Troy, son of Jesse, son of Evette, I anoint you with the oil of blessing to become king over all the creatures in the Orange Elevator. Mighty Troy of Salem, I anoint you to be a strong leader among your people. To be kind and yet bold, gentle and yet firm, to be gracious and yet just.

I have asked the Creator to take your physical infirmities and transform them into your greatest assets. Mighty Troy, may your ears be able to hear what your eyes cannot see. May your feet give you assurance, strength and balance as if you were walking with Logos Himself. May you love the Great Creator with all your heart, all your mind, and all your soul. In the Logos' name we pray, amen." At that very moment, the Spirit came powerfully upon Mighty Troy of Salem.

When the wise Old Seer finished his prayer, Jesse and Evette bowed before him. "Thank you so much for coming to our humble home, Socrates. We never expected this honour or this blessing. Please know you are welcome here any time, sir."

Evette gave the Seer a big hug and kiss on the cheek. He

went to the door, opened it to leave, but then looked over his shoulder and gave her a quick wink.

Evette closed the door and picked Troy off the floor. "You're going to be a great king someday, young buck, what do you think of that?"

Troy just held his toy mouse up for all to see and said, "Papa, Papa" over and over again.

Jesse smiled as he took his son from Evette and placed him on his shoulder. Troy wrapped his arms tightly around his papa, closed his eye and went to sleep.

Jesse headed back up the stairs and placed Troy in his crib while Evette went to check on the other pups who were supposed to be asleep. With all the pups settled, Jesse and Evette got ready for bed, dug in under the warm wheat chaff and cried themselves to sleep with tears of joy.

The main water supply was a small well in the basement floor

CHAPTER 4

THE CLAN WAR

RELATIONSHIPS ARE COMPLICATED,

ESPECIALLY IN THE MIDST OF CONFLICT.

THE MYSTERY OF LOVE IS HOW IT SEEMS

TO DEEPEN WHEN BATTLING THROUGH

THE STORMS OF LIFE — TOGETHER.

Jesse Durum

Troy greatly admired his Papa Jesse for passing on his love and commitment to the Great Creator. He taught Troy the meaning of true love and respect for all creatures great and small. Papa Jesse would often tell his little munchkins, "Strong faith motivates hard work and discipline."

Jesse's character and work ethic came from time spent in the army. He was a war strategist and combat instructor for the Durum clan until his retirement.

Jesse also said, "War was to be a last resort and then only from a defensive position." He joined the army just before his 10th birthday because his papa told him it was an honour to defend the clan and a military experience would build character.

As Jesse walked along the main road toward the army recruitment office to enlist, a few young does swooned and flirted with him. Mouse flirting occurs when a doe taps her foot on the floor as fast as possible, while wiggling her wet nose.

Jesse was tall, lean, and very handsome. His hair was greased back, and parted in the middle. He sported a large moustache curled up at the tips with hot wax, which made him look very distinguished.

Two years after he enlisted, the clan wars began because of an elevator shut down. The water supply was seriously low and everyone panicked. Rumours spread quickly that the giants were fighting and didn't want to store wheat in the Elevator any more.

As days turned into weeks, it became clear the grain bins

were nearly empty. Jesse was worried because he'd seen what happened when a crisis threatened families. Everyone would begin fighting over the crumbs left in the dusty, dirty corners of the elevator. It also meant their mortal enemies, the Rafter Rats, would also be competing for the last remaining morsels. Tensions increased when the Bulgur, Kamet, and Graham clans began to hoard what little food was left.

In response, the Durum and Spelt clans decided to place guards around the water sources in the Orange Elevator. Jesse said they had hoped this would encourage the others to share the remaining food supply. Needless to say, the plan didn't work. The very next day, the three opposing clans attacked the main water supply, which was a small well in the basement floor. From then on fighting erupted in every corner and on every floor, except level five where the Rafter Rats lived.

The battle continued for weeks and the clans were becoming weaker and more exhausted. No one ever imagined peace would finally come in the dead of night through a pretty little doe named Evette Spelt.

EVETTE SPELT

E VETTE WAS BORN INTO THE SPELT CLAN WHO fought alongside the Durum clan. She wasn't officially in the army, but she volunteered to assist in the war effort. Jesse happened to be one of the guards stationed at the basement well and this is where he met the lovely Evette.

She came out of a dark corner one evening with three of her doe friends bringing delicious food for the soldiers on patrol that night. She carried herself like a princess and when she talked, her voice was soft and confident. As she moved into the glowing light of a small fire, Jesse noticed her beauty and thought she could be the one. His foot began to tap and his nose wiggled quite vigorously. Evette's fur was pure white, except for a long thin streak of red combed up to the back of her head. As she smiled at Jesse, a piece of fur curled in front of her bright blue eyes.

She stood on top of the well pounding her staff on the metal lid. "Thank you for your service, my brave bucks! The Spelt Clan thought you might be hungry so they asked for volunteers to bring our warriors some nourishment."

Jesse was the first in line to receive the much-needed energy. He eagerly held out his paw as Evette handed him a small piece of rare blue cheese and a few crushed wheat kernels. Later that evening he tried to thank her for the food, but all that came out was a pathetic little squeak. Someday he knew he would marry the beautiful Evette Spelt.

BATTLE OF THE CLANS

THE ATTACK CAME SUDDENLY JUST AS EVETTE AND her friends handed out the last bit of food to the soldiers. The Bulgur, Kamet, and Graham clans knew if they could control the main water supply and the emergency food rations, their own families would have a better chance of surviving the winter.

It was close to midnight when Candor, leader of the Bulgur Clan, came running out of the dark and attacked Jesse. His sword swung from side to side until he was close enough to lift it above his head and bring it down for a fatal blow. But Jesse swung around, his gold sword of justice clashed against Candor's sword, shattering it into tiny pieces. Defenceless, Candor ran into the darkness to find another weapon calling for reinforcements.

Ten more large bucks charged out of the dark towards Jesse and his buddies, swords drawn. Fighting broke out around the well. All you could hear was shouting, screaming, and the clanging of metal.

YOUNG LAMI AND SAPH'S BAIT

EVETTE AND HER FRIENDS HUDDLED TOGETHER IN the dark corners of the wall and watched the battle ensue. They hadn't noticed two sets of red eyes peering out from a small hole in the wall watching the cheese lovers fighting over the well. Two teenage Rats had been sent to the basement to fetch water for their Papa Goar, king of the Rafter Rats. They sat in silence and couldn't believe

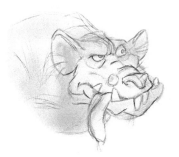

their luck when a few tasty does came to hide right beside them.

Prince Saph's large tongue hung to one side and drooled at the thought of snatching a little tasty. He lived for the hunt and loved to eat.

"I'll give you the two brown ones, if you let me take the white one, Lami. I find the white ones more sweet and juicy."

Young prince Lami was papa's choice to be next in line to the throne and loved to remind his older brother of that fact. He slapped the back of his head. "Not yet, doofus! Don't you see all those bucks by the well? If we take their does, they'll stop fighting each other and attack us! That is why papa chose me to be the next king and not you. I have half a brain."

"Awww, that hurt, Lami," Saph protested, rubbing the sore spot on his head. "I just thought the cheese lovers might be too busy fighting and wouldn't notice if we take just one snack."

Lami could see the bucks were quite distracted. "Okay, okay, we'll grab the white one, but that's it. Here's the plan; I happen to have some peanuts I stole from the giants' cupboard the other day and if there's one thing I know, cheese lovers adore peanuts almost as much as cheese. So, all we have to do is lead the white one into the tunnel by using my peanuts as bait."

Saph nearly clapped his paws in excitement. "May I have the peanuts and lay them down, Lami, huh, may I?" He was beaming as if it was his first visit to the Salem garbage dump.

His older brother reluctantly agreed and handed Saph four pieces of irresistible mouse bait.

"Okay, okay you can have them but they're not a snack and lay them down at least three feet apart. Make sure the last nut leads the white doe inside the hole, we'll snatch her and be gone before they even know the girly cheese lover is missing."

Saph took one more look at the four peanuts in his open

paw and made his way toward the three does as silently as possible. Evette and her friends were so busy watching the battle they didn't notice the young Rafter Rat placing the first peanut right beside their feet.

THE FIGHT CONTINUES

CANDOR CAME BACK INTO THE FIGHT AFTER ACQUIRING a new sword. He went after Jesse with a vengeance.

"Now it's my turn, little buck. How can you even lift that gold weapon of yours?" The clan leader struck Jesse's sword with a hard blow driving him to the floor. "And why are the Durums sending out a baby to fight a buck's war?"

Jesse flipped over backwards, bounced off the wall and swung the gold sword, striking Candor's heel.

"I am Jesse Durum, son of Methuselah the Adventurer, and I will not be mocked by the likes of you. Now go home and let us all work this out in a civilized manner. We can share what is left and come up with a solution together instead of fighting one another."

Candor's sword fell to the elevator floor as he cried out in pain and clutched his wound.

Jesse knelt down to help his enemy, but before he could, another warrior attacked him from behind. The spear came out of nowhere and nearly struck his shoulder, but Jesse's gold sword of justice sensed the danger and brushed it harmlessly to one side.

Before Candor could speak, one of his warriors pulled him to safety and went back to continue the battle for control of the well. The fighting continued for sometime until everyone was totally exhausted.

THE TRAP IS SET

BY NOW EVETTE HAD SEEN ENOUGH AND WAS THINK-ing about how she could stop the fighting. Lowering her head in deep thought she noticed something hard beneath her foot. She stepped back and her nose caught the scent of something heavenly.

"What is that wonderful smell?" thought Evette as she bent down, picked the peanut off the floor then popped it in her mouth. "Mmmm, it tastes so good. I haven't had one of these in such a long time I forgot how good they were." Before she finished chewing the first one, her nose caught the scent of a second nut and then a third. She ate them both before noticing one more lying at the entrance of a small hole in the wall. She was about to pick it up, when she stopped. Something was wrong. Her tail tingled, and she knew it could be a warning that danger was imminent. But she shook off the instinct to run. "Maybe this feeling is not indicating danger but guilt for not sharing with my friends." She was just about to call them over, but it was too late. The trap had already been tripped and the bait taken.

Lami placed his paw over Evette's mouth before she could call her friends and dragged her into the tunnel. Her eyes opened wide as she tried to scream but nothing came out. "Hurry, Saph, grab the cheese lover's legs and let's get out of here before they figure out she is gone."

Saph bent down to grab Evette's feet but she kicked him in the nose.

"Owww! Hold still, little cheese lover. If you keep resisting, it will just make matters worse."

Lami shook his head. "What's wrong with you, Saph? If you can't even control a little, tiny mouse how would you ever command an army of rats? Now get her under control so that we can get outta here before all the bucks come looking for her."

"I'm trying, I'm trying," responded Saph as he finally jumped on top of her legs and held them tightly. When she was finally still they began moving her further into the tunnel. They rounded a corner and were almost out of sight when Lami tripped over a piece of wood and landed on his back. Evette fell to the floor and let out a scream so loud he was sure the roof would cave in.

Saph reached out in the dark trying to grab hold of his tasty prize but Evette would have no part of it. She felt his arm and bit down as hard as she could. Saph fell forwards and his face came within inches of Evette so she grabbed his large tongue and gave it a good pull. Pain shot through his arm and his mouth was so sore he couldn't talk very well — not that he ever could. Saph frantically tried to find the mouse in the dark.

"I can't believe you bit me, cheese lover! You'll pay for this when I finally get a hold of you."

Evette saw an opening and wasted no time. She picked herself off the floor and ran towards the entrance. The two other does had heard Evette's scream and were already at tunnel entrance when she dove into their arms.

Lami brushed the dust off his shirt and whacked Saph with his Staff.

"You're such a poor excuse for a prince. I thought you were hungry."

Saph placed his sore tongue back in his mouth and rubbed his arm. "I lost my grip when you dropped her, Lami! Wait until I tell papa how you fell and let my cheese lover go. It wasn't my fault, it was yours!"

"Well, she's gone now," complained Lami, "and we still have no water. Papa Goar will not be pleased if we bring this bucket home empty. Come on, let's get outta here and find another water source."

Saph nodded and followed his big brother down the tunnel.

Evette scurried back to the wall with her two friends and shared what had happened a few moments ago. They made her promise not to be lured by any more peanuts no matter how "heavenly" they tasted. They had a good laugh when she told them how she escaped but she knew it was a close call.

The fight was continuing at the well and suddenly she had a plan.

Just as the fighting was at its worst a voice pierced the darkness, "Stop this fighting! Stop this senseless violence right now!"

Every soldier stopped as if frozen in time and just stared at the well. Jesse noticed a lovely doe standing on the well covering, her face red with anger and her front paws flying in every direction as she spoke.

"Clans, please, we must stop this senseless violence against each other and begin working towards a solution. Greed and fear have taken hold of our civilized behaviour and our vow of peace and community. We all have families that are suffering and are at risk. We will not survive very long if we do not learn to work together towards a solution in a crisis. We have enough water for all the clans and the Creator will help us find food for all of us if we work as a community. This senseless fighting must stop, now." Evette placed her hands by her side and slowly stepped off the well. She took Candor's paw, held it forward and placed it into Jesse's. "So, shake paws, stop this senseless war and let's figure a way out of this mess. What do you say?" She winked at Jesse and went back to stand with her friends.

Jesse took his enemy's paw and gave it a hardy shake.

"She's right, Candor, we must learn to work together. This fighting is not good for any of us."

Candor agreed to stop fighting and they all went home that night arm in arm to find a solution.

To their surprise a small amount of food was eventually found in the dump bin on level one. The clan wars ended that same day and as soon as the giants went back to work food was plentiful once again.

Papa walked home that night with Evette Spelt, the love of his life. They were married a few days later and there was great rejoicing. Everyone still talked about the wedding of Jesse and Evette Durum. They would say it was an amazing time of peace and love shared by every clan in the Orange Elevator of Salem.

Cat Hill was in the middle of his path.

CHAPTER 5

THE LAW OF ISOLATION

WE WERE CREATED TO BE SOCIAL

CREATURES. TO LIVE, LOVE, LAUGH, PLAY

AND EXPERIENCE THIS MAGICAL WORLD IN

THE PASSION OF COMMUNITY.

THERE IS NOTHING NATURAL ABOUT

LIVING IN ISOLATION.

WHEN TROY SHARED WITH ME THE LIFE STORY of his Grandpapa Methuselah, I was drawn to his grandpapa's fearless character and amazing sense of adventure.

His story begins with the Law of Isolation. The mouse clans never ventured outside the Orange Elevator—ever. In fact, isolation became the law in order to keep themselves and future generations safe. The elders believed there were enough dangers within the walls of the elevator. They already had to avoid giants who walked around everywhere and dangerous machines operating on most floors. Traps were set with deadly temptations and poisons strategically placed around every food source. Yes, there were many dangers existing inside the Orange Elevator, yet not even close to the horrors that were surely lurking outside. These facts generated fear among all the clans and so the elders voted to enact what became known as, "The Law of Isolation."

In order to discourage disobedience, the elders created false stories of mice that disobeyed the law and were never seen or heard from again. According to the elders' information no one had ever left the elevator until a young buck named Methuselah had an unfortunate accident.

He and his friend Alex were on their way home after a hard day's work at the storage bins when they both noticed a bright light shining in through a hole in the wall. The young Methuselah was curious and so he went to check it out. As he got closer he noticed two boards were missing and could see outside. It was so beautiful. The sky was blue and the green grass looked like a soft carpet. Flowers of every colour were in full bloom and the scent was heavenly.

"Methuselah, come back," Alex warned. "It's not safe to be so close to the open wall."

"It's so beautiful!" exclaimed Methuselah, beckoning his friend with a paw to come look for himself. "You must come and see how magical the outside world is, Alex."

His friend and work mate turned his head from side to side, paranoid that someone was watching them. "The elders don't want us to look beyond the elevator walls. They know we might be tempted to break the law of Isolation. Let's just go home, Selah, our families will be wondering where we are."

"Okay, okay. I'm comin'," whined Methuselah. He turned to walk back to his friend but slipped on a loose board and went backwards through the open hole. He fell three storeys, hit the ground and everything went black.

Alex saw Methuselah fall and ran to the hole. He peered over the side.

"Selah, Selah! Are you okay?" Alex called over and over, but there was no answer.

Methuselah had hit his head on a rock as he landed and was unconscious the rest of the day and most of the night.

Alex kept searching for his friend but finally had to give-up and find help. He arrived home, called Selah's wife, Edna, and told her what had happened. She immediately called the elders and begged them to look for her husband outside the Orange Elevator but they refused.

"We're sorry, ma'am, but we can't break the Law of Isolation, even if it occurred by accident. Leaving the elevator could endanger all the clans for future generations. All we can do now is ask the Creator to protect Methuselah and to bring him home safely."

After a month had passed and he hadn't come home, the elders declared him missing or dead. They had a funeral and everyone came to say their goodbye to Methuselah and pay their respects to the widow Edna and her young pups.

But one day, to everyone's surprise, Methuselah actually showed up. He had been gone from the Orange Elevator for two years and had many stories to tell. His amazing adventures are told in "The Chronicles of Methuselah."

It is believed that Selah was the only mouse that had ever been outside the Orange Elevator and returned safely home. His family thanked the Great Creator for returning their Papa safely to them. Grandmama Edna prepared a large feast and invited all the clans to join in the celebration of Methuselah's miraculous return.

Stories spread regarding the world beyond the elevator. Selah told of wild hunter cats on the lookout for a quick meal, owls and hawks watching for food from above and coyotes hunting mice in packs. In fact, there were rumors that Methuselah was nearly eaten by a family of cats in a place called Cat Hill. Stories also circulated of fire breathing dragons with four wings and blue metallic armor. The young buck told about the unholy creatures from the Dragon Forest and that they lived deep within the Red Crystal Caves.

The many adventures of Methuselah were told throughout the clans until more and more mice began to question the Law of Isolation. The elders knew they needed to act quickly and so they forbade the clans to speak of Methuselah's adventures for fear others might follow his example. They arrested him in spite of the loud protests that followed. The elders had a trial and found him guilty of breaking the Law of Isolation, spreading lies and encouraging a clan rebellion. As punishment they banished Methuselah to the dungeons below the Orange Elevator for the safety of the clans.

No one was allowed to visit Methuselah and many years passed until the stories were forgotten by most. Even at the mention of his name, the elders denied his existence. Various rumours circulated about a crazy old man wandering about the elevator. Troy told me some of his friends had witnessed someone running up and down the shaft late at night meowing like a cat and screaming like a bat. He also heard some talk of strange sounds coming from a forbidden part of the basement when everyone was sleeping. Those who claimed to have seen him said he was very

old and had the Wisdom of Solomon. They claimed he had wild curly hair, a long grey beard and sparkling green eyes that seem to look into your soul. They said that he walked bent over and carried a large staff.

The truth was, Methuselah was very much alive and ventured outside the elevator on occasion. Then, without anyone knowing he would sneak back in, in the dead of night.

I want to let you in on a secret... Methuselah, Troy's Grandpapa, and Jessie's Papa still loved his family dearly and covertly watched over them from the shadows. He's never given up hope that one day he would be pardoned by the clan elders and allowed to reunite with his family.

VISITING SOCRATES

THE DAY AFTER TROY'S ANOINTING, METHUSELAH was invited to dinner at the house of Socrates the Seer. He left the elevator through a secret exit in the basement and travelled across Potter's field to visit his friend. It was a dangerous journey for any mouse, let alone one as old as he. Cat Hill was in the middle of his path and he had to skirt around their city hiding in the grass and keeping a sharp look out for The Hunters. These cats were trained by the city officials to gather food for the mayor and his household. They were all large tomcats chosen for their killer instincts.

Methuselah left early in the morning in hopes of arriving in time for dinner, but a large cat named Brutus who had smelled his scent delayed him. The feline wandered into Cat City one day after escaping an abusive giant owner. His grey hair was long and wild. He had large golden eyes and a black collar surrounded by numerous silver spikes.

Methuselah had caught the scent of his enemy and so instinctively stayed as still as possible. He readied his staff in case he had to defend himself. Cats were quite predictable, but they were fast and their sharp claws were always deadly.

Brutus crouched as low as possible, slithering through the grass like a snake heading towards its prey. He knew the cheese lover was close because his whiskers began to tingle somethin' fierce. Suddenly he saw a glimpse of the big-eared mouse, and growled with anticipation, "I've got you now, rodent."

Selah heard the cat and bolted underneath a large rock just as Brutus pounced a second later.

"Come out, come out, wherever you are," taunted Brutus, as he circled the rock over and over looking for a possible entrance. "I know you're in there my little sugar plum."

"I can stay in here all day, you overgrown fur-ball," answered Selah defiantly. He'd hoped his comment would show the cat how fruitless waiting for him would be, but it didn't work.

Brutus stuck his paw into a small opening he had found after digging a bit. "I want you now more than ever and it's only a matter of time until I you're mine mousy."

Selah noticed the paw blindly fishing around in the dark and he saw this as an opportunity to bait the large feline. Maybe if he could aggravate Brutus, he could keep him swiping blindly in the dark. "Hah, you're not even close, sunshine, or should I call you, Catnip?"

"My name is Brutus, cheese lover, not Catnip! Not that it makes any difference 'cause soon you'll be my breakfast." The cat continued digging frantically and then stuck his paw back into the hole hoping to snag the little creature with his sharp claws.

Methuselah said a quick prayer to his Creator and removed the large staff from behind his back. He reached into his backpack and pulled out a small fish hook. Selah attached it to one end of his staff and waited until Brutus's paw came close enough to snag it.

"Meoooww!" Brutus frantically tried to pull it out of the hole.

Selah hung on to the staff and quickly jammed it against the side of the opening. This made Brutus panic as he pulled harder and harder to get free, but the hook pushed deeper into his paw.

The wise old buck saw his opportunity and dashed out of a small hole under the rock. He took one last look at the poor tomcat rolling around in the dirt still trying to pull his paw out of the hole to no avail. He turned away and ran, knowing that eventually Brutus would figure it out. Once he calmed down and stopped pulling, the staff would naturally drop to the ground, allowing him to escape.

The rest of the journey was less traumatic for Methuselah. He loved the freedom of being outside the Orange Elevator and enjoyed the sunshine and the song of the birds. He loved adventure and walking through a field of grass in the crisp spring air.

HOME OF SOCRATES

FINALLY REACHING THE LARGE TREE WHERE HIS friend Socrates lived, Selah climbed up fifty feet or so and hopped on to the porch. He stood in front of the door for a while, then gave a hard knock.

"Socrates, are you there? It's your old friend, Methuselah."

The Seer of Salem heard the banging. "Selah, I'm so glad you could make it, my dear boy."

The wise owl opened the door and gave his friend a big hug.

"Good to finally see you, Old Chap," he said in his strong English accent. "Come in, come in, Selah. We have much to talk about. But first we'll sit, have a warm cup of tea and some biscuits and cheese. They both sat down on large chairs filled with hay from Potter's barn. "So you must tell me, how was your long journey to my humble abode, Selah? Hopefully it was uneventful. I do know how risky the travel from the elevator can be, even if one circles around Cat Hill. Hopefully those pesky Hunter Cats didn't bother you, my friend?"

Methuselah took a bite from his delicious biscuit and a long sip of tea before he spoke. He looked up with a smirk. "I did run into a rather large Hunter Cat by the name of Brutus. He was fast but not too bright I'm afraid. Hopefully, he has released himself from my staff's hook by now so that I can retrieve it on my way home." They both laughed as they took another sip of tea. "Other than that small incident, the walk through Potter's field was divine my friend. It is just so good to be free from the confines of the Orange Elevator. I don't think we were created to be isolated for too long. We become agitated and lose our sense of wonder and adventure. Don't you agree, my dear friend?"

The owl lifted his tea in agreement. "Quite, quite, my dear old buck. Life is far too short and time moves much too fast. The word that comes to mind is 'Carpe Diem.' We must all learn to 'seize the day,' Selah. It is rather unfortunate that your kind cannot as yet understand that to create an absolute law of isolation means that it can only be enforced temporarily. You see, all creatures were created to be social in nature and to explore our surroundings no matter what the risk. We all want to see what is beyond the known world."

Selah lowered his head and contemplated the wise words of his old friend.

They both finished their tea and Socrates took on a more serious tone. "I hear the Rafter Rats are beating the drums of war again and there is more unrest among all the creatures in the Orange Elevator. Is there a food shortage again, Selah?"

Methuselah looked intently at his old friend. "You have always been so perceptive, Socrates. The Creator has given you a great mind and you always use it to help others and make this world a better place." He stood up and paced the room with his front paws behind his back. "You are absolutely right, the clan's emergency storage bins are nearly empty and if we don't find enough food for all the creatures, war will come. I have scarcely enough food left for myself otherwise I would do what I could to help.

The Seer was concerned, and rubbed below his beak with the tip of his right wing.

"We will have to keep a close eye on this situation, my dear buck. This time of year has always been extremely difficult. The winters are long and cold and for some reason this year there were fewer grains left over. Do you have any idea where we could find enough food for a few weeks, Selah?"

The old buck tapped a paw on his lip, showing that he was in deep thought. "Have you checked Potter's barn and inside the giant's home, Socrates?"

The Seer shook his head. "Sadly, Old Chap, there is

nothing left in the barn. I'm sure king Og of the Loft Rats has taken every available food source for himself. Even the resources we used in the past have come up empty. Now, we do know the giants inside Potter's home will have food, however it is too risky to raid now, because the colder it gets the more time they spend inside."

"Right, you're absolutely right, old friend." Methuselah rubbed his paws together. "We must ask the Creator to help us find a solution and quickly."

"Yes, yes, I do agree, my dear boy. However, you have come to see me for another reason, Selah, have you not?" The Seer sat back down in his old chair and smiled.

"Yes, I do have a couple of important questions to ask you, sir." The old buck sat back down beside his friend. "As you are well aware, since my exile I have been watching and protecting my family from afar. I was in the shadows when my grandpups took their first steps and said their first words. I was there at Troy's birth, Socrates. I was even there when my little Troy was bullied on the way home from school and secretly protected him from being hurt by the Rafter Rats on many occasions. When Troy, together with his brothers and sisters, graduated from RAMS school, I was in the crowd disguised as a clan official. I know each grandpup's special gift and talent and yet they do not know I exist. Do you think it is time for me to defy the law and come out from isolation? Do you think it is time I let the pups know that I am their grandpapa?"

Socrates stood up and placed his hand on his long-time friend and confidant's shoulder. "Selah, I have known you for many years, dear boy. I am amazed at how you have not allowed the clans' imposed isolation hinder you from loving your family from afar. However, I do believe that it is time for you to play a greater role in the lives of those you love. You must reveal yourself to them as soon as the opportunity comes knocking. Your grandpups need you now more than ever, especially little Troy, he is going to need your wisdom, protection and support. You have so much you could teach him, Selah."

The old mouse began to cry. "Thank you, my friend. I feel more empowered and even excited to become acquainted with them. I will first find Troy and tell him who I am and then tell the others."

Socrates knew there was another question gnawing on his friend's heart. "Selah, you still seem full of questions. You can ask me anything, you know? I am your best friend, remember? Would you like another spot of tea?"

"You sometimes scare me with your amazing gift of discernment, you Old Hoot." He held out his cup to be filled. "Forgive me if I am being intrusive, but you know how I find ways to be involved with the lives of my family. Anyway, I noticed that you went to Jesse and Evette's home and anointed little Troy with oil. I also observed that you believe the Creator has chosen him to be king and bring peace to all the creatures of the elevator. I am curious, though, why did you choose Troy? He is such a sensitive pup and has many challenges to overcome, as you know. Kingship is a heavy mantle to place on one so small and vulnerable, don't you agree?"

Socrates smiled at the old mouse; his blue eyes twinkled with glee as if he was about to share a great secret.

"I saw a Watcher, Selah, I saw a real Watcher from the Great Creator Himself. He came to me just before I went to see Troy and his family. Jesse just wanted me to come and bless their son and ask the Creator to protect him despite his many disabilities. I anointed Troy with oil and prophesied over him because that is what the Watcher commanded me to do. He told me Troy was chosen to bring order and justice to the clans and all the creatures in the Orange Elevator. He told me Troy would be mighty. The Watcher said the Logos chose Troy because he is weak in the world's eyes. Since he has nothing in this world, he will be more faithful in his service to Logos."

Selah shook his head in protest. "Still, Socrates, Troy is so small and vulnerable. The evil world will eat him up, literally!"

The owl lay back in his big chair. "My friend, I learned many years ago that much is expected from those who've been given much and nothing is expected from those who've been given little. Yet, why is it that those with nothing always seem to give the most? Why does the Great Creator always choose the weak to do the work of the strong? Tell me, Selah, why does the Logos choose the last to be first and the first to be last? The Creator will show His power through this tiny, seemingly insignificant, little mouse that has a pure heart and a just soul. This is why, after the anointing, the Spirit came upon Troy in a powerful way and why he will be known in all the land as "Mighty Troy of Salem."

That evening, Methuselah journeyed back to the dungeons of the Orange Elevator and marvelled at what he had just heard. He vowed to keep all these things in his heart and to be reunited with his family—soon.

CHAPTER 6

RAMS: TRIPPIN' TRAPS

THERE IS A THEORY THAT LARGE

FAMILIES ARE LIKE BIG DREAMS.

THEY USUALLY BEGIN WITH GREAT

EXPECTATIONS BUT END UP CARRYING US

THROUGH UNPRECEDENTED JOURNEYS.

TROY WAS THE YOUNGEST OF EIGHT BROTHERS AND five sisters and he had big dreams.

Each of the newborn pups had unique personalities, gifts, powers and abilities, all of which would be used to their fullest potential in the future. When Troy came into the world, he appeared to have more disabilities than abilities, more problems than solutions and more sorrows than joy. Those around him thought his future didn't look promising. Yet, there is a saying, if you dig a little deeper behind the flesh of an ordinary oyster, you just might find a pearl of great price.

The eight male pups born to Jesse and Evette Durum were: Elijah the Risk Taker, Joseph the Strong One, followed by Samuel the Sneak, James the Wise One, Joab the Fighter, Judah the Builder, Jacob the Flash, Shaun the Gentle Giant and, of course, 15 minutes later Mighty Troy of Salem.

Troy was also preceded by five beautiful sisters who were known throughout the Orange Elevator as wild, fearless experts in the art of war and strategy. The first-born was Frey the Lover of Freedom, then Ava the Fearless, Olivia the Leader, Evalyn the Planner, and Tammy the Jumping Bean.

The Durum brothers and sisters developed a close bond over time and used their weapons to fight as individuals and as a unit. They all graduated with honours at the Royal Academy of Mouse Survival (RAMS).

Troy's Family Life

As Troy grew up with his large family, they all encouraged him to overcome his disabilities, except for his brother, Samuel. Samuel would constantly tease Troy about what he couldn't do, which made Troy focus on his disabilities and not his gifts.

Samuel would sneak up on Troy's blind side and yell, "Troy Durum is a little blind bat, a little blind bat that'll be eaten by a rat. A Rafter Rat, a Rafter Rat, Troy will be eaten by a Rafter Rat, ha, ha, ha." There were times when he even made fun of Troy in front of his friends. Samuel would call Troy "elephant ears" or mock his big feet by pretending he was a kangaroo. On these days Troy would go to bed early and cry himself to sleep.

Troy always knew he was different from his siblings, yet he never imagined those differences would one day become his greatest assets. Troy would soon discover that his ears were more highly tuned than others'. His lack of sight was compensated by his extraordinary sense of hearing. If he focused intently on a particular sound, he could even hear the whistle from a rat's nose, a cat purring in another room, or a fly buzzing on the third floor.

Tammy the Jumping Bean was not only Troy's older sister but also his best friend. They were close to the same size and did everything together. They walked to school together, played in the flour bin together, and even hunted ants together. Yet, there were a few things that Troy did not like doing with his sister Tammy like playing hide-and-go-seek and tag. She would always disappear like magic and he could never find her. Playing tag with her was like playing the loneliest game ever, so they usually went back to hunting ants.

ROYAL ACADEMY OF MOUSE SURVIVAL (RAMS)

RAMS HAD EXISTED IN THE ORANGE ELEVATOR FOR as long as anyone could remember. The school motto was "Survive and Thrive."

Every young pup went to RAMS. Here they learned to hone and develop their special abilities and avoid dangers of every kind. Pups went to school every day for two long years, learning basic defensive and offensive fighting skills to use against their predators. They were taught how to outwit a Rafter Rat, avoid being detected by an Orange Bat and outrun any cat. They learned how to avoid human traps and render them useless by tripping them using a variety of methods. There was even a class on detecting poisons, black boxes and sticky tapes.

When the new school year began, all 14 of Jesse and Evette's pups were eager to learn from the clan's best and brightest educators. Troy didn't sleep very well the night before the first day of school. He was way too excited to begin his new adventure. He was looking forward to learning all he could about the world around him and how to protect his family and those he loved.

The Durum's breakfast bell finally rang along with his Papa's voice.

"Come get it while it's hot! We can't be late for the first day of school, my precious pups!"

Troy could almost taste the old cheese and freshly warm oats as the aroma wafted up the stairs and into the pups' bedrooms.

After getting dressed and cleaning themselves, they were told to place their school supplies in the backpacks Papa had placed at the foot of each bed. Samuel and Olivia were the first to rush downstairs and into the arms of Mama Evette.

Hardly able to contain her excitement, Olivia exclaimed, "I can't wait for school, mama!"

"I just hope it won't be boring and the teachers aren't too mean," complained Samuel. "My friend Ham says that Postmaster Piggly is teaching a class on how to run a small business and that it's a snore."

"And I heard from my friend Annabelle that one of the elders actually spanks his students for just looking at him the wrong way," whined Olivia as she looked at mama with a frown.

Evette stopped stirring the oats simmering on the stove. She bent down and placed her hands on their shoulders, "I wouldn't worry too much about what you've heard, my loves, just mind your manners, respect your elders and you'll be fine."

Before Evette finished talking, the rest of the pups bounded down the stairs accidentally tripping over Troy. He rolled the rest of the way down and landed with a thud at the bottom, his school supplies scattered all over the floor.

"Hey, hey, hey! Be more careful, my little munchkins," scolded Jesse as he picked Troy up and brushed him off.

"Are you okay, Troy?" Papa asked, the fur above his nose wrinkling.

"I'm all right, Papa!" answered Troy as he picked up his supplies and put them away in his new backpack. "What's for breakfast? I'm starving!"

Everyone laughed as they sat down to eat. Papa Jesse bowed his head and prayed a blessing over the food and for the protection of his pups.

When they were finished eating, Evette handed each pup a bagged lunch and kissed their cheeks.

"Bye, Mama and Papa!" they chorused as they ran off to RAMS, which was located in the wood room on level two.

When they finally arrived at school, the headmaster divided them into various classes. Frey, Ava and Olivia went into class number two where they learned about poisons. Shaun, Samuel, Elijah and Joseph were in class three where they studied how to evade giants. James, Joab and Judah were not too pleased to be in Mr. Piggly's small business class.

Troy, Jacob, Evalyn and Tammy all held paws as they entered the RAMS main hall. They were in the first class learning about various traps. All four siblings sat down beside each other and waited for the lesson to begin.

CLASS #1 AVOIDING DEADLY TRAPS

THEIR TEACHER WAS AN EXPERT IN MOUSETRAPS OF all kinds. As the bell rang to begin classes she tried to get the students attention. "Young bucks and does, may I please have your attention. My name is Miss Von Trap."

A few bucks in the back row snickered as their teacher

turned and wrote her name on the chalkboard. She turned around and looked directly at the naughty bucks.

"This morning, I will show you ways to avoid, disable, or in some cases totally destroy a trap. Receiving a passing grade in this class will save your life and possibly those around you." She looked up and pointed to the bucks who snickered in the back row, "and a failing grade could very well be your demise."

Miss Von Trap wrote the names of the most common mousetraps on the blackboard.

"Students, today we are going to look at the snap or bar trap, however there are many more. Other examples are the electric trap and the sticky trap."

SNAP TRAP TRIPPING

"NOW THEN, LET'S BEGIN LEARNING ABOUT OUR first trap shall we?" She turned and wrote SNAP TRAP in large letters on the blackboard. "How many of you have seen or heard of this particular trap?" A few hands went up. "Who would like to tell me what this trap is and how it works?" Troy's hand shot up first eager to show his teacher what he knew. "Yes, you in the back"—she pointed to little Troy—"give us your name and stand up when you speak."

Troy stood, his chin tilted up proudly. "My name is Troy Durum. The snap trap is usually made of wood and metal. It has a bar in the shape of a square coming out of a tightly wound spring. This is attached to a rectangular wooden base with a food platter nailed to it at the front. There is an arm with a hook loosely attached to the spring. Bait is

The snap trap is the oldest and most common of all mouse traps

carefully placed on to the plate and the bar is pulled back. The arm is hooked into the front food plate and it's locked and loaded. A mouse comes to eat the bait, the arm is released and snap, the head is caught in the trap and the poor mouse is dead." Troy smiled and sat down.

"That was a very good description, Troy, thank you," praised Miss Von Trap, then she continued her lesson. "Bucks and does, the snap trap is the oldest and most common of all mouse traps. Statistics say that this type of trap has taken the lives of more of our relatives than any other snare the giants have made." There were gasps and the occasional cry from her young students. "This is why I am here, my little pups. Listen closely to each lesson, put them into practice and your chances of survival will improve greatly.

"Now, let me show you some methods of tripping a snap trap. If there is only one trap, disabling it can be quite simple. First, you must find a large heavy object like a rock or a long stick. Next, throw the object onto the food plate or tap it with the stick and snap, it's rendered harmless. Then go and retrieve your free food.

"If you find two or more traps in a row, disabling can become more difficult. The method used to trip consecutive traps is called 'the jumping method.'"

She waved a paw at the two large traps at the front of the room loaded and ready to go. "To trip these traps you must run directly towards the front." She sprang off her hind paws sprinted, instructing as she went. "You must hop over the food tray—like this." She cleared half the trap and landed on the trigger arm. The trap snapped and fell harmlessly to the floor. Without missing a beat, she then jumped on the trigger arm of the second trap. It also snapped, as she landed safely to the side.

All the pups hopped up and down cheering and clapping with glee as their teacher took a bow. When the accolades died down she asked her aid Henry, a rather large buck, to reset the trap. She turned to her students and asked for a volunteer.

Jacob eagerly put his paw up. "I will! I will!"

Miss Von Trap pointed to Jacob. "Are you fast, little pup?"

"Yes, ma'am, I am. My Papa says I'm the fastest pup this side of Salem. In fact, they call me Jacob the Flash."

"Swell, young buck," she responded, as she clapped her paws, "then come up here and show us how it's done."

Jacob ran to the front, overjoyed at the opportunity to show his friends what he could do.

"Be careful, Jacob! I know you are fast but this is a live trap," warned Troy. "I don't wanna tell Mama that we had an accident on your first day of school."

Their teacher smiled. "Don't worry, pups, this trap is loud when it snaps, but it's not powerful enough to hurt anyone." Then she turned back to Jacob. "Are you ready to do this, Flash?"

Before she even finished asking the question Jacob had already tripped the first trap, which snapped, then the second and stood beside her with his arms crossed.

His teacher just looked at him, mouth slightly open and nose twitching. "Wow! That was fast! Where did you learn how to do that Jacob?"

"Oh, that's nothin', Miss Von Trap," Tammy bragged, as she hopped on her feet in a kind of vibrating rhythm.

"Jacob the Flash tripped two live traps in a row one day as we explored the caves down in the dungeon."

Miss Von Trap rested her paws on her hips and looked at Jacob. "Do you think you could do three in a row, my speedy little pup? That's the clan record, you know? No one has done it again for many years and so the record still holds."

Before Jacob could answer, Troy broke into the conversation. "Miss Von Trapp, who currently holds that record?"

"Actually, Troy, it's me. I still hold the record of tripping three traps in a row," she responded with pride, the fur on her chest puffing out slightly. "I did it when I was a young pup like you. The clan was so impressed that they called me when they needed someone to trip traps that were set in the tunnels they were working on. In fact, that is how I became to be known as 'Von Trap.'"

All the pups laughed until she turned her attention back to Jacob. "Well, little pup, are you willing to try for three and tie my record?"

Jacob smiled the biggest smile. "Actually, ma'am, do you think I could try to beat your record and trip four, and do it in under three seconds?"

Everyone cheered and began to chant, "Go, Flash. Go, Flash. Go, Flash."

"All right, all right," Miss Von Trap waved her paws in the air to regain control of the excited pups. "Quiet down now. Quiet down, my eager pups." Then turning back to Jacob with concern, she bent down and looked into his eyes. "Are you sure you want to try this? The dummy traps are not deadly, however tripping four at once is dangerous and could injure you if something went wrong."

Jacob just looked back at her, grinned and motioned to the teacher's aide. "Load 'em up, Mr. Henry, sir."

The class stood as one and began to cheer. Young Jacob bent down in a racing stance and said a quick prayer to the Great Creator as the large assistant loaded all four traps. He arranged them in a row, set the timer and said, "Ready when you are, Jacob the Flash." He stepped back and leaned against the wall to watch the show.

Jacob closed his eyes, opened them again and with a stare of determination, took off. He arrived at the first trap, jumped in the air and landed on the loaded arm. He ducked, snap, dashed to the next, snap, snap, snap. He landed after a perfect somersault at Henry's feet.

The large teacher's aide picked Jacob up and held him in the air for all to see. "Bucks and does, may I present to you our new snap trap tripping champion and record holder, Jacob the Flash!" The class erupted in cheers and foot thumping as Henry continued, "This young buck has successfully tripped four consecutive traps in a record time of two point nine five seconds."

More cheering came from Jacob's classmates as he ran into Miss Von Trap's arms.

"Did you see that, teacher? I did it! I did it!" exclaimed Jacob as his whiskers twitched with excitement.

"Why, yes I saw you," answered his teacher, "and I am so proud of you. You are the new record holder, Jacob." She put him down and he ran to Troy and Tammy.

"Four in a row, Troy! I tripped four snap traps in a row. Can you believe it? I honestly didn't think I would make the last one, cause I slipped on the bar of trap number three."

"That's okay, Jacob," answered Troy as he adjusted the rag patch over his eye to a more comfortable position, "you're a legend now and I'm so proud you're my brother." Troy, Tammy and Evalyn hugged Jacob as the bell rang to end their first day of school.

In the next few months Miss Von Trap would teach them all to become experts at disabling traps of every kind.

Professor Venom knew his poisons.

CHAPTER 7

RAMS: POISONS AND EVASIONS

EDUCATION IS A POWERFUL TOOL WHEN

USED TO BETTER ONESELF AND IMPROVE

THE SOCIETY IN WHICH WE LIVE.

YET IT IS MOST BENEFICIAL WHEN

KNOWLEDGE AND TRADITION ARE

PASSED DOWN FROM GENERATION TO

GENERATION.

TRAP COURSE GRADUATION

SIX MONTHS LATER, TROY, TAMMY, AND JACOB GRAD-uated with honours from Miss Von Trap's course. The mice became experts on how to trip every kind of snap-trap the giants created. They even learned how to unstick or cover the dreaded glue trays and sticky tape. Their teacher was so proud when Troy came up with a new method of completely disabling sticky tape with just a thin piece of wood. He placed a portion of the wood onto the sticky tape, leaving a small piece to use as a handle. As the wood stuck to the paper, Troy kept flipping it over until he could roll it up like a scroll, rendering the tape useless.

For that new invention he received the official RAMS "Certificate of Invention" signed by Dean Winchester himself. The day Troy brought the award home to show his Mama, and Papa was the first time he actually believed the Great Creator might have a plan for him. Still, his early successes in life did not mean growing up with disabilities was easy. Troy believed that if he worked harder than everyone else, his classmates would overlook what he couldn't do, but he was still bullied every day. The Durums would fiercely protect their little brother, but soon learned Troy could hold his own in a war of words or during a fight. The bullies usually waited until Troy was somewhere alone, but they would make it look like an accident. Troy would walk down the hall with his arms full of books and four large young bucks would come towards him. They would "accidentally" bump him, knocking the books to the floor. Yet, even in those situations Troy would always try to make peace first and only fought back in self-defence.

DISCOVERING BUBBLE GUM

EVERY MORNING THE YOUNG DURUMS WENT TO school together. Along the way they would share jokes and play with the interesting objects they found lying on the floor. One day while on their way to class, Samuel discovered something that looked like a strange pink blob. It was kinda sticky to the touch and yet it smelled so divine. Sam didn't dare taste it because he was still suspicious, so he decided to circle it a few times, sniffing it along the way.

"Hey, what did you find there, Sam?" asked Ava, who was always curious.

"I don't know, but it sure smells good. There's a picture beside it showing a giant swinging a big wooden club, and it says O-Pee-Chee on the package. Hey, maybe it's some new kind of food for the giants." He got closer and gave it a quick lick.

"No, Samuel! Don't lick it," warned Ava. "It could be poison. You should let Troy smell it. His nose can pick out any toxin from the other end of the room."

Samuel placed his hands on his hips. "Troy's not the only one with a good sense of smell you know. I can sniff out cheese even if it's in the dungeons below. Besides, why is Troy always chosen as the one with the greatest gifts, I mean, he can't even see straight."

Tammy jumped up and down as she came to Troy's defence. "Samuel Durum! You know that mama doesn't approve of us pointing out the things Troy cannot do. Now say you're sorry and speak to him with words of encouragement." She stopped scolding her brother and tried to encourage him. "Sam, you may not be able to smell as well as Troy, yet when I lose something I would always ask you to help me find it. There is no one better at sleuthing than you."

Samuel smiled at Tammy and looked down. "Sorry, Troy, wanna give this sticky ol' rock a sniff? I'll bet it smells real good to your super nose. Oh, and while you're at it, bro, could you make sure there is no poison on it?"

Troy came over to his brother and hugged him. "Swell, let's check this thing out, Sam." He ran over to the pink blob, took a big whiff and grinned. "You were right, Sam, there's no poison on this food and it smells very sweet." He bent down and began to pull off a piece, but it stretched and stretched until suddenly—snap! It came loose and Troy was on the floor holding a sticky mess.

Everyone laughed as Troy got up, put a small piece in his mouth and began to chew. They watched as he kept on chewing and chewing.

"Hey, this stuff is a blast," he said as bubbles began to come out of his mouth. "I can't swallow this food, but the flavour doesn't stop and it's so much fun to chew. C'mon, guys, dig in!" Troy's invitation was all they needed to dive in and take a piece of this heavenly bubble food that lasted forever.

The Durums went into their classes that morning chewing loudly and blowing bubbles. It didn't take long to be surrounded by their friends who asked them where they found this magical food. The Durums passed out pieces to anyone that asked.

Class #2 Poisons

Tammy, Troy and Jacob and Evalyn went into their first class on detecting poisons. Their new teacher greeted them as they entered the room smacking their bit of sweet pink blob loudly.

Professor Venom knew his poisons. He knew everything there was about the black box, cyanide, pellets, and sprays. They all had one thing in common—death. Mouse lore said the professor got his name after surviving a deadly bite from a poisonous snake. After his brush with death he spent time studying poisons of every kind. His lessons became invaluable to the mouse clans of Salem and everyone wanted him to teach their young pups what he knew. He had categorized each poison by its particular odour and collected pictures of every bait created by the giants.

His students found their seats and waited for class to begin.

Professor Venom sat in his chair slowly tapping the yardstick on his hand. He rubbed his chin and crunched his fur between his eyes. Finally he stood, and slammed the yardstick on the desk—crack!

"What is that incessant noise? You know it is forbidden to eat during class time. And why are you all chewing at the same time?"

One of the school bullies pointed at Troy. "It was the Durum freak with one eye. He told us that his brother found the strange food that makes bubbles and then shared it with everyone before class."

Tammy jumped out of her seat and landed right beside the bully's desk. "You need to apologize to Troy, right now, Steven Spelt. He may only have one eye, but he could spot danger long before you would know it's there."

Professor Venom's forehead wrinkled and his eyebrows rose as he approached the bully. "Master Steven, we do not name call or belittle our schoolmates in my classroom. Is that clear? Now apologize to Troy so that we can get on with our lesson."

"Yes sir." Steven got up from his seat, went over to Troy and held out his hand. "I am sorry, Troy. Your eye cover is actually pretty cool." The young buck smiled at his teacher and went back to his seat.

Dr. Venom grabbed the garbage pail from beside his desk and gave it to Troy. "All right Mr. Durum, since you began this chewing fad you will have to end it. Go between the isles and have everyone spit the pink bubble chew into the bucket." Without waiting for Troy, Dr. Venom turned around and began to write the word "Cyanide" on the blackboard. After each of his classmates deposited their treat, Troy placed the bucket beside his teacher and went back to his seat.

"All right," began Dr. Venom, "Today, we are examining a poison known as cyanide. This deadly toxin can be placed onto any food and liquid. To some it can be odourless and tasteless but to others it smells like burnt almonds." The professor held up a bottle of liquid. "Now, my young pups, you might ask, 'Professor Venom, is it possible to accurately detect and safely avoid poisons?' First, you must be aware the Great Creator has built amazing poison detectors into our bodies. He has given us an extra sensitive nose that is capable of smelling untainted food at great distances but this is not all. We have sensitive whiskers, which are more commonly used to navigate around the elevator, to assist in detecting poisons. Any questions so far?"

Evalyn's hand shot up as if she could hardly wait to gain this knowledge.

The professor smiled and pointed his finger at the raised hand. "Yes, Miss Evalyn, did you have a question?"

Evalyn was thrilled Dr. Venom had noticed her and stood beside her desk. "I did, Professor Venom. I heard from my Papa that all mice have an extra odour detecting organ or a second nose. Is that true? And if so, can it be used to help us detect poisons?"

"Wow! Evalyn, that is a great question. The answer is, yes. It is true. This special organ is actually located deep inside the nasal cavity and is able to detect the personal smell of other mice among other things. Yet, I also believe we can learn to use it to discover who has touched the food, a giant or another mouse. As you already know, if a giant's scent is on the food, do not, under any circumstances, go near it."

Tammy's hand shot up.

"Yes, young doe," acknowledged Dr. Venom. "Tell us your name and your question?"

"My name is, Tammy Durum." Her feet began to tap on the floor faster and faster. "My brother, Troy, has an amazing sense of smell and when my brother Samuel found the pink chewing food, it had a giant's smell, and yet he didn't detect poison. Is it okay to eat food the giant has touched if we know it is safe?"

"My dear, I'm so glad you brought this up because I was

going to mention it later." The professor placed his hands on his hips. "It is always a risk to take food that has been left by a giant. Even if it smells heavenly, you must avoid the temptation at all costs. It still may have been a trap."

Dr. Venom addressed Troy. "Tell me, young buck, what if you made a mistake? What if there had been a new kind of poison you were unable to detect? You may have killed yourself, your siblings and many students in this class. No matter how sensitive your nose is, Troy, a giant's scent is always dangerous. My Grandpapa had this saying:

If you do smell a giant he can't be too far.
He may very well smell you and know where you are.
So run from his scent, turn away from his lure,
or you will be caught in his trap that's for sure.

Troy slowly put his hand up half way. "I mean no disrespect, sir, but what if the giants are nice. What if they mean us no harm? Does not the Creator love all of His creatures? Is it not possible for us to all live in peace?"

Dr. Venom looked at Troy as if he had just made the most sacrilegious statement ever. "What? Troy, the giants have always been our greatest enemies and they want nothing more than to destroy us completely. To them we are nothing more than pests. They will kill you and me the first chance they get!"

Troy looked a little puzzled and cocked his head to one side. "But, sir, what about the passage in the Book of Truth that commands us to '...love our neighbour as ourselves.' Are not the giants our neighbours? Maybe, if we loved

them, they would love us."

"Nonsense, my young buck, nonsense!" replied the professor. "The giants will never love us. Just as the Rafter Rats will always hate us. Just as their king, Goar, will always enslave the mouse clans and worship their false god Dreck. And what about the Orange Bats, do you think they will someday love us as their neighbours as well? Do you think they will miraculously stop hunting us?" Dr. Venom finished answering Troy just as the bell rang to end the class.

Tammy and Jacob went and stood beside Troy's desk. "Don't worry about ol' Doc Venom, Troy. He doesn't know about your anointing and your special gift of love the Creator has given you. If anyone can bring peace to the Orange Elevator it's you." Tammy grabbed both her brother's paws and changed the subject. "C'mon, guys, let's go up to the sifting machine and catch some ants. I'm starving." They said good-bye to Dr. Venom and ran outside arm in arm.

As they headed for the sifting room, Troy couldn't help thinking about what the professor had said regarding the creatures in the elevator. "Maybe he is right." Said Troy to himself, "maybe there is no hope of peace in a violent world." Yet, in his heart Troy knew someday he would find a way to make friends with the giants. Someday he must bring all creatures together in a common bond of love.

ZIGZAG REVERSE SURPRISE

IN THE MONTHS THAT FOLLOWED, THE DURUMS learned how to detect and avoid poisons of every kind. They learned many evasion strategies that would be effective during a giant's pursuit. They learned how to stay clear of a cat's dangerous claws. They were taught how to stop moving when chased by an Orange Bat so the bat could not hone in on their location. They even learned how to outsmart a Rafter Rat by using their size against them.

After one of his classes Troy invented a unique method of evasion called "The Zigzag Reverse Surprise." This technique was useful for evading giants, Rafter Rats, Orange Bats and even most cats. Troy actually discovered it by accident one day while they were practising Dr. Venom's favourite Zigzag evasion method.

Jacob was paired together with Troy and because of his brother's amazing speed Troy was easily caught even when he zigzagged as often as he could. Nothing seemed to work until one time Jacob caught the edge of Troy's foot and it accidentally flipped him over so Troy just kept zigzagging and zoomed underneath Jacob's legs. He suddenly stopped and turned around to see where Jacob had gone and realized he was going in the opposite direction. Troy had evaded his brother even when he couldn't out run him. This gave him an idea. He asked Jacob to chase him once again as fast as he could. They began a yard apart.

"Ready or not, here I come." Troy ran as fast as his little legs could carry him zigzagging as he was taught. Just as he could hear Jacob nearly upon him he did a back flip and reversed his direction and then continued zigzagging. He went in the opposite direction, underneath Jacob's legs and was free. From that time on Dr. Venom would teach what would be known as "Troy's Universal Method of Evasion" (TUME) aka "The Zigzag Reverse Surprise."

That evening Troy came home with yet another RAMS certificate recognizing his new technique, which was signed by Dean Winchester himself. The whole family celebrated Troy's success, except his brother Samuel. He told everyone he wasn't feeling well and went to bed early. The real reason was because he was jealous that his "freak of a brother" always received the attention and awards.

After the Durum pups graduated from RAMS they were officially recognized as young adults. It was late winter and the clans were running out of food so the school year ended with the elders strictly rationing the grains left in the storage bins on level four.

The sword has amazing power for those chosen by the Creator.

CHAPTER 8

GOLD SWORD OF JUSTICE

SURVIVAL CAN BE RATHER IRONIC.

ON THE ONE HAND ALL LIVING THINGS

NEED NOURISHMENT TO SURVIVE AND YET

ALL NOURISHMENT COMES FROM LIVING

THINGS. STILL, NOT ALL NOURISHMENT

IS PHYSICAL IN NATURE. CREATURES NEED

SOUL FOOD — JOY AND HOPE

FOR THE FUTURE.

ROY SHARED WITH ME THE amazing story of how he received his papa's gold sword of justice, but first we had a great discussion regarding a creature's need to survive.

Troy sat on my worktable eating a piece of chocolate I had given him.

"When food is scarce, Mr. Wolfe, all creatures are in panic mode. I find survival to be rather ironic, don't you? On the one hand, all living things need nourishment to survive and yet all nourishment comes from living things."

"This is very true, my friend." I poured him a small bowl of water and continued, "Yet, we must always remember where the source of our nourishment comes from. All things are from the Great Creator. The Book of Truth says, 'He gives food to every creature. His love endures forever.'"

Troy smiled at my statement of faith and added, "I have also learned that not all nourishment is physical in nature, Mr. Wolfe. Creatures also need food for their soul—joy and hope for the future. The Book of Truth says to not worry about your life, what you will eat or drink; or about your body, what you will wear. Is life not more than food, and the body more than clothes?"

I was so proud of Troy and couldn't believe how much he had grown in his faith since the last time we met. "You're right, Troy. It is called trust. We must learn to trust the Logos to provide for us. So, how did your family come up with the idea to steal my oats? The Great Creator would surely not approve of theft, would He?"

The young buck laughed as he scarfed down another piece of chocolate. "To be honest, Mr. Wolfe, I'm ashamed we did not trust the Creator to take care of us. I guess we thought that desperate times called for desperate measures."

Troy sat down with his legs crossed and told me how his family came up with The Oats Mission.

"Well, Mr. Wolfe, it began, like many family discussions do, around the kitchen table. We discussed some possible solutions to the current food crisis. The winter storage supply had nearly run out again and so the clans were beginning to panic. The last thing they wanted was another clan war to break out in the Orange Elevator.

THE OATS MISSION

"I HAVE AN IDEA," EVALYN THE PLANNER SUGGESTED. "What if I assemble a search party to venture outside the elevator. They could look for spilled wheat kernels around the base of the building and between the steel tracks?

"Good thought, Evalyn. There actually may be food in that area, but venturing outside the elevator would be in direct violation of the elder's isolation law," stated Mama Evette.

"But these are extenuating circumstances, Mama," objected Evalyn. "Everyone needs food and as you know I can be quite convincing." The rest of the pups cheered loudly in agreement with their sister's great idea.

"Quiet, quiet down, my little munchkins," interrupted

Jesse. "There may be another solution to this problem. Last week, I was in the storage shed attached to the office and discovered a large bag of fresh oats on the second shelf. Why don't we send our boys on a mission to retrieve those oats? They can strap on their burlap backpacks and carefully make their way to the lunchroom before the giant comes to work in the morning. When they return we can distribute the food to the clans in the emergency storage room on level four.

"I don't like that plan, sweetheart," responded Evette in a worried tone, the fur bunching above her nose. "Don't you think the little bucks are too young for such a dangerous mission?"

"They are quite young, my love," agreed Jesse, "however, I strongly believe the Creator wants them to accomplish this mission. He will be with them, Evette."

Evalyn's eyes brightened at the possible need for her organizational skills. "Papa, what if my sisters and I go on our very own mission. We could notify the clans and plan a time for them to pick up their share of oats."

"That's the spirit, my girl," praised Jesse. "You are such a great planner, Evalyn. That bag of oats will tide all of us over until the wheat begins to flow again."

Troy was the first to respond. "We'll do it, Papa! May I bring my toy sword? You never know when it might come in handy."

"How can a one-eyed baby mouse use a sword?" mocked Samuel. "You'll probably stab yourself before we even get to the oats."

"Stop it, Samuel," scolded Tammy, jumping up and

down in protest. "If you have nothing nice to say, don't say anything at all. Mama, Samuel's always so mean to Troy. Make him stop."

Evette turned to face her son. "Samuel, say sorry to your brother. You know he has many gifts that far outshine his weaknesses and someday you may have to depend on him to get you out of trouble."

Samuel hung his head in feigned shame. "Yes, Mama. I'm sorry, Troy." He looked at his little brother so that Evette couldn't see him and promptly stuck out his tongue.

THE SWORD AND SHIELD

JESSE REACHED INTO HIS GOLD VEST POCKET AND pulled out an old key. He scurried over to the dining room.

"Bucks, come over here and help your papa move this old china cupboard."

When it was finally moved away, they noticed a large a hole in the wall. Jesse carefully bent down and pulled out an old chest with brass hinges and a padlock at the centre. Papa carefully placed the brass key into the lock and turned it to the right. The lock popped open with a loud click. Jesse slowly opened it, reached in and pulled out a bright red blanket. He placed it on the table and looked up. "Now this, my dears, was entrusted to me by your grandmama Edna. It belonged to your grandpapa who died many years ago." Jesse unwrapped the blanket to reveal a gold sword and a large brass shield.

The pups' eyes were as big as saucers. "Cool!" they exclaimed in unison.

"How did Grandpapa get the sword, sir?" asked Troy with excitement. "And why is it glowing?"

"Well," answered Jesse, "papa found it in the basement. It appeared to have fallen from an old plaque, which was made to commemorate the construction of the Orange Elevator. As he lifted it from the floor, he found it was light as a feather and began to glow. The sword has amazing power for those chosen by the Creator.

"Do you know the last time I used this sword?" He asked his pups. "I was standing guard outside our home while your mama was giving birth. It was a cold night and I was on my way in to fetch a warm blanket, when Dr. Agrarian suddenly appeared at the door. He handed me one of my beautiful pups. I'm still not sure who it was, however, I thought it might have been Jacob because his legs never stopped kicking. I remember my heart filled with joy as I held him to my chest. Suddenly, I heard the faint sound of leather wings coming closer and closer. I quickly handed Jacob to the Doc and told him to get him inside. He brought him to safety just before an Orange Bat nearly snagged him. I swung the gold sword of justice at the beast and struck him twice. I never saw him again."

"Wow," exclaimed Samuel, as his paws touched his cheeks, "if I had that sword no one would ever want to mess with me."

"Now, now, Sam, the sword cannot be used for personal gain," Papa explained. "In fact, only the one who is chosen may use its powers."

Samuel stepped forward. "Papa, give it to me. Maybe I'm the chosen one."

"Okay, son, hold out your hands." Papa gently placed the gold sword in Samuel's hands, but it was too heavy and fell to the floor.

"Why doesn't this stupid thing work for me, Papa? I'm a good mouse and I love the Great Creator."

Mama placed her arms around her son. "And He loves you as well, Samuel, but He is the one who chooses those who will serve His purpose. It is not for us to know all things but to follow Him in full obedience."

Olivia cocked her head to one side and traced her finger inside the strange letters carved on the front of the shield. "What about the shield, where did Grandpapa get it? Oh, and what does 'L-e-v-i' mean?"

Jesse looked up and smiled at his daughter. "Good question, my little princess. My mama said she wasn't sure where he found the shield. When the clans told her Papa had died they brought her all his things and one of them was the shield. It must have belonged to someone named Levi because his name is carved on the front."

Jesse picked up the gold sword and held it with both hands in front of him. "Troy, I want you to come forward and try to take the sword, my son."

"What?" Samuel looked down at his tiny brother. "If I can't even lift the sword, how in the world is Troy going to do it?"

Tammy had been quiet this whole time, but couldn't take it anymore. "Samuel, are you saying that our Creator wouldn't choose Troy? Are you saying that He wouldn't use a mouse with disabilities for His will and purpose?"

Troy hung his head. "Samuel's right, Papa. I could never

hold that sword. I'm too small and I do have a little trouble seeing everything."

"Nonsense, Troy," answered Mama, "The Creator loves to use our weakness to reveal His power. In fact, He says, 'My grace is all you need. My power works best in weakness.'"

Papa smiled and held out the sword once again. "Troy, come forward and hold your head high, my son."

James snickered as his little brother came forward to take the gold sword from his Papa. Troy glanced back and forth at his siblings and reached out his paws with apprehension. Even before it touched his paws the sword began to vibrate and glow.

"It's so light," exclaimed Troy as he wielded the weapon around in a full arch with ease. "Wow, this is fun." He stopped and looked at the glowing sword and listened to the noise emanating from it. "Does this mean I'm chosen, Papa?" Everyone stood there with their mouths open, awestruck with wonder in witnessing the Creator's power working through their little brother.

Jesse was proud of Troy and remembered the Old Seer's prophecy. "My dear children, it is time that you all know why I believe the Creator has chosen Troy to lead the Oats Mission. You must know that we were worried about Troy when he was born, so we decided to ask Postmaster Piggly to send a message to Socrates the Seer who lives in Potter's barn.

"The Seer anointed your brother with oil and blessed him. This is why Troy must lead the Oats Mission. He has a heart after the Logos' heart and will one day unite the entire elevator."

His little mousekins gasped and doubted they would ever be friends with the Rafter Rats. Surely those pagan rodents would never leave their false god Dreck and follow the Creator of all things.

Jesse continued to explain why Troy is so special. "The Creator has chosen Troy to hold the power of the golden sword of justice. He will also carry the brass shield of Levi because of his unswerving love and unshakable faith."

Jesse leaned forward and pointed at the glowing weapon now in Troy's hand. "Troy, when you hold this sword may you have the strength of the Spirit. May you cut through the lies of the enemy and have wisdom to discern the Book of Truth."

His papa took the brass Levi shield from the red blanket and placed it on Troy's small arm. "Troy, may this shield of faith deflect the flaming arrows of doubt and the forces of darkness that will try to destroy your gift of love. Go now, my son, bring home the oats and may our Great Creator be with you and your brothers."

By now all of Troy's siblings were staring at their little brother with astonishment. His biggest supporter, Tammy, was the first to respond.

"Troy, I'm so proud of you. I always knew you were special and that the Great Creator had His eye on you."

With that, the whole family encircled Troy and prayed for His blessing and protection.

THE MISSION BEGINS

"**A**LRIGHT THEN, IT'S SETTLED," SAID JESSE, AS HE gathered the backpacks and placed them beside the exit. "Bucks, you'll be heading out bright and early. It's going to be a busy day tomorrow, so get some sleep."

The morning did come early for the Durum bucks. Troy was the first one out of bed, dressed and ready to go before any of his brothers even moved.

"Come on, you guys, get up!" encouraged Troy. "We won't have the element of surprise if we don't leave immediately. Has anyone seen the gold sword and shield Papa gave me last night?"

Elijah slowly turned over in his straw bed, stretched his arms and yawned loudly before he responded to his brother's rude awakening.

"Yeah, I have them right here beside my bed. I hid them under a blanket for safekeeping. Troy, aren't you sure it wouldn't be wiser for me to hold on it during the mission?"

"Right, Elijah," mocked Samuel, "you can't even lift the sword and it doesn't glow for you. You're obviously not the chosen one."

Elijah reluctantly lifted the blanket and watched as Troy easily picked up the sword and swung it around with lightning speed. He handed his brother the shield and began barking orders to the rest of his brothers.

"Warriors, you heard Troy. It's time to get up, so put on your uniforms, strap-on your backpacks and meet us downstairs by 0400 hours for our O-plan (Operation Plan)."

As they got ready, Troy took the opportunity to practice his fighting skills. The sword began to glow and hum with

anticipation. He copied defensive and offensive moves he'd
seen Papa use countless times
as he rehearsed for battle.

"Stand guard, you nasty
Rafter Rats, your pathetic god
Dreck cannot save you." Troy
thrust the point of the sword
forward, swinging it back and
forth and ducking behind the
shield. He jumped side to side
and turned in a beautifully choreographed dance. A weak
growl came from his throat as he curled his upper lip.
"You'll never catch me, King Kappa, you leather-winged
devil. The Great Creator is with me and I am Mighty Troy
of Salem."

He hadn't noticed Papa at the door watching him.
"Great footwork, son."

Troy startled at his papa's presence.

"Those Rafter Rats will never stand a chance. And King
Kappa will cower in fear."

"Papa, I-I didn't see you. How-how long have you been
there?" asked Troy.

"Long enough to see that you are ready for this mission,
my son. Don't ever underestimate yourself." Jesse walked
over and held Troy's face in his paws. He looked intently
into his eye and said, "Remember, my pup, centre on what
you can do, not on what you can't do."

Troy responded with a big hug as the rest of his brothers
ran past them and bounded down the stairs. They all lined

up in a straight row awaiting papa's O-plan for the Oats Mission.

They took great pride in their first undercover, covert operation. Dressed in black and covered in charcoal dust made them feel like elite marines on a special mission.

Troy tucked the sword into an old shoelace he tied around his shoulder so that the sword rested on his back.

"Bucks, be brave," Jesse began with as much authority as he could muster. "Follow Troy. His nose has become his strength and compensates for his lack of vision. He will guide you to the oats. Stay close to the walls and don't be tempted to take short cuts. It could mean the difference between life and death. Go down through the pipes that lead to the main floor and do not take the stairs under any circumstances.

"Find the oats, climb up the side of the giant's shelf and push the bag of oats over the edge to the floor. Fill your backpacks as quickly as possible and come straight home. No matter what happens, do not look back. Remember, your mission priority is to go in, get out and come home safe and sound. Now, off you go and may the Great Creator be with you, my brave young warriors."

The Durum brothers gathered around in a circle, placed their paws in the centre and recited the Durum bucks motto: "The Durum bucks are not dissuade, we're stronger together we're not afraid. We fight for freedom, we fight for love, but look for peace from the Logos above— Durum bucks rule!"

CHAPTER 9

MISSION IMPOSSIBLE

FEAR MAKES WHAT IS POSSIBLE SEEM

IMPOSSIBLE BECAUSE FEAR CREATES DOUBT

AND PARALYSES HOPE. THE OPPOSITE OF

FEAR IS FAITH, WHICH LEADS TO COURAGE,

WHICH LEADS TO HOPE, WHICH LEADS TO

LOVE, WHICH LEADS TO OUR CREATOR.

TROY AND HIS BRAVE BROTHERS STOOD OUTSIDE
THE door and peered into the darkness of night. Troy
held up the golden sword of justice.

"For the King of Kings and His revolution of love!"

With that declaration, they began the impossible Oats
Mission. The only thing standing in their way was fear.
Troy sensed his brothers' apprehension in his leadership
and fear of the impending mission.

"Bucks, I know this is our first mission and it will be a
dangerous one. I also understand that some of you doubt
my ability to lead. Yet, I believe the Logos is with us and
if we follow Him we will succeed. He has revealed to me
'there's no fear in love, because perfect love casts out fear,'
therefore our victory is sure!"

They left the light of the front porch and hugged the
walls of the gleaning room just as Papa suggested. Their
sense of smell became heightened and their pupils dilated,
enabling them to see perfectly in the night. They arrived at
a hallway and Troy raised his paw in the air, signalling for
everyone to stop. He lifted his head and sniffed for danger.
He could clearly smell sour breath and hear a wheezing
sound.

"Arnie." whispered Troy.

ARNIE THE PATROL CAT

SURE ENOUGH, AS TROY CAREFULLY PEERED AROUND
the corner he found himself face to face with Arnie the
night patrol cat. He jumped backwards; old Arnie jumped
two feet in the air and screamed.

"Meowwww."

The brothers used the chaos to run and hide underneath
anything they could find. Troy
wasn't too worried about old
Arnie. He couldn't hear very
well, his sense of smell was

gone and his sight was nothing but a blur. Old Arnie had
cataracts and one of his eyes tilted outward a bit. Due to
many catfights, his ears had a few pieces missing and most
of his claws had worn off. His fur was dirty white, his teeth
were mostly gone and his breath reeked of rotten sardines.

Arnie landed on the wood floor, quaking with fear. He
sat down and started licking his front paws one at a time.
The longer Arnie licked the calmer he became until the
quaking stopped. He looked to see if anyone had noticed
his obvious fear, stood and hacked up a fur-ball.

Troy watched as Arnie turned his head first one way and
then another, eyes squinting as he searched for the mice.
The cat didn't appear to see them because he never moved
from his spot, but just smiled.

He probably thought he'd scared them away.

Arnie stretched, shook out his fur from head to tail until
everything fell back in place. Then, he held his head high
and cat-strolled off to continue patrolling the Orange Elevator.

Troy waved for his brothers to stay where they were for a
few more minutes. Once he was sure Arnie had gone, Troy
broke the silence and whispered to his brothers,

"I think he's gone, bucks. And don't worry, old Arnie
couldn't hurt a fly. Papa told me he isn't very dangerous

unless he gets a hold of you, so let's move out and get those oats."

Troy waved his paw forward and they all dashed across the hallway, which led to the main leg of the elevator. The hall was long and dark and once again they hugged the wall to avoid the Orange Bats who were out for their evening hunt. Troy's hand tightened around the brass Levi Shield close to his chest. Then without warning the sword of justice began to vibrate behind his back and Troy's nose caught a strange, yet familiar scent.

He stopped, held up his hand again and placed a claw to his mouth, "Shhhh."

THE TRAP

"WHY ARE WE STOPPING THIS TIME, TROY?" complained Samuel. "We're almost at the pipe entrance, so let's go already!"

James, who always had words of wisdom, spoke sternly to his brother, "Samuel, Papa told us to trust Troy and his special gifts the Creator gave him. These gifts could save our lives on this mission." Then he turned to Troy. "Do you hear or smell something? Do you sense danger, Troy?"

"I definitely smell cheese, James, and yet there's also the scent of a giant and Papa's sword is vibrating. When I was at RAMS they taught us that those two scents together are always dangerous. I'll take Shaun with me and check it out, the rest of you stay here. If we don't come back, you're in charge of the mission, James."

James nodded. "You had better come back, Troy. We are not doing this without you."

I definitely smell cheese, James, and yet there's also the
scent of a giant and Papa's sword is vibrating.

Troy and Shaun moved slowly along the wall as the cheesy smell grew stronger and stronger with each step.

"Mmmm, it smells so cheesy and sweet, Troy," cooed Shaun, as his mouth began to water.

"Don't be fooled, Shaun," warned Troy, as they arrived at the end of the hall. "The cheese smells too strong and it has a slight chemical edge to it. I think it might have been poisoned."

Shaun was hoping it wasn't bad. "It smells just fine to me, but I know your nose is much more sensitive than mine."

Troy came to the edge of the hall and peeked around the corner. There it was, the biggest piece of cheese he'd ever seen. It was twice the size of Shaun and covered in a creamy sauce.

Shaun stood next to Troy rubbing his eyes, which had gone to about the size of Troy's shield. "Wow! Look at that, Troy! If it's safe, can we take it to our brothers and have a snack before we begin the mission? I'm hungry."

Troy creeped up close to the cheese and shook his head. "Sorry, bro, that would not be a good idea. I'm afraid this cheese is covered in a sweet and yet deadly poison. I'll mark it with a red flag that Papa gave me to mark any poison we came across on our mission. This will warn others that this cheese, as wonderful as it smells, is not safe to eat."

They turned around and scampered back to where they left their brothers. Shaun quickly told them how Troy knew the cheese was bad even before they saw it.

"You should have seen the size of it, bucks!" Shaun held his paws up wide. "It was the biggest piece of cheese we'd ever seen and was smothered in a creamy sauce. It had me fooled but not Troy. He took one sniff and knew it was poison."

Jacob came over and put his arm around Troy. "I'm sure glad we have you on our side. Lead on, little brother, we're right behind you."

Raising his nose in the air Troy sniffed to the left and to the right. It wasn't long before he caught wind of the oats two floors below.

"It's this way, guys," he said, pointing them in the direction of the leg pipe. They arrived at the gleaning pipe and peered down the dark hole, which would take them to the main floor. "Well, what are we waiting for?"

Troy jumped in the hole, first, followed by his brothers. They popped out at full speed, landing on top of one another with Troy on the bottom of the pile.

"Get off of me! Get off of me! I can't breathe!" He screamed.

Everyone leapt off the pile until Troy was free. Then they started complaining and bickering about whose fault the pile-up was and fights began to break out among the siblings.

RED EYES WATCHING

As SOON AS TROY AND HIS BROTHERS SLID DOWN the pipe on top of one another, four red eyes honed in on them. Watching the Durum boys from the floor grates which led to the grain pits below were two young Rafter Rats. They hungrily licked their lips and salivated at the possible meal that had seemingly come out of nowhere.

Their uncle Goar had sent them on a mission to search for some food in the wheat pits. The Rafter Rats' storehouse was also empty and they were looking for scraps to restock it anywhere they could. They silently waited for an opportunity to attack.

"Quiet, quiet down everyone," Shaun shushed. "We don't want to alert the Rafter Rats. Remember, they aren't deaf like Arnie, they have super hearing and they are much faster than cats."

"Well, I've got super hearing, too," said Troy. "And I've got my sword. If those Rafter Rats try anything I'll cut them down."

"Yeah right, Troy!" mocked Samuel, "You're such a baby you'd probably wet your self if a real Rafter Rat attacked you! Besides, you wouldn't even see him before he'd have you in his grasp."

"Samuel, stop that right now!" Shaun snapped in Troy's defence. "You're always against Troy, and I for one will not stand for it anymore. He's your brother and I have never heard him say anything negative against you. We are all special in the Creator's eyes. We have to stick together, especially now. Our priority is to complete our mission and save the clans from starvation. Now, I want you to apologize to Troy so that he can continue to lead us to the oats."

Ashamed, Samuel looked at his brother. "I'm sorry, Troy. I had no right to speak to you that way. I don't know why I am so mean."

Joab took Troy's hand, which was holding the sword, and held it up. "Now lead us to those delicious oats, Mighty Troy of Salem!"

CHAPTER 10

THE GOOD NEWS OP

GOOD NEWS IS MEANT TO BE SHARED

WITH OTHERS BUT NOT ALL MESSENGERS

ARE RECEIVED AND THERE ARE NO

GUARANTEES THOSE WHO HEAR WILL

LISTEN, ACCEPT OR BELIEVE THE MESSAGE.

A T THE DURUM FAMILY HOME, THE YOUNG DOES and their parents were preparing for a very important mission of their own.

"Would you be able to take charge of 'Operation Good News' and delegate responsibilities to your sisters, Olivia?" Jesse asked his daughter with pride.

"Sure thing, Papa, I'd be honored to do my part to fulfill this operation, but I would rather be out there with my brothers, where the action is," declared Olivia. "Why can't I go with them this time? Is it because I'm a doe, Papa?"

"No, of course not, darling!" he responded, hugging her. "Your mama and I have always believed you are capable of doing anything you put your mind to. We just think your gifts are more suited to this particular operation."

"Okay," responded Olivia with a frown, "but promise me, next time I get to go along with my brothers, okay?"

Evette shook her head before Jesse could say a word. "Not on my watch, young lady! I know you are very talented with your staff, but you've only had a year of combat theory and no real-life experience."

"But, Mama, those defence classes at the Royal Academy used real scenarios of what could happen. I feel I am ready to outmanoeuvre any attack," Olivia pleaded.

Evette smiled and looked deep into her daughter's blue eyes. "Someday, sweetheart, you and your sisters will have the chance to work with your brothers, but for now you have a very important operation of your own. So let's get busy."

Jesse set out the girls' O-plan.

"Olivia, I want you and Frey to inform the Bulgur and

Kamet clans that we have discovered a large bag of oats on the main floor. Tell them to bring enough jars for their own families and to meet at our storage bins on level four tonight at 7 p.m.

"Evalyn, Ava and Tammy, my does, you are to inform the larger Graham and Spelt clans of the same news."

Evette stepped back so she could see them all and looked from one to the other. "I want you to prepare for the party, tonight, and Olivia's in charge, understood?"

"Yes, Mama, you can count on us," agreed Tammy, as her sisters nodded.

Evette continued, "I want you to move the spare tables to the centre of the floor. Find the torches and place them on the walls. Oh, and don't forget the fire sticks inside the top drawer, beside bin number one.

"Now, remember girls, do not let anything distract you from your operation. There are many dangers lurking around every corner. Stay close to the walls and never allow your noses to become tempted by free cheese or peanut butter. These are red flags that signal a human trap. Also, watch for Rafter Rats. Their vision may not be as good as yours, but never underestimate their cunning ways. Assume they are watching you at all times."

Evette lifted her head for dramatic effect. "Finally, my does, you must always look up when you hear the sound of flapping leather wings. The Orange Bats on level seven will swoop in from above. Remember, they are always on the hunt for unsuspecting little mice. Bats can't fly along the walls and their sonar cannot find you through objects. Do you understand everything I have told you?"

"Tell them to bring enough jars for their own families..."

"Yes, Mama," they all chimed at once.

Jesse went to the front door and gave each of his little does a big hug. He knelt down and began to bless them. "Olivia my sweet angel, may the Great Creator give you the courage to lead."

Olivia had shiny blonde fur that was soft as silk. Her large, bright blue eyes sparkled when she talked and she always had something to say. She loved to read and would often sneak away to her secret spot high on a dusty shelf filled with old books. A worker who loved to read left them behind one summer. Her favourite book was penned in 1877 by English author, Anna Sewell, about a horse named Black Beauty, which she dreamed of riding one day. Olivia was also a fierce fighter and learned to master the staff at the academy.

Jesse continued, "Olivia, lead your sisters with strength and courage. Use your staff wisely and bring them all home safely."

Papa gently placed his arm around the lovely Evalyn. His second daughter had light brown fur and wore a black collar around her neck. She was solution minded and therefore wasn't one to complain. Being somewhat sceptical she would question everything. At the academy she became known for her well-planned battle strategies and demanded proof before she would trust. Her friends said her life was an open book and yet she had concealed a big secret until today. She had told her papa she loved cats, their mortal enemies and dreamt of one day meeting old Arnie.

Jesse looked into her eyes. "My sweet Evalyn, I surely don't understand or approve of your love of cats. Still,

I truly hope someday you will meet Arnie, but on your terms, not his. My daughter, I'm counting on you to be the voice of reason. The Creator has blessed you with the gift to planning and strategy. May you be wise in all your decisions, but remember to listen to your sister's advice. A good planner always listens to the wisdom of others before committing themselves to action."

Jesse moved towards his tallest daughter Frey and placed his paws over hers. "Frey, my dear one, you never stop smiling and always stand up for justice. Remember, nothing can keep you from being free in your heart. You have always been able to escape from locks, cages, traps and ropes. If you ever find yourself in a trap where you cannot escape, know that the Logos has already made you free in Him through His love for you."

Papa moved his paw to her head and began to bless her. "Frey, my happy freedom fighter, you have been given a heart for the oppressed. Your love for those in need is unmatched by anyone I have ever known. May the Great Creator grant you success in your mission. Young ones from every clan are depending on you for food."

Ava looked at her papa as he came towards her and began to cry.

"Ava, Ava, my sweet, fearless little bug, don't cry. Remember that fear is also there to protect you from harm. Your sisters need your confidence and courage that comes from your Creator, but also listen to the wisdom of your sisters. Heed the warnings of that still small voice inside your head. It will tell you when it is time to run or move forward, so that you can live to fight another day."

Ava had the curliest black fur ever on a mouse, and her smile would melt the coldest heart. She loved to run—everywhere—and she feared nothing except losing one of her family. She had an amazing gift of faith in the Great Creator. She was not afraid to ask Him for miracles and to help those who were unable to help themselves. Ava was gifted with the bow and arrow. She could split the end of a rat's tail in two at five meters. One other thing that separated Ava from the rest of Mama's babies is that she loved vegetables and cream cheese. She could never get enough. She would go to great lengths to steel a celery stick from a giant's lunch box. If Ava ever discovered cream cheese, she would become dizzy with excitement.

"Tammy, my little jumping bean," continued Jesse with a smile, "may the Creator grant you joy, so you can share the healing power of laughter and happiness to those around you." Little Tammy was small and could never sit still, but could that girl jump! When she was only one week old Tammy hopped over objects a meter high. In fact, she was able to jump and balance on almost anything, even if it was moving. She had long white fur, usually tied back in a ponytail with a bright blue ribbon.

She also had an amazing ability to change her white fir to match the colour of any object, like a chameleon. In other words she could pretty much disappear into thin air.

"Tammy, use your gift with confidence," added Jesse, "calculating each jump with advice from your sisters. Do not allow your emotions to dictate your decisions. Use your ability to appear and disappear to protect your sisters and help those in need." When Jesse was done blessing

MIGHTY TROY OF SALEM | THE OATS MISSION

their mission, he and Evette began to cry and hold on to each other for strength.

Olivia put down her staff and gathered her four sisters around in a circle. They placed their hands together and chanted the Durum does' motto. "The Durum does are not dissuade, we're stronger together, we're not afraid. We fight for freedom, we fight for love, but look for peace from the Logos above." They cheered, and then stepped out into the darkness of night.

Olivia glanced back at her parents and blew a kiss.

"Good-bye, Papa. Good-bye, Mama! We love you! And we'll see you at the party very soon." Her voice faded as they disappeared into the shadows.

CHAPTER 11

THE RAFTER RATS

LEADERS KEEP MOVING FORWARD EVEN

IF THE ROAD IS ROUGH OR THE WAY IS

BLOCKED. THEY NEVER LOSE FAITH OR

FOCUS ON THE PROBLEM BUT STRIVE FOR

A SOLUTION.

KING GOAR

GOAR WAS A VERY RICH RAT WHO LIVED ON THE upper rafters of level five in the Orange Elevator. He owned a large junkyard full of all kinds of useful products and shiny trinkets that would be the envy of any rat with good taste. Goar declared himself king over all the Rafter Rats when he was very young and dared anyone to challenge his right to the throne. He wore a gold bottle cap

as a crown and had a long white beard, which he tied in knots. He was heavy set due to his high fat diet and lack of exercise.

Goar's eyes looked like two red-hot coals and his teeth were brown and as crooked as a thief. He had three long scars on his face where the wounds were so deep his fur had never grown back in those places. Some say Goar had a fight with three cats when he was just a rat pup.

Goar was born on a hot summer day in the basement of the Potter's farmhouse. He was a member of the Loft Rats who were ruled at the time by the ruthless King Og. Those that have seen Goar say he proudly wears a thick mouse-tailed necklace and his ear is badly torn from battles fought with the Orange Bats on level seven. They also report that Goar is carried around on a golden litter by 12 skinny mouse slaves, all with their tails missing.

He was married to Noam and had five sons: Benob, Saph,

Lami, Joab, Jonathan and an adopted daughter named Abigail. Some say Abigail was stolen from a large mouse litter when she was only a baby. He wanted her to become one of his wife's servant girls. Noam, however, fell in love with the pretty little mouse, and claimed her as one of her own brood.

Goar and Noam were busy celebrating the wedding of their son Benob who married Lilith the daughter of King Og from the Loft Rat Tribe.

KING OG

OG WAS MARRIED TO THE LOVELY JAIR OF SALEM. She felt honoured to not only be the wife of a king but also to a wizard of the rat god Dreck. Og was known to have mystical powers, which he used to control his people. They had two evil sons, Bashan and Rapha, who were very large and constantly getting into trouble.

Og the wizard became King of the Loft Rats and dwelt in Potter's barn. At one time Goar was the captain of king Og's army. One day, they had a huge disagreement over territory and Goar's family was banished to the Orange Elevator. Some of King Og's tribe followed Goar and made their home on level five. He soon made himself king of the Rafter Rats and became very powerful. Goar fought many battles against King Og of the Loft Rats but now they wanted peace.

King Og was known as the tallest rat in all of Salem. He had many gold chains around his neck and rings on every finger. Og was very rich and he wanted everyone to know it, so he held his head high as he walked about. Many believed his wealth was ill-gained, however, and that Bashan and Rapha were his henchmen.

They were all feasting at the wedding table, gorging on the best garbage Salem's dump could offer, all while the rats from both tribes were on the brink of starvation.

THE ATTACK

An hour earlier King Goar had sent his two grandsons Chuba and Rodney (sons of Lami), on a scouting mission to see if there was any wheat left over underneath the grates of the dump pit below level one.

They were on their way back to let Goar know the bad news. The pit was completely empty.

Rodney was tall and skinny with a long pink nose and a brown coat held together with staples. He never went anywhere without his gold cane made from the arm of an old mouse-trap. Rodney was very much the brains of the operation and would constantly remind his younger brother of that fact.

Chuba knew his place and was quite happy in that role. He was mostly the opposite of his older brother. He was short, overweight and wore a green sweater much too small for his over-sized belly. He had large close set eyes, messy fur and an earring made from a

King Goar owned a large junkyard full of all kinds of useful products and shiny trinkets.

paper clip, which he'd found in the Salem dump. Food was on his mind constantly which meant he had trouble concentrating on the mission at hand.

Rodney was the first to see a nest of mice tumble to the floor 10 yards in front of him.

Chuba peeked his head out of the floor grate, noticed the mice and looked back at his brother.

"Can you believe our luck, Rodney? Here we are searching for food and nine tasty cheese lovers pop out of a pipe and on to our plates."

"Yeah, thanks to lord Dreck," whispered Rodney. "Grandpapa Goar will be so proud of us when we bring home a large nest of tasty treats for dinner. Let's get 'em!"

The two young Rafter Rats bolted out of the loading grate at full speed toward the unsuspecting mice.

Hearing the noise the Durum boys turned their heads and saw two Rafter Rats bearing down on them. Shaun instinctively looked for Troy and noticed his distracted brother swinging his papa's gold sword back and forth attacking some imaginary rats.

Shaun had just enough time to warn his little brother of the coming battle. "Run, Troy, run! It's the Rafter Rats."

They all yelled and scurried away in all directions assuming that Troy would follow. Shaun looked back and noticed Troy frozen in place. He was in shock or maybe, more confused as to what was happening.

Troy turned around and held his shield and sword instinctively in front of him. Rodney came to a sliding halt and Chuba who had been following close behind banged into him. This pushed Rodney to within a hair of Troy's

sword. This tiny little mouse stood firm, his one eye on fire with anger and his brow arched in determination.

Rodney's eyes were wide. He stood perfectly still and his wet nose was only a few millimeters from the tip of Troy's glowing sword. Chuba cowered behind  his brother staring over his shoulder at this tiny mouse that didn't run away like all the rest. Then as if waking up from a trance they looked at each other and began to laugh hysterically.

Still laughing, Rodney exclaimed, "Chuba, do you see what I see? We have in front of us a little freak of nature, a mouse with only one eye and a dirty rag over his face. His sword looks like a glowing toy! And his shield is a giant's old button, ha, ha, ha!"

Chuba continued to mock in his usual raspy voice, "Are you sure this is a real mouse, Rodney? No wonder his brothers left him. He's like their little sacrifice, although I don't think it would be right to eat only half a mouse, would it, Rodney?"

Rodney just kept laughing. "You're right, Chuba, he's not even half a mouse, in fact I don't think he is a mouse at all. He looks more like a bat with no hair and no wings, ha, ha, ha, ha."

Both little rats dropped to the floor laughing so hard they didn't notice the eight Durum boys sneaking up behind them. Troy's brothers had large staffs in their hands and were prepared for a major fight. Shaun the Gentle Giant was in front of his brothers and glared at the two rats with anger and determination.

"Let's get 'em, boys!" he yelled as they took off towards the two young Rafter Rats swinging their staffs in a figure eight pattern of war.

Rodney and Chuba never expected Troy's brothers to come back and were totally taken by surprise. They peered over their shoulders at the oncoming mob.

"Chuba, let's go. This little freak is too bony to eat anyway."

Elijah the Risk Taker stuck out his foot as Chuba ran by and he stumbled a bit. The rat recovered, turned back and lunged towards Elijah, stopping within inches of his eyes. Chuba snarled, spit flying from his mouth, "You'll pay for that someday, you little flea bitten cheese lover."

Elijah turned his face away in disgust at Chuba's dirty mouth and the rancid smell of his breath. Then, as the rat turned to leave, Elijah called after him, "What did you have for dinner anyway, rotten fish, frog eyes, or mouse poo?"

Meanwhile his brother Joab threw his staff at Rodney as he ran towards him and hit him squarely in the face. He screeched in pain and immediately began rubbing his nose.

He turned towards Troy and sneered, "I'm coming back for you, you little freak!" then he scampered after his brother and disappeared into the dark shadows.

"Wow! That was a close call," exclaimed Joab, "You're lucky we came back for you, Troy, or you'd surely have been a goner."

Troy held up his papa's gold sword. "Actually, I was just about to finish them off when you guys showed up, but thanks for coming back for me, I do appreciate it." He lifted his nose in the air and soon caught the scent of those delicious oats. Troy pointed the sword of justice towards the ancient tunnel, which would lead them to the lunchroom. "This way, bucks, we're almost there."

Olivia led the way towards "the leg," a long pipe that carried wheat to the top of the elevator and then flowed into bin separators.

CHAPTER 12

THE LEG PIPES

A JOURNEY INTO THE UNKNOWN IS A

WINDING PATH FRAUGHT WITH DANGER

AND FEAR. ARRIVING AT THE DESTINATION

REQUIRES PURE WISDOM AND COURAGE

FROM THE GREAT CREATOR.

OLIVIA KNEW THIS SPECIAL OPERATION WOULD NOT be easy and yet it needed to be done for the clans to survive. She knew fear could lead to careless mistakes and so she lightened the conversation.

"Isn't this exciting, does?" Olivia giggled as she led her sisters along the wall and through the doorway of the gleaning room. "Like our brothers, we too are on a dangerous mission. You heard, Mama, we may even see a real live Orange Bat." They rounded the corner of the great room housing the large storage bins that went up the centre of the elevator for five levels.

"Have you even seen a real Orange Bat, Olivia?" questioned Evalyn with a tone of doubt and sarcasm. "I heard that every night they hunt for mice in the elevator. Some even say they go outside under the light of the moon to eat flying insects and birds. I, for one, do not want to see one tonight."

Tammy, who followed behind Evalyn, couldn't hold her excitement in any longer. She kept jumping up and down squealing with delight.

"We are on an adventure that could change the whole course of our lives forever, ladies." She stopped jumping for a moment and looked up in a dreamy stare. "I wonder if Rodger Spelt will come to the Town Hall Park when we let the Mayor know about the party? He's got such a cute smile and big blue eyes. He could even ask me to marry him on this very night. Can you imagine that? I could be Ms. Rodger Spelt by tomorrow morning."

Olivia rolled her eyes, turned to Tammy and chided her. "Right, Tammy. You stare at Rodger all through dinner and he doesn't even know you exist. Why would he suddenly notice you and marry you tonight? Besides, we have more important things to think about then cute bucks and we must get back before too long or Papa and Mama will worry."

Olivia led the way towards "the leg," a long pipe that carried wheat to the top of the elevator and then flowed into bin separators. She pointed straight ahead. "Let's crawl under that wheat grinder. It'll protect us from our enemies and give us a rest before we continue with phase two of our Good News Op. Evalyn, like Mama said, "you get off on three with Tammy and Ava to inform the Spelt and Graham clans. Frey and I will climb to level four and let the Kamet and Bulgur clans know about the party."

Olivia knew that her sister loved to explore so she added, "Evalyn, don't take any shortcuts and stay close to the walls. Do not wander into back lanes for any reason. The Rafter Rats love to hide there and humans place their traps in these locations."

Ava the Fearless pointed her staff in the air and waved it back and forth shouting, "I'm not afraid, Olivia! My staff will render any human trap useless and the Rafter Rats are too slow, besides I heard most of them will be attending a wedding for Goar's son Benob."

Evalyn jumped into the conversation. "Don't worry, Olivia, we'll stick to the operation and be at the storage room in no time."

"I'm still not really sure we should split up," Olivia muttered, "and yet mama said it's the only way we can inform all the clans and make it to the storage bins before our brothers get back."

Evalyn led the Durum girls from under the wheat grinder and straight to the leg pipe, which would take them to levels three and four. They left one at a time so as not to attract any attention. When they safely arrived at the entrance Evalyn pulled out a large map showing the maze of pipes flowing through the centre of the elevator.

"Listen up, does. We don't want to take the wrong turn and get lost," whispered Olivia. "As you can see, this pipe will take us to the clans but there is one problem—the entrance is too high and the door is bolted shut." She pointed to a metal nut located two feet above where she was standing. "Tammy will use this wrench"—Olivia held it up for all to see— "and loosen the nut each time she jumps until it pops open."

Tammy, who was standing close to the pipe, took the wrench from Evalyn, took a bow and then jumped two feet in the air and on her way down hooked the wrench around the nut and gave it a quick turn. She did this three times until the cover suddenly popped open with a snap. It opened just enough for a mouse to enter through.

Ava looked confused. "How are we supposed to climb up two feet along this slippery pipe, Evalyn? None of us have the amazing jumping skill Tammy has and even if we could get up there, we'll slip down to the bottom once we climb in."

"I have a plan for that," answered Evalyn with confidence. "Tammy is going to carry each of us in her arms as she jumps the height of the opening. As soon as she reaches the door, you jump through it and crawl in. Once inside, turn to the left and you will notice a ribbing that holds the pipe together all the way from the bottom to the top. The bumps will enable you to easily scale the leg to the top of the elevator if you so desired."

Tammy stood beside the leg pipe waiting to take the girls up to the door. Evalyn was the first to volunteer. She enthusiastically hopped on Tammy's back.

"I love it when she gives us rides. I get to know what it feels like to fly like an Orange Bat, even if it is for just a moment."

Tammy crouched low, wiggled her nose for good luck and took off like a rocket. The two young mice squealed with delight as they flew into the air. Evalyn had wrapped her arms around Tammy's neck and when she reached the open door she jumped through with perfect timing. Ava went next, followed by Frey and then Olivia. By now Tammy was extremely tired but she easily made one last jump to join her sisters in the leg.

"Are you okay, Tammy?" asked Olivia, as her sister bounded through the opening.

"Yes, I'll be okay. I just need to rest a while," panted Tammy as she crawled up to join her sisters.

"I think I remember how to navigate the way to level four," said Olivia. "Tammy, you can stay behind with Evalyn and Ava, and when you're ready, take them to level three to inform the Spelt and Graham clans with the good news."

"You won't get any complaints from me," assured Tammy with a grateful smile.

"We'll probably still beat you to the meeting room and

have half the tables set up before you arrive," teased Ava placing her arm around her exhausted sister.

"You could be right," agreed Olivia. "The Kamet and Bulgur clans have twice as many mice than the Spelt and Grahams do, I'll give you that."

Leaving their three sisters behind, Olivia and Frey began the long and winding journey to the fourth level. Up and up they went, around the corner to the left and then the right and then up again. Finally, they arrived at level four and squeezed through a small opening in the pipe and then through the floor.

"Where do we begin?" asked Frey as they both sat against the wall catching their breath.

"With prayer, sis, with prayer."

Olivia didn't tell her sisters, but she had a feeling something bad was about to happen and so she asked the Creator for protection.

CHAPTER 13

THE ANCIENT TUNNEL

OBSTACLES ARE MEANT TO BE

OVERCOME, YET FAILURE IS SURE IF ONE

NEVER TRIES. SUCCESS IS NOT DEFINED BY

BEING THE BEST BUT IN DOING YOUR BEST.

THE SMELL OF DELICIOUS OATS GREW WITH EVERY step. Troy knew exactly where he would find the bag of oats once they were inside the giant's pantry.

"We're almost there," Troy exclaimed excitedly as they entered the large lunchroom. He stopped and pointed at a small opening in the wall. "Here it is, my brave warriors—the ancient tunnel, which will take us safely across the lunchroom and to the oat bag. Papa told me our ancestors created this passageway shortly after the giants built the elevator. He told me they chewed holes through every wooden stud for nearly twenty feet. It ends up at the other end of the lunchroom and into the giant's pantry."

James scratched his chin. "But, Troy, why wouldn't they just run across the lunchroom and under the pantry door. Wouldn't that be much faster?"

"Well," answered Troy with a smile, "it would be way too dangerous to cross the lunchroom floor. When the elevator is open the giants are in and out of this room all the time and when they are gone the bats and Rafter Rats are on the look out for anything moving. So, they built the tunnel to avoid predators and have access to the giant's pantry. Papa told me this is where the most delicious food is stored. When the elevator is busy the pantry is full of bread, cheese, jam and even sweet cakes and cookies." He noticed his brothers begin to drool and smack their lips.

"Do you think they'll have cookies today, Troy?" asked Elijah, rubbing his stomach. He thought back to when he found some cookie crumbs on the floor one Christmas and remembered how delicious they were.

"Sorry, Elijah, but I don't think we'll find any crumbs in

the room, today," Troy stated with disappointment. "Most of the workers won't be coming in until the harvest. However, there is one giant who has been coming in every year and on this very day. He walks all over the elevator and checks the machines, so we must be very careful as we enter the next phase of our mission." Troy began to enter the tunnel but then held up his hand to stop.

Samuel scowled. He wanted to get on with the mission. "Why are we stopping again, Troy? Let's keep moving."

TRIPPING THE TRAPS

"WE MUST MOVE MUCH SLOWER AT THIS STAGE OF the mission," explained Troy. "Around the next corner there could be Rafter Rats, poisons or even snap-traps. In fact, I suspect a number of traps have been placed near the entrance. This is why we've stopped moving forward, Samuel."

Upon hearing there could be snap-traps, the Durum brothers moved back from the tunnel entrance and left Troy standing there alone.

Joab began to cry. "I don't want to die in a snap-trap, Troy."

"You're not going to die in a trap, Joab," responded Troy with confidence, "I have a plan. First of all, we don't know for sure if there are any traps in there. Secondly, if any traps are found, I suggest we ask Jacob the Flash to use his incredible speed to trip all of them."

"I am very fast," responded Jacob, "but first, why don't we see if there are any traps. In fact, I'll go with Troy and check it out."

Troy and his brothers climbed over the mound of disabled mousetraps.

His brothers agreed and so Troy and Jacob entered the tunnel. They hadn't gone more than a few feet when Troy smelled old cheese and his eye caught a glint of metal in the darkness. He put up his hand, "Don't move, Jacob. Look over there, you see what I see?"

"Oh no!" exclaimed his brother. "How far back do they go? I can see at least four snap-traps. How many do you see?"

Troy had only one eye, but he could see much clearer in the dark than any of his siblings. He climbed up one of the wood beams and squinted his eye. "I can see nearly to the end of the tunnel before it cuts to the right, Jacob."

"Well, do you see how many traps I have to trip?" asked Jacob impatiently.

Troy climbed down the beam and stared at Jacob with a worried look. "I've seen you trip four traps in Miss Von Trap's class, but they were not the real thing. How many real loaded traps have you tripped at once, Jacob?"

Jacob was cautiously optimistic, "Ummmm, well, I've done three real ones no problem. The four mock traps I tripped were difficult but I could probably trip four real ones. Why? How many traps did you see, Troy?"

Troy put his head down. "There are five snap-traps set with old cheese and ready to fire, Jacob." He looked up at his brother and asked, "Do you think you can do five?"

"I don't know, but I sure could try." Jacob had tears in his eyes and he looked kinda scared.

Troy shook his head back and forth. "I don't like this, Jacob. If you're not absolutely sure you can do five traps without getting caught tell me. It's ok we'll find another way in. I'm not willing to risk losing you. There are other options. We could get to the bag of oats by going through the centre of the workers' lunchroom or we could enter the pantry through the giant's office."

"No, Troy" Jacob responded, "You and I both know those routes are far too risky. At this time of night the Orange Bats will spot us for sure and we'll have nowhere to hide. We could lose at least two warriors or more before we reach the pantry door and if we go through the office the giant will kill us. We have no choice, I have to try."

Troy put his hand on his brother's shoulder. "Come on, Speedy, let's go and tell our brothers the bad news."

They walked out of the tunnel putting on a brave face for the sake of their brothers.

"Well, bucks, we have some good news and some bad news. The bad news is there are five snap-traps lined up in a row, baited, locked and loaded, three feet from the tunnel entrance."

"So, what's the good news, Troy?" asked Samuel, as his brothers nodded.

Troy looked down unable to speak.

Jacob took the cue and responded, "Well, the good news is I will run as fast as I can and try to trip all he traps without getting caught."

"That's the 'good' news?" Samuel shouted, his eyes wide. "Are you crazy? This isn't a game, Troy. Jacob could die and it would be all your fault."

"Bucks, I don't think this is a good plan," Shaun said, as he placed his arm around Jacob. "We all know the gift of speed the Creator has given to you, Jacob, but I know that you have never tripped five traps before." Shaun turned to Troy. "Do you think we should let Jacob try this? I think it's too risky. Isn't there another way we can enter the giant's pantry without going through the tunnel and sending Jacob on a suicide mission?"

"Why don't we just go through the workers' lunchroom?" asked James. "There are no workers there now and it would be faster anyway."

Troy raised a paw for quiet. "Jacob and I actually discussed that option, however we both agreed it would place more lives in danger. The lunchroom has no tables to hide underneath at this time of year. We would be out in the open and totally vulnerable to an aerial attack by King Kappa and his hunters. We could lose two of us or even more with that option."

Joseph had been quiet until now and his emotions got the best of him. "I don't want Jacob to die! I mean, I don't want any of us to die. Both ideas are bad. What do we do, Troy?"

Jacob answered before Troy could, "Bucks! It is my decision. Logos has given me peace about this. He will be with me because tripping snap-traps is the safest option. Remember, Papa asked Him to help us fulfill our mission."

James knew what they needed to do. "Well, then let's all bow our heads right now and ask our Creator to do a miracle today. Troy, Papa has placed you in charge of the Oats Mission and so it is only fitting you lead us in prayer for our brother Jacob."

"Sounds like words of wisdom, James," said Troy as he knelt in front of the tunnel and leaned against the handle of his papa's sword. He bowed his head and began to pray as Papa taught him, "Our Creator, I know we are just tiny mice. I know that we are a small piece of Your great creation. Yet, Papa has told me you still care for us. We are asking you to help Jacob do something he has never done before—trip five traps. I know it is a lot to ask, Logos. You have already made him very fast, but he needs to go faster today. We are only doing this to save our clans—thanks a lot—Amen!"

"Amen," all the brothers agreed together.

"Let's form a circle and say the Durum bucks battle cry one more time," Jacob said. They gathered around and recited in unison, "The Durum bucks are not dissuaded, we are stronger together, we're not afraid. We fight for freedom, we fight for love, but look for peace from the Logos above—Durum bucks rule!"

They gave Jacob one last hug before he entered the tunnel with Troy to prepare for the run of his life. He knew he had to be faster than ever before, stepping through five traps and releasing all five springs.

Troy walked with Jacob as far as he could to the opposite end of the cave to give him room for the run. Jacob bent down into a runner's stance.

"All right, Jacob, you can do this!" encouraged Troy. "Are you ready?"

Jacob responded with a grin, "Ready as I'll ever be, Troy."

Troy tapped his brother on the back and said, "Then run, Jacob, run!!"

Almost instantly it seemed to Troy, his brother turned

into a blur and then he heard five loud consecutive snaps. Each trap flipped in the air hitting the walls of the tunnel in every direction and when the dust settled Troy ran to the tunnel entrance where his brothers had already gathered.

"Well, did he do it?" asked Samuel.

"Is he dead?" wondered Judah

"Can you see him, Troy?" asked Elijah

Troy squinted his eye but the dust was too thick, so he waited for a few more seconds, moved closer and looked again. "I—I—I think I see a hand waving at me, guys! I think—it is, it's Jacob! He did it! The Creator has done a miracle, bucks!"

A voice came loud and clear through the dust and debris from the flying mousetraps, now disabled and lying in heaps all over the tunnel floor.

"I think I did it, guys! Did you see that? I tripped all five traps! It was amazing! I felt as though I was on fire and my feet they've never run so fast. I know that the Creator helped me run faster. If only Miss Von Trap could have been here to see this."

When the dust finally settled the brothers went and stood beside Troy. They couldn't believe what they saw. There was Jacob casually leaning against a wooden two-by-four with his legs crossed and the biggest grin on his face.

"C'mon, guys, get over here and give me a hug. Don't worry, it's safe!"

Troy and his brothers climbed over the mound of disabled mousetraps and joined Jacob. They put their arms around him, knelt down and thanked their Creator for saving their brother and the mission.

When they'd finished praying, Troy stretched out his arm and with the gold sword, pointed in the direction they should go.

THE WALL

THEY HEADED DOWN THEIR ANCESTORS' TUNNEL single file. For the most part, the mission was going as planned, except for running into Arnie the patrol cat, finding poisonous cheese, the small incident with Chuba and Rodney, and the five deadly snap-traps inside the tunnel. They moved quite quickly and without incident for the next 10 feet or so, until they ran into a wall—literally. Troy held up his hand.

"Hold up, bucks! We have a problem."

"What now, Troy?" Samuel complained as he ran up beside him. "We don't have much time until the giant comes to work."

Troy hit the edge of the wooden stud and pointed to where the hole was supposed to be. "It appears as though a large piece of gyp rock has been pushed in and is blocking the hole. I need Shaun to come and break through this wall. Where's Shaun?"

"Shaun!" yelled Joab. "Troy needs your muscles, big buck!" Big Shaun had been taking up the rear and because of his size he had to squeeze by all his brothers to get to where Troy and Joab were. When he arrived, Shaun saw that breaking through the hole would not be easy. In fact, he would have to ask the Creator for extra strength.

Shaun bowed his head for a moment then lay on his back. He placed his large feet in the air, looked up with a fierce determination and yelled, "For the clans and for the mission." Then with all the determination he could muster, struck the barrier blocking the hole. It cracked slightly but didn't break.

"Awww!" cried Shaun in pain. "I think I broke my foot."

"Are you able to stand up, Shaun?" asked Troy.

"I... I'm not sure. It just hurts awful bad."

Troy bent down to help his brother stand, however his foot could not bear any weight.

"Let me try again," begged Shaun. "The barrier is cracked, so I could easily break it with my head."

"Sure you can, big boy," mocked Elijah who had come to the front so the giant mouse could lean up against him for support. "What would Papa say if we brought you home with a broken skull?"

Meanwhile, Troy was poking at the cracked gyp rock with the point of his sword and the vibration made it crumble. This gave him added incentive and he stabbed at it harder and faster until he could see a hole forming in the middle. The brothers noticed what was happening and began to cheer for Troy.

"You can do it, Troy," they coached. With every poke and slash they chanted louder in unison, "Go, Troy! Go, Troy! Go, Troy! Go, Troy!"

Troy kept stabbing the gyp rock until finally there was a hole large enough for them to squeeze through. He stood in front of the opening and ushered each mouse through one by one. Then he pointed to Elijah with his sword.

"I want you to stay here with Shaun and wait until we return, okay? Give me your empty backpacks, we'll need as many oats as possible to bring home."

"Aye, aye, captain." Elijah saluted with a smile. "Don't worry, I'll look after the big fella."

With that, Troy slipped through the hole and led his brothers down the inside of the door jam, which led to the pantry door. When they reached the bottom, the bucks were loudly chattering with excitement, so Troy held up his arm to quiet them down.

"Do you want everyone in the elevator to know that we are here?" Troy chided, holding on to the edge of the opening. "Besides, I can't listen for danger when you're making so much noise." This silenced them. He peeked around the corner of the hole to see if the coast was clear. The pantry appeared to be empty and his sensitive ears only heard the winter wind blowing outside. His sensitive nose wiggled back and forth until he picked up the exact location of the bag of oats.

The brown burlap bag filled with heavenly food lay on the top shelf next to the office manager's door. He pulled out his pocket watch and looked at the time.

"We have to hurry, men. We only have a few minutes left before the human comes in to work."

James tapped Troy on the shoulder and whispered, "Do you think it is wise for all of us to go out at once or should we divide into teams?"

"That's a great idea, James," exclaimed Troy as he turned towards his brothers. "Joseph, you go first and take Samuel and James with you."

Troy handed Joseph the rope and relayed the plan. "Take the rope to the top shelf where the oats are located, tie one end to the bag and drop the other end down to me. The three of you push the bag from the back and the rest of us will pull it from the front. When it falls over the edge, come back down and help us fill the knapsacks with the oats.

"Jacob, since you are fast, I want you to go under the office door with Judah the Builder and warn us as soon as the giant unlocks the door."

Troy held up his sword. "So, are you ready to do this, bucks?" They all nodded. "Then, let's roll," he said with a grin.

Joseph led the way, followed by Samuel and James. They scurried along the corner of the pantry until they got to the bottom of the shelf. Shortly after, Troy, Joab, Jacob and Judah followed behind. They arrived at the office door just as Joseph was making his way to the top shelf with the rope dangling from his mouth.

Evalyn pulled the small rug back revealing three carved letters in the middle of the door.

CHAPTER 14

CAUGHT BY OLD ARNIE

SILENCE AND DARKNESS SEEM TO BE

PARTNERS WRAPPED IN A COMMON

CAUSE. THEY ALERT THE SENSES AND

YET CONFUSE REALITY. WHEN UNITED,

DARKNESS BRINGS FEAR OF THE

UNKNOWN AND SILENCE HEIGHTENS THE

IMAGINATION.

LEVEL THREE

EVALYN, AVA AND TAMMY BROKE THROUGH THE OPENing and scurried against the wall for protection.

"Did you hear that?" Tammy's right back leg tapped nervously on the wooden floor. "I have a bad feeling about this, does. It's dark and quiet … too quiet."

Ava agreed and hugged closer to the wall. "The sooner we arrive at the Mayor's house the better. This space is creepy and too wide open. It leaves us vulnerable to a bat attack."

Evalyn was also nervous but kept her feelings to herself. She drew her sisters' attention to the map lying on the floor.

"According to Mama's map we must first cross a bridge." She pointed to a dark corner at the end of the hall where a piece of wood spanned a water trough. "Once we cross over all we need is to find a small trap door in the floor, climb down the stairs and we'll arrive at the Spelt and Durum village."

Ava and Tammy seemed more at ease once they heard the plan and saw that Evalyn was calm.

"Let's move out," commanded Evalyn. "The sooner we cross the bridge the safer we'll be."

Ava went first and tentatively stepped out into the open. The floorboards creaked with every step and that set the sisters into a panic.

They dashed towards the bridge, all except poor Tammy. She was beside herself with fear and instinctively, blended herself into the floor like a chameleon. While she was still invisible she jumped three feet in the air, hopped forward three more times and landed in front of the bridge just ahead of her siblings. They bounded around the corner and banged into Tammy just as she reappeared.

"How did you get here so fast, Tammy?" questioned Ava, who was the first to collide with her.

"Oh, you know, I just thought I'd take a short cut," joked Tammy with a crooked smile.

"All right, ladies," Evalyn stated firmly, "let's get across this bridge so we can get on with our mission." She began to slowly walk across, followed by her two sisters. Suddenly, out of nowhere a large furry paw slammed on top of Ava, pinning her down without mercy.

"Help me! Help me!" cried Ava, as she kicked and pulled, to free herself from the weight bearing down on her chest. She couldn't breathe and yet looked fearlessly into the eyes of her attacker.

Old Arnie, the night patrol cat, had accidentally caught Ava. A look of shock and glee spread across his face.

"Wow, I haven't caught a mouse in five years. What do I do now! What do I do?"

Even before old Arnie could decide what to do next, Tammy jumped on top of his head.

"Let go of my sister, kitty cat!" She pulled on his ears and thumped her left foot up and down in a nervous twitch.

Arnie shook his head back and forth trying to remove her. "You're hurting my ears, you nasty little mouse!"

Tammy was mad and knew she had to do something drastic so she reached down in front of Arnie's face and pulled out one of his whiskers.

"Meowwwww!!" The old cat jumped in the air and landed

in the water.

Tammy jumped off Arnie's head and rolled onto the floor. She stood up and ran to where Ava was lying unconscious on the bridge. She knelt down beside her sister, stroking her head. "Ava, Ava, wake up!"

Arnie hated water and jumped out as if it was full of snakes. Once he landed back on the floor, he immediately began to shake off the water. He was on his way back to his catch but Evalyn stood in front of the bridge blocking his way.

Tammy noticed the cat coming toward her sister and tried to warn her, "Evalyn, run! This way, quick!"

Evalyn just stood there looking at the strange cat. "Uh, uh, hi, Arnie!" She had dreamt about this moment all her life and here he was, live and in person. Yet, somehow she imagined he would be much better looking than he was.

Arnie was annoyed, cold and in no mood to have a chat with a cheese lover. "What are you looking at, mouse? Haven't you ever seen a wet cat before? Now get out of the way so that I can eat my catch."

Evalyn stood there with her mouth agape, staring at the large cat. "Now, Arnie, you don't want to eat my sister. Trust me, she'd taste terrible, besides I have been wanting to meet you for as long as I can remember."

"You have wanted to meet me? Why would you want to do that? I'm a cat and you're a mouse. We can never be friends. It's against the natural order."

Evalyn smiled, reached into her backpack and pulled out

a brown package. "I've been saving this just in case I'd meet you." She held the gift towards the cat.

Arnie cocked his head to one side, his ears twitching. "For me? You have a gift for me? No one has ever given me a gift before. Are you sure this isn't a trick, little mouse?"

"This is no trick, Arnie." Evalyn opened the brown package and revealed a piece of dried fish. "I knew your favourite treat was fish, Arnie. If you promise to let us go free, you can have it and maybe we could even be friends."

The cat's nose twitched as it smelled the fish. He closed his eyes, taking in the aroma.

"You have a deal, mousy! The fish for your freedom, but we will never be friends."

"Okay, here it is." Evalyn placed the fish down on the floor and stepped back with Tammy and Ava. "It was very nice to meet you."

Arnie didn't respond as he took the fish in his mouth and trotted away with his head held high in victory.

As the Patrol Cat disappeared around the corner, Evalyn sat down with Ava, tears flowing from her eyes. "Ava, Ava, are you okay?" She was beside herself with worry. What would Mama and Papa do if something happened to brave little Ava? She bent down, took hold of her sister and shook her, trying to get her to move but Ava stayed completely still. Her front legs spread wide apart and her head slumped over to one side. Evalyn held her sister in her arms.

"How is she?" asked Tammy. "She doesn't look so good, Evalyn."

Evalyn couldn't see her sister through her clouded eyes as she continued to try and awaken her. "Ava, wake-up, wake-up, we aren't finished our mission yet. We need you, Ava. I-I'm not going on without you." She bowed her head and asked the Creator to heal her little sister. "Oh please, Logos, don't let Ava die."

Tammy bent down and stroked Evalyn's ears to comforting her. "What are we gonna do? Should I go find Olivia and Frey while you stay here?"

Before Evalyn could answer, Ava opened her eyes. "What's everyone cryin' about? Did someone die?"

Tammy bent down and kissed her. "Ava, you're alive."

Evalyn punched her shoulder. "I thought you were dead. Don't ever scare us like that again!"

Ava jumped up, hugging both sisters at once. "I think I just passed out from having the wind knocked out of me, you guys, and ol' Arnie, well he couldn't hurt a fly. He's got no teeth left and his paws are about as dangerous as a foam pillow. Speaking of which, where is that dangerous feline anyway?"

Evalyn and Tammy looked at each other and laughed. "Let's just say he'll be busy for a while." Tammy then turned and winked at Evalyn.

Ava just stood there confused. Her two sisters grabbed her arm as they scurried across the bridge.

It wasn't long before they found the entrance to the Clan's village hidden under a small rug. Evalyn pulled it back revealing three carved letters in the middle of the door.

"Way cool," blurted Ava as she pointed at the letters D.S.V. "What do they stand for?"

"Durum and Spelt Village," exclaimed Tammy with a

grin. "Papa told me they were hand-carved by our very own grandpapa."

Ava placed her hands on her hips, "Hey, how come we've never met him, Tammy? Did he die or somethin'?"

Tammy shrugged her shoulders. "I'm not sure, I think so, Ava. I overheard Mama and Papa talking late one night when they thought we were asleep. They mentioned Grandpapa died right before their wedding day. Apparently he broke the Isolation Law and became quite a world traveller."

Evalyn bent down and opened the trap door so her two sisters could crawl down into the hole first. It made a creaking noise, reminding her of a scary story she'd once heard.

"I should remind the Mayor to oil this old door when we see him today."

She closed the cover with the leather handle and followed her sisters to the village below.

TEA WITH THE MAYOR

As SOON AS THE DOOR WAS SHUT, TAMMY, EVALYN and Ava heard the sounds of a bustling city located between the two floor joists. They made their way down the long staircase, which led them around the corner from the Graham and Spelt City Hall. Ava was first down the stairs and jumped for joy at the sight before her.

"Wow, Tammy and Evalyn! You have to see this! The whole town has come out to celebrate something."

"We're coming! We're coming!" shouted Tammy. "Wait for us, Ava!"

The does ran down the last few stairs and joined their sister. It was a fair-like atmosphere. Mice danced in the streets and sang lively traditional mouse tunes. There were musicians on every corner and actors surrounded by cheering spectators. Marching in front of them was a grand parade with signs that read "Happy birthday Mr. Mayor."

Oh, how Tammy loved a good parade.

Leading the procession was Mayor Smore and his lovely wife, Ginger. They knew it was him because Papa had said to look for a round mouse with a large moustache and a fringe of grey hair circling his balding head. To Tammy, His eyes looked rather large behind the thick round glasses, which seemed far too big for his small face. For today's celebration he carried a wooden cane with a gold handle in his right hand, which moved up and down to the rhythm of the marching band.

Evalyn knew they had to get his attention so the clans would know where to pick up the oats. Assuming of course Troy and his brothers accomplished their mission.

She called out, "Mr. Mayor, we need to talk to you!"

The mayor took one look at the three does on the side of the street and yelled, "Stop the parade!" He made his way towards the Durum sisters. "Are you three daughters of Jesse?"

"Yes, we are, Mr. Mayor," replied Tammy. "We come bearing great news, sir! Troy and our brothers found a bag of oats in the giant's cupboard and are retrieving it as we speak. My sisters and I were sent by Papa Jesse to inform your two clans to meet at the community storage bins tonight at 7 p.m. After we have distributed the rations, there will be a Great Rejoicing."

Upon hearing the news, Mayor Smore hugged his wife. "See, I told you the Creator would take care of us, my dear. Thanks to some brave young warriors we will all have food this winter."

While the Mayor and his wife continued to chat with Ava and Evalyn, Tammy was in her own world. She had spotted her dreamboat, Rodger Spelt, in the marching band. She couldn't believe her eyes. There he was in living colour, her future husband and the papa of her pups. Everything seemed to happen in slow motion, as he looked her way. She couldn't be sure but she thought she saw him wink at her.

Ava and Evalyn noticed why she wasn't paying attention to their conversation with the Mayor and his wife.

"Tammy, Tammy, snap out of it," chided Ava. "You can sort out your love life later, but right now we have a mission op to accomplish."

Tammy's fuzzy cheeks turned a shade of pink as she tried to use her gift of camouflage. "I—I'm sorry, Mr. Mayor, I was just admiring your talented musicians."

They all laughed as Mayor Smore began to address the crowd. He turned to the Durum girls. "On behalf of the Spelt and Graham clans, we thank you for risking your lives to bring us good news, daughters of Jesse." The Mayor pointed to the three Durum sisters. "These three brave young does have informed me that their brothers are retrieving a large supply of oats from the giant's cupboard. They've also let us know that we are invited to a Great Rejoicing up on level four tonight at 7 p.m. The oats will be distributed in the emergency storage bins after which there will be a celebration dance."

A cheer arose from the crowd and the band began to play louder than before. Mayor Smore held up his hands for them to quiet down.

"My good citizens, let us bow our heads as we give thanks to our great Creator for providing for us once again. Let us ask Him to bless Mighty Troy and his brothers and to bring them home safely."

The birthday party ended and most of the clans went home to prepare for the Great Rejoicing. Mayor Smore and Ginger treated the three sisters to a small amount of delicious cheese and a cup of tea.

When they finished the Mayor and his wife walked with the Durum sisters to the staircase.

"When you reach the top of the stairs," he said, "you will find a long tunnel. It will lead you directly to the door of the emergency storage room on level four."

"Miss Ginger, I think it's swell that you are named after a wonderful spice. I would be very interested in how you received that name?" Ava asked.

The mayor's wife smiled at the little doe's inquisitive spirit.

"Well, Ava, I was the only mouse in the Graham clan that did not have a name until my first birthday. My parents decided to wait until I exhibited more personal characteristics before giving me a name. My Papa said they chose to call me Ginger because of an event that occurred one day just before my first birthday. I went missing and Mama had the whole clan searching for me. Within a few hours someone spotted me in the giant's lunchroom underneath the Christmas tree. There I was lying on my back eating all the worker's gingerbread cookies. Do you know the funniest thing? That night I got so sick I haven't touched a gingerbread cookie since."

They had a good laugh as they arrived at the base of the staircase, and then bid their farewells.

Before they made their way up the stairs, Tammy had one last question.

"Mr. Mayor, sir, could you make sure that Rodger Spelt and his family come to the party tonight. Tell him I will even save a dance for him."

Miss Ginger grabbed Tammy's hand. "Don't you worry, dear, I will personally see to it that he attends."

Tammy was over the moon as she joined her two sisters who were already halfway up the long staircase. Finally reaching the top they stood on the landing and gazed into a dark tunnel.

"We are almost there, girls," encouraged Evalyn. "We must move cautiously through this tunnel which ends in front of the storage bin doors. When we arrive we will have a great deal of work to do, so let's move."

As they walked in the darkness, hugging the sides of the walls to avoid traps, Ava was already in prep mode. "I was just thinking. Olivia and Frey are probably already in the room and if our brothers had no problems finding the oats they should be there as well."

"I hope so, and with a large pile of yummy oats," said Evalyn as she rubbed her tummy and licked her lips. It wasn't too long before they arrived at the exit and stood in front of the bin room doors. Moving quickly, they slipped underneath.

"It's sure dark in here," Evalyn said. She suddenly remembered what her mama said about lighting the torches. Reaching into her backpack, she pulled out a small flashlight and turned it on. She went straight for the fire sticks that Mama said were inside the top drawer beside bin number one.

"Here they are," exclaimed Evalyn as she struck the stick on the floor igniting the flame. She took one of the torches off the wall and lit it. "C'mon, ladies, bring me the rest of the torches and let's get this show on the road!"

Soon the room was shining as bright as the sun revealing just how large it was. "Wow, they weren't kidding! It's so-o-o big!" exclaimed Tammy while jumping up and down. "We really are out of food, aren't we? The bins are totally bare."

For a moment the sisters gazed at the large space before them. They'd heard Mama and Papa talking about the room before, yet they never expected it to be so cavernous. At the far end facing them were two large hopper bins with small doors at the bottom. There were belts and motors and pipes of every size protruding from the floor.

Tammy pointed towards a stack of wooden tables that were leaning up against the far wall to her right. "Look, does, we need to set those tables up for our guests." Her brother Judah had built them in the wood shed at home one summer and some of the clan elders had come and taken them away as soon as they were finished. She had always wondered where they had gone.

"Let's move it, girls," ordered Ava as she placed her hands on her hips. "We have half an hour before our brothers come back with the oats and Olivia and Frey should be walking through that door at any moment now."

CHAPTER 15

DEFEATING
THE GIANT

FACING YOUR GIANTS CAN BE DAUNTING,

ESPECIALLY WHEN YOU ARE VULNERABLE

AND UNPREPARED. THEY COME TO

DESTROY YOUR CONFIDENCE AND ROB

YOUR JOY; YET THE BIGGER THEY ARE THE

HARDER THEY FALL. —TROY

RETRIEVING THE OAT BAG

TROY AND JOAB STOOD CLOSE TO THE OFFICE DOOR, watching Joseph climb the shelves with the rope in his mouth. Samuel and James followed close behind to help their big brother push the bag off the shelf. When they arrived Joseph tied the oats shut.

"Look out below!" He threw the rope down to Troy and Joab and ran behind the bag to help his brothers.

"Shhhh! Do you guys want the whole world to know we're stealing the giant's oats?" scolded Troy.

Samuel ignored his brother and said in a loud whisper, "One, two, three, go!" They pushed and pulled the bag until it suddenly moved forward too fast teetering on the edge.

Troy noticed the bag was beginning to fall and told Joab to take cover. They both dove out of the way in the nick of time just as the oats landed with a thump, splitting open and scattering everywhere. Little Troy and Joab were completely covered in the precious food.

Joseph, Samuel, and James laughed as they scurried down the side of the shelf.

"Where are you, Troy?" questioned Joseph. "Are you okay?"

Troy drove his sword upwards through the oats and popped out.

"It smells soooo good in here." He sat up straight, shook his head and spit out pieces of dried oats from his mouth.

Joab was busy stuffing as many into his mouth as he possibly could.

James, usually the wise more mature brother, unchar-

Troy noticed the bag was beginning to fall and told Joab to take cover.

acteristically jumped into the pile of oats on his belly and flapped his arms and legs.

"Look, I'm making oat angels, you guys!"

They all laughed, took off their backpacks and joined in the fun.

IN THE OFFICE

MEANWHILE, JACOB AND JUDAH ENTERED THE GI-ant's office. Their mission was to inform Troy as soon as the giant unlocked the door.

Jacob dashed under the potbelly stove at the centre of the room and waved his brother over.

"Come on, Judah, this is the perfect place to watch the front door."

Judah looked both ways and cautiously ran under the stove to join Jacob.

"Do you know what Papa says the first thing the giant does before he opens the door?" asked Jacob. "He jingles his keys, starts a fire in the stove and makes a cup of joe."

Judah could hardly wait to get out of the office.

"Well, I suggest we run under the door and tell Troy as soon as we hear the sound of the keys. I don't want to be under the stove when the giant lights the fire or we'll be roasted like wieners on a stick."

Jacob nodded. "I agree with you, brother. We run even before he comes in the door."

THE GIANT ENTERS

TROY FINISHED FILLING HIS BACKPACK WITH OATS and placed the two extra bags from Shaun and Elijah on the floor. He took a break to check on Jacob and Judah's stakeout.

Peeking under the door he called out in a soft voice, "Is there any sign of the giant yet, Jacob?"

Troy noticed Jacob crouched beneath the stove with his brother who was shaking with fear. "The giant hasn't arrived as yet, Troy, but he is due any moment."

Judah came out from his hiding spot. "I'm scared, Troy. What if the giant comes in and catches us stealing his oats? I think we should all go home now before it's too late. We have enough oats, don't we?"

"Just keep your eyes on the door, you two," commanded Troy, "we can't leave until all our bags are filled. Besides we're almost finished."

He slipped under the door and joined his brothers who were filling the two remaining backpacks. Suddenly, Troy's super sensitive ears heard the jingle of keys.

"Oh no, the giant's arrived!" He ran to the door and yelled at the top of his voice, "Judah, Jacob, get out of there, now! He's here. The giant is coming." But, before Troy could slip under the door, Jacob bolted past him in a blur. Troy took hold of his front leg as he went by. "Where's Judah? Is he still in there ... with the giant?"

"I-I-I don't know," stammered Jacob. "The last I saw him he was right behind me." Jacob pointed towards the door. "Oh no, he's still in there, Troy! I have to go back and get him." Troy grabbed his brother by the shoulders and looked intently at him. "Stop and think, Jacob. Where was Judah when the giant entered the room?"

"Well," Jacob explained through his tears, "we ... we

were under the stove when the giant placed his key in the lock and opened the door. I looked at Judah and told him to run to the door. He was right beside me when the lights came on. I heard the giant yelling something as I slipped under the door but Judah wasn't with me. What are we going to do, Troy?!"

"It's okay, Jacob," consoled Troy, "Let's go and see where he is." They went back to the office entrance, slipped halfway under the door and lay flat on the floor. Troy surveyed the room and spotted Judah hiding behind a corn-broom about four feet from where they were standing. The giant was lighting the stove and placing a pot of joe on the black iron top. He turned around and began walking towards the counter. His feet stopped right beside the broom where Judah was hiding. The giant turned on the radio and rested both his hands on the table top, while tapping his fingers to the beat of the music.

Judah turned his head to the side and noticed Jacob and Troy under the door. He was shaking and tears flowed down his whiskers.

They frantically waved their paws for him to run towards them but he shook his head in protest. Judah seemed to freeze for just a moment and then bolted towards their location. Troy grabbed him and they dashed under the door.

Judah and Jacob quickly went over to the small pile of oats and quickly filled their backpacks.

"Let's go, men," Troy commanded as soon as they were done. "The giant is here." Troy and his brothers scurried under the shelf and were halfway through when they heard the office door opening with a slow creak. "Be very still."

The human entered the lunchroom, turned on the light and walked to the shelf where the oat bag had been stored. It was missing, so he looked down and noticed the empty bag on the floor. He scanned the room and began to yell something in a loud booming voice.

"Quickly, under here," Troy whisper-shouted, as he led his brothers inside a key closet 10 feet from the tunnel. As they entered the darkness of the small room Troy immediately knew they had made a mistake. They were trapped and the giant seemed angry.

The Durum brothers huddled closely in the dark corner of the room and shook with fear. They all heard the giant shouting but couldn't understand him.

Troy worried that his brave warriors may not make it home tonight after all. Suddenly, he had an uneasy feeling that he was missing someone. He quietly whispered, "Joab, Joab, are you there?" He didn't answer. "Any of you see Joab come in with us?"

James tapped Troy on the shoulder, "I think I saw Joab hiding behind a leg under the cupboard where we got the oats."

"Oh no," muttered Troy, "Joab's in trouble."

DISCOVERING THE MICE

I JUST STARED AT THE BAG OF EMPTY OATS. "How could a few tiny mice bring down such a large bag of oats?"

Suddenly, I heard a skittering sound, and a blur running towards the key closet.

"So there you are, you little rascals. I've got you now."

THE DARK CLOSET

BACK IN THE CLOSET, TROY AND HIS BROTHERS MOVED away from the door and squished themselves in the corner.

"He heard us move, Troy!" whispered Judah, wiping the tears from his eyes. "We should have run for the tunnel sooner, now we're all going to die."

"I want to go home," whined Samuel.

"I want to know whose backpack was left behind," questioned Troy.

"I miss Mama and Papa," cried James, hiding his face under Troy's arm.

They sounded like a wailing family at a funeral. Even Mighty Troy was worried, so he did the only thing he could—pray.

"My Creator and friend, this is Troy again. The clans are depending on our Oats Mission to succeed. I know your eye is on the little sparrow and that you're watching us right now. As You know, our clans are running out of food, and my papa and mama are depending on me to bring us home safely, so please help us. Amen—oh and also protect Joab." When Troy was finished he noticed his brothers had quieted down and seemed more at peace.

CLOSING IN

I TIPTOED TOWARDS THE DOOR WHERE I THOUGHT those pesky mice were hiding. Placing my hand on the old brass handle I slowly pulled open the door, but before I could look inside I heard a loud squeak. I snapped my head towards the sound and noticed a mouse streak across the floor.

"Trying to get away, are we?" I said with a grin as I shut the door and looked around for the mouse.

I spotted him racing in the direction of the garden tools, which hung in a row along the side of the wall.

If that rodent went there, he's trapped, I thought, keeping my gaze focused on where I had seen him disappear. "I've got you now, you little runt," I said, hoping he could hear me. "You can't steal oats from Lyle Wolfe and get away with it." I came around the corner, slowly lifted the broom and couldn't believe what I saw. The mouse was looking straight at me with his beady little eyes. He appeared to have a smirk on his face. I shook my head and rubbed my eyes. Yep, the little guy was still there, staring at me—not moving a muscle.

The mouse was standing upright, legs apart and hands up as if ready for the fight of his life.

"Okay," I said with resolve. "If that's the way you want it, little guy, bring it on."

The mouse was approximately three feet away. I lunged forward, but that's when everything went black. All I remember was the shock of something coming out of nowhere and hitting me square in the middle of my forehead.

JOAB IN SHOCK

JOAB WATCHED THE GIANT FALL FLAT ON HIS BACK. HE was completely still.

Is he dead? What just happened here? Did the Creator knock him down to save me? He closed his eyes and tried to remember what happened.

He remembered hiding behind the leg of the shelf and his brothers running under the key closet door with the giant in hot pursuit. When the human opened the door and knew he had to do something quick, but what? He decided he needed a distraction so the bad ol' giant would follow him instead.

Joab had yelled as loud as he could and dashed for the tunnel entrance. It worked. The giant shut the closet door and ran after him instead. His voice boomed and his feet shook the floor as the giant ran towards him.

He knew he wouldn't have made it to the tunnel in time so he headed for the garden tools hanging on the wall. From that point on, everything seemed to happen in slow motion and yet he was ready to face the giant. He would be the sacrifice for his brothers, for his family, for the clan. He was hiding behind the broom but then the giant moved it away exposing him to the enemy.

At first Joab froze in fear. He was trapped with no escape. The giant stepped towards him and right on the rake's teeth. It came up like a hammer and hit him between the eyes. The bad ol' giant just stood there for a moment, his mouth open in shock, then he fell like a tree with a loud THUMP! The floor shook so hard Joab nearly fell down with the force of the impact.

THE KEY ROOM

A FEW MOMENTS BEFORE THE DOOR OPENED THEY heard Joab scream and the door close again. The giant's feet pounded as he ran after Joab.

Run, Joab, run! thought Troy.

In the darkness Jacob was still shaking. "Are we safe? Is the giant gone?" He looked up at Troy with wide, hopeful eyes.

Troy closed his eyes and thought of what was happening outside the door.

"The Creator must have told Joab to distract the giant so that we could escape," replied Troy with a reassuring smile. "We should seize this moment and head for the tunnel as quickly as possible, guys."

Samuel looked down and realized that in the midst of all the panic he was the one who had left his backpack beside the oats.

Troy noticed Samuel without his pack and consoled him. "It's okay, Sam, take Joab's bag until we see him again."

Everyone grabbed their bag of oats, slid under the door and ran single file towards the tunnel.

The brothers slipped under the door one by one with Jacob the Flash leading the way. Troy took up the rear to make sure no one was left behind. He knew there was no time to lose, the giant could notice them escaping, so they had to hurry. Soon the frightened Durum brothers arrived safely inside the hole. Shaun and Elijah greeted them with open arms excited to see all the bags filled to the brim with delicious oats.

As the bucks hugged each other, Troy moved to the tunnel opening and peeked around the corner to see what had happened to Joab and why he wasn't coming to join them. It was quiet—too quiet.

Something must have happened to poor Joab. But then he noticed the giant lying on the floor face up. Joab was standing on his chest, holding his staff up in triumph.

Troy waved a paw to his brothers.

"Hey, guys, come here! You've got to see this. I think Joab killed the giant! " They joined Troy who was standing in the middle of the tunnel opening, laughing and laughing.

Elijah the Risk Taker, seeing the giant was dead, ran out to see his brother—the hero. Troy and the rest of his brothers followed him. Even Shaun hobbled out of the opening with a relieved smile on his face.

A miracle, he thought. It's a miracle.

Joab shook his head as he came out of shock. He saw his brother Elijah coming towards him so he dropped his staff, hopped off the giant and threw his arms around him.

Troy and the others followed close behind screaming and cheering with joy at what appeared to be a great victory that would go down in clan history. Everyone in Salem would chant, "Joab the Giant Killer! Joab faced a mighty giant and struck him down with one blow."

James was overjoyed to see that Joab was okay.

"You saved us from certain death, Joab. You killed a mighty giant of Salem. How did you do it? Tell us what happened from the beginning and don't leave anything out." They all stopped talking as Joab told them how he killed the giant. When he got to the part where the Creator spoke to him, his brothers' ears perked up.

Joab walked beside the giant's head. "I hid behind one of the shelf legs and heard the giant open the door. Then all of you suddenly ran past me and into the key closet. I stood in my spot until I saw the giant open the closet door where you were hiding. I didn't know what to do, but suddenly I heard a voice telling me to create a diversion so you could escape.

"I ran out and screamed as loud as I could. To my surprise the giant saw me dash across the room and so he closed the closet door. I ran behind a broom, which was leaning against the wall, but the giant noticed. I knocked the rake loose and it fell to the floor in front of me. I took my staff, held it up and faced the giant. He pushed the broom aside and exposed my location. Then, smiling, he took one step forward and BAM! The rake rose up and hit him square between the eyes. He fell to the floor like a logged tree."

Jacob pointed at the giant with a wide grin. "And there he is, bucks, stiff as a board."

Troy climbed onto one of the giant's mukluks and pulled out his papa's sword of justice. "C'mon, guys, let's check him out. I've never seen a giant before, have you?"

Joab was quick to protest. "No, Troy, that wouldn't be a good idea. What if he's only asleep, wakes up and eats us. I think we should go back into the tunnel, pick up our bags of oats and head for home. Papa's instructions were not to be distracted by anything, even a real giant. Besides, Papa will worry if we're not home soon."

Troy placed the sword behind his back and crossed his arms. "Okay, you guys go ahead. I'll be right there. I just want to see the giant's face up close."

Suddenly, the creature's yellow eyes opened wide and stared directly at the little mouse.

CHAPTER 16

SAVING BETA

KINDNESS IS A VIRTUE EVEN IF THE ONE

IN NEED SHEDS CROCODILE TEARS. ITS

REWARDS ARE FAR GREATER THAN THE

SACRIFICE.

THE HUNT

OLIVIA AND FREY ARRIVED ON LEVEL FOUR TO IN-form the Kamet and Bulgur clans of the precious oats that were hopefully on their way from the giant's cupboard.

"Let's get moving, Frey," said Olivia, as she searched around the dark void of the rafters with wary eyes. "We must stay close to the wall and stop every few yards to watch for incoming bats."

Frey was visibly trembling. "I don't understand, Olivia. Why do we have to stop and look up? Why can't we just run for the control room door?"

"Because the bats would take us before we could duck underneath, sis." Olivia responded. "Papa told me just be-cause the Orange Bats can't see very well, doesn't mean they don't know where we are. Bats can sense motion, so when we're moving, their radar can track our location with pinpoint accuracy. If we stop-start, stop-start, it confuses their echo locator and allows us to get away — if we're lucky."

They sprinted along the wall, stopped, sprinted again and stopped. Frey gazed up for any signs of danger — so far so good. They had 20 feet to go until they reached the control room door. Suddenly, there was a soft swoosh.

"Olivia, did you feel that? I felt wind over my head and I heard what sounded like a wing flap. I'm scared," said Frey with a shaking voice.

"Stay quiet and still," whispered Olivia. "Did you see anything?"

"N-no," stuttered Frey. "I just felt something fly over my head."

Olivia knew they had to move fast because if Frey was right and there was an Orange Bat chasing them, they had to get to the door before it circled around for another pass.

Olivia tapped Frey on the shoulder. "Are you ready for one last sprint to the door?"

"Well, I'm really scared but we have no choice. We're too vulnerable if we stay here. What if it really was a bat trying to get me, Olivia? It could be waiting for us to move again." Frey started to cry.

"If it was an Orange Bat, Frey, it would have to turn around and try to find our movements again, and by that time we'll be safely under the door."

The does stayed absolutely still for a few more seconds just to be sure the bat was gone. It was a good thing they did because soon they heard a sharp whistle and the awkward flapping of leather wings above their heads. They waited as the Orange Bat flew round and round trying to hone in on their last known whereabouts. As soon as it was silent once again, the sisters made a final run for the control room. They sprinted as fast as their tiny legs could carry them. Twisting and turning, they skillfully used bat evasion strategies from RAMS.

Olivia arrived in the bin room first, followed by Frey who slipped under the door just as she heard a flap of leather wings above her head.

"That was close, Olivia," she panted as she pointed to an opening in the ceiling. "Is that where we are heading next?"

"Yes, it is, sis." Olivia was both relieved and confident the worst was behind them. "We have a ways to go, but it shouldn't take too long. All we have to do is climb the black desk, scurry up the wall, pass through a small tunnel, cross a rafter and find the entrance to the village."

Frey laughed. "Ha, ha, is that all? I hope the rest of the journey is less stressful, don't you?"

Olivia was worried. "I do, Frey, but something tells me things are going to get interesting around here very soon."

BETA THE ORANGE BAT

AFTER CATCHING THEIR BREATH, THE SILENCE WAS interrupted by a loud crash, thud and the flapping of wings.

"What was that?" asked Frey as she backed away from the door.

"Never mind that now, Frey," exclaimed Olivia as she continued towards the desk. "We must not get distracted from our mission."

The banging continued but was followed by a loud screech and a then soft cry.

"Help me! Help me!" A high but raspy voice cried out in pain.

"Did you hear that, Olivia? Someone is in trouble. Maybe we should slip under the door and see if whoever it is needs our help."

"No, Frey," chided Olivia, as she pulled her sister away from the door, "it could be a trap. Papa says the Orange Bats are very cunning. It could be waiting right behind that door and then when we come out— BAM! Before we know it, we'll be up on level seven being served on a platter to a family of hungry bats."

Frey was stubborn especially when it came to protecting someone's freedom. Being a "lover of freedom" was her greatest gift, after all, and so Frey began to reason. "We don't even know if it is a bat, Olivia, and besides what if it's trapped and needs our help. I for one am going under that door!"

Olivia reluctantly gave in. "Okay, okay! We'll go and see what all the commotion is about, but only if we can do this my way—with caution, agreed?"

Frey respected Olivia's wisdom during a crisis. "All right, so what's the plan?"

Olivia pointed to Frey's backpack. "Did you happen to bring your favourite mirror with you, Frey? The one Mama gave you on your birthday last year? And while you're at it, look for some tape, we'll need that too."

The mirror was the most beautiful thing Frey owned. Mama had found it one day on the first floor of the dumping grate. It must have fallen out of a truck that came in to deliver grain.

Frey smiled a big smile as she took the sack off her back and began to dig around for her prized mirror. "Here it is! And I have tape too!"

Olivia took the mirror and tape from Frey and found a small stick on the floor. She carved a notch on one end and placed the mirror carefully inside, wrapping the tape around it nice and tight.

"There, this should work," exclaimed Olivia with pride. "Now, we just slide it under the door and see if we can find out if that cry for help is real or not."

Olivia held the stick and turned the mirror from side to

side while Frey bent down low and looked to see where the noise was coming from.

"Stop, Olivia." Frey held up her paw. "I see something moving." The banging continued and the cries for help became more frantic. "It's coming from the grain sifter right next to the door." She squinted her eyes and took a closer look at the large sifter. It was shaking violently. "There's definitely something in there, Olivia. We must help whoever it is. Papa says that the Creator wants us to help the helpless and to free those in bondage. We can't just look the other way."

"Well, we have no choice now that it appears to be legitimate," replied Olivia after a few long moments of silence. "You're right, Frey, the Creator wants us to help the vulnerable." They gave each other a high five, scurried under the door and headed for the grain sifter. It was still shaking and banging as they stood at the base of the large machine. "Hello! Is anyone in there? Is there something we can do to help?"

The noise stopped for a few seconds before a nasally voice chirped inside the sifting box. "I–I seem to be caught inside this ghastly grain sifter. I had m-m-my radar honed in on two scrumptious little cheese lovers but they scurried under the door before I could snatch them. I never saw the sifter 'til it was too late. The screen must have been broken and I flew right into it."

Holding their paws over their mouths Frey and Olivia just looked at each other and gasped, then mouthed the words "Orange Bat!" They ran back under the door.

When they arrived inside the control room they remembered the words of the Creator reminding them to love their enemies. *"You have heard the Law, Love your neighbour and hate your enemy. But I say, love your enemies! Pray for those who persecute you! In that way, you will be acting as true children of your Father in heaven."*

The Orange Bat suddenly broke the silence and began crying for help again. "Hello? Are you still there? I need some help here! Hello!"

The does shrugged their shoulders in unison then Olivia responded, "All right, just hang on. We're coming."

Frey scurried up the leg of the grain sifter followed by Olivia who said a quick prayer for safety and wisdom. Arriving at the top of the machine they peeked over the edge and were filled with fear at what they saw behind the broken screen. Lying in the corner of the loading basket was a medium sized female Orange Bat nursing a broken wing and a few cuts, which were bleeding. She had pearly white teeth, piercing yellow eyes, a wet pushed-in nose and a jet-black face. The bat's orange streaked hair was sticking up in every direction and quite matted with blood. Both wings had orange flecks sprayed down to its claws.

Olivia stood in the open and waved for Frey to join her. She placed her hands on her hips and spoke as gently as possible. "You-you don't look so good, you big ol' bat."

The creature was startled and lifted her head. She couldn't believe who was standing there looking at her with pity. "You're-you're a cheese lover," she managed to say with a raspy voice.

"Actually," said Olivia pulling a reluctant Frey into view, "it's two 'cheese lovers.' I'm Olivia and this is my sister

Frey. We were the ones you almost 'snatched' for dinner."

The bat just stared at them in disbelief for a few seconds and then with a slow wicked grin lunged at them without warning. The girls slipped back under the basket just as the injured creature bounced off the screen and lay still. She looked up at them as they peered over the edge.

"Why did you come back?" But before the mice could answer, the bat fell still.

Frey crossed her arms and sighed. "What should we do now, Olivia? The bat's lost too much blood, if we don't help her now she'll die. On the other hand if she wakes up before we're done patching her up she could eat us."

"I know, I know," responded Olivia with a worried tone. "But you heard what our Creator wants us to do, Frey. We must help our enemies and trust Him no matter what happens."

Frey agreed with her sister and started pulling back the broken screen.

"You're right, Olivia. Let's go in there and see what we can do." They squeezed through the opening and cautiously walked towards the injured Orange Bat.

Frey went around the bat's side where she noticed a tear in her left wing.

Olivia checked the deeper cuts around her face and head. She opened her backpack and was glad Mama remembered to pack an emergency kit.

Frey carefully examined the extent of the injured wing. "I'm going to need some thread and a stitching needle."

"The cuts to her face and head seem quite bad, especially around the ear," Olivia reported. "I'm going to need to do some stitching as well."

The sisters began mending the wounds of their worst enemy.

"Okay, I'm nearly done here," exclaimed Frey as she finished a couple more rows, closing the torn wing quite nicely.

Olivia continued to wipe blood from the bat's face and hair, stitching together the worst cuts. She finished wiping down the head and sat down to rest beside it. Olivia had never been this close to an Orange Bat before and so she closely examined her dark skin and the curious orange dye in her hair. Suddenly, the creature's yellow eyes opened wide and stared directly at the little mouse.

"She's awake!" cried Olivia, jumping up. "Run!"

"No wait," pleaded the bat with a weak voice. "I-I won't hurt you. I just want to know, why would you help me? I was going to eat you and still you risked your life to help an enemy. I just want to thank you for your kindness. My name is Beta. What's yours?"

"Hi, Beta," responded Olivia, "my name is Olivia and this is my younger sister Frey. She fixed your wing and I cleaned and stitched the cuts on your face and head. I'm afraid you will not be able to fly for a while."

Beta felt the room begin to spin as she tried to speak.

Frey noticed the bat's disorientation and placed a paw to her lips, "Shhhh, Beta, you must not talk now. You've lost a lot of blood and should rest."

The does continued to clean Beta up as best they could and sat down to wait until she woke up. Frey pulled out some cheese snacks mama had packed.

"We're way behind, Olivia, if we don't show up at the storage bin on time, our sisters will worry that something has happened to us."

Olivia waved her hand and calmly answered, "They know whoever arrives at the bin first is to begin preparations for the Great Rejoicing. I suggest we take a short nap while we wait for Beta to wake up." They both laid down on their side and went to sleep.

A few minutes passed and the does were awakened by a loud groan as Beta began to stir and moan. "I don't feel so good. My head hurts and I can't move my wing."

"Well, Beta," Olivia began to explain, "you did tear a major ligament in your wing and have lost a lot of blood."

"And you also have a large bump on your head, Beta," Frey added.

The Orange Bat tried to stand to no avail. She just flopped back down.

"I can't thank you enough for what you have done for me. How can I ever repay you? I don't think I would have survived if you hadn't come back. I feel so bad I hunted you. You are the bravest little creatures I've known and I promise never to hunt mice again."

Tears had welled up in Beta's eyes and she looked down in shame.

"You must go now. It is not safe to be with me much longer. I'll be fine. My brother Zeta will come looking for me if I don't come home for dinner. Thanks again for your help. We are best friends forever."

Frey smiled. "We were just following our Creator's example. He tells us to help those in need and love our enemies. Maybe we'll meet again someday and you could bring Zeta along."

"I don't think that would be a good idea, Frey." Beta shook her head. "Zeta hates all cheese lovers. In fact, he would never, ever allow me to have you as my friends, even if he knew what you did for me."

While Frey and Beta were talking, Olivia was busy pushing open the broken mesh, which was the result of the bat's miscalculation.

"There, that should do it," she grunted and then turned towards Beta. "I must say, I have never met an Orange Bat up close before. You looked quite scary, however I love your hair—it's so modern."

Frey went up to Olivia and grabbed her paw, then spoke to Beta, "We'd love to stay longer, my friend, but we have a very time sensitive mission to complete before dinner."

"Yeah, it was great to meet you, Beta!" replied Olivia as she gave Beta one last look. "We will pray that you recover quickly. Hey! I have an idea. If you feel better tonight maybe you could come to the dance at the emergency storage bin on level four."

As her little friends scurried away Beta smiled and with a little chuckle yelled after them, "I'll see how I feel tonight and if I can get away without my big brother finding out. Anyway, you guys better get going. Good luck, my cheese lover friends!"

Their home was a comfortable, open concept wooden cave, situated between two upper rafters on level seven.

CHAPTER 17

DELTA AND IOTA

TRUTH BECOMES MORE ELUSIVE
WHEN CLOUDED WITH EMOTION AND
CONSEQUENCES. TELLING JUST ONE LIE DOES
NOT EXIST. IT MULTIPLIES FASTER THAN
TWO FRUIT FLIES IN AN APPLE ORCHARD.

FINDING LITTLE BEE

IT WAS A GOOD THING OLIVIA AND FREY LEFT WHEN they did because Zeta's radar had already located his baby sister and was flapping his way towards the sifter.

"There you are, little Bee," said Zeta as he swooped down and landed less than gracefully on top of the broken mesh. He peered in through the opening and looked upside down at his sister.

"You're kind of banged up, sis. You don't look so good? How did this happen?" He pushed back the mesh and hopped inside the sifter plate before his sister could reply. "Hey, looks to me like someone patched you up, little Miss Bee." Zeta came close and began examining her wounds. "Did your girlfriend Tau patch you up? By the way, where is she anyway? I'd like to thank her."

Beta just laid there, her eyes gazing down. "Ah, ah, Tau didn't come with me today, Zeta. She had chores at home, so I went hunting alone. I was circling around listening for movement and heard two cheese lovers scurrying towards the door beside the wheat sifter. I dove down and nearly caught them before they disappeared. I was in mid-flight and never saw the sifter tray until it was too late. The wire mesh tore through my wing and cut my face. I just lay there dazed, not fully aware of what happened."

Zeta was looking more and more worried. "So if Tau wasn't with you, who came to help you, Bee? And why aren't they still with you?"

"Just let me finish, will ya? You won't believe what happened in a million years." Beta was nervous to tell her brother the truth. "It's actually quite funny. When I got over the shock of smashing into the sifter tray, I desperately attempted to find my way out but the more I tried the more I became entangled in the wire. I called for help over and over and at first no one heard me. Then, when I lost hope, a small voice answered. To my surprise two little cheese lovers peeked around the corner."

"What? Beta, no!" Zeta was infuriated but then began to mock his sister. "You allowed two baby cheese lovers to come to your rescue? Ha, ha, ha! You're right, I don't believe you. How could you accept help from — from our prey?"

"Well, I didn't accept it right away, Zeta," she answered in defence. "At first I was angry and embarrassed that these rodents saw me in a vulnerable position and that they might laugh at my misfortune. I actually lunged at them but the pain in my wing was so great I passed out. When I came to, these little cheese lovers had stitched my torn wing and cleaned my wounds. I must admit, I totally misunderstood their intentions. I didn't expect them to show kindness to me. I'm their mortal enemy. Yet, they chose to help me, even at the risk of their own lives. So, I—I owe them my life, Zeta."

Her brother didn't respond. He was still angry. She could see it in his eyes. She slowly crawled on top of his huge back and hung on to his neck as Zeta carefully manoeuvred his way out of the gleaner. He stood on the edge for a moment, spread his large wings and took off into the darkness.

"Hang on, little Bee. We'd best be getting home. Mama and Papa will be worried sick by now." As they neared home on level seven he whispered, "Beta, I don't want you speaking a word of this to anyone, you hear? As far as our parents are concerned I found you, I stitched your wing, I cleaned you up and I brought you home. Understood, little Bee? We cannot be having the Orange Bat tribe thinking they can become friends with their dinner, now can we?"

Beta just stayed silent, put her head on his back and closed her eyes.

BETA'S FAMILY

IT WASN'T LONG UNTIL ZETA SWOOPED IN AND LANDED on the front porch of their family home. Papa Delta was worried sick.

"Where have you been, little Bee?" Papa's special nickname for Beta had stuck ever since he held his little girl at birth. She was sleeping so soundly that her snore sounded like little buzzing bees.

"I just wanted to go on a hunting trip with my friend Tau and surprise you, Papa," cried Beta with tears in her eyes, "but she had to stay home and do chores, so I went alone to prove I am just as good as any male hunter."

"Little Bee, I know you can hunt well. I taught you. But you know there are many dangers in the Orange Elevator. If something were to go wrong you would be on your own. I mean, look what happened. If Zeta hadn't spotted you in time we could have lost our little Bee. Therefore, until you are old enough, you must always take Zeta with you. Do you understand?"

She stared at the floor saddened by her Papa's rebuke. "Yes, Papa." She ran to Mama for comfort.

Iota held tightly to her little "whelp" (young bat) as she looked over her shoulder and smiled at her husband. "Now, now, my little Bee, I'm just glad you're all right. I was scared something happened to you." Mama let go and noticed Beta's wounded wing. "Baby Bee, how did this happen?"

Beta glanced at her brother for permission to tell the truth. He just gave her a cold stare and a slight shake of his head, as if warning her not to do it.

She was silent for a moment, thinking about what she would say. "I was circling around just as Papa taught me, using my whistle for echolocation when I honed in on two little … cheese lovers. I dived down and was about to snag one of them when they slipped under the doorway. When I looked up, the wheat sifter was right in front of me and I slammed into some wire mesh. I tried my best to get loose but the more I struggled, the more entangled I became."

Mama Iota placed an edge of her wing over her mouth in shock. "What did you do, sweetheart? Were you scared?"

Zeta was sitting on his special perch nervously awaiting his sister's response. Once again she looked up at him for consent but he turned away, pretending he wasn't interested in her story.

She continued, "I cried out for help, over and over until suddenly I heard a tiny voice calling back, 'Hello! Is anyone in there? Do you need our help?' It sounded like a little cheese lover."

Papa Delta gasped. "You were saved b-by cheese lovers? Zeta, is that true? I thought it was you that saved her."

Zeta waited until his parents were looking away for a

moment and then gave Beta a serious look of disappoint-ment. "What she means to say, Papa, is that she thought she heard a mouse. Bee hurt her head as you can see and when I found her she was not herself."

"But, Zeta —"

"It's okay, sis, I'll tell them what really happened." Now he had the full attention of his parents. "I was flying every-where looking for Beta. Suddenly, I heard a cry for help. The sound appeared to come from the grain sifter below, so I went to check it out. Well, there was our little Bee all banged up, just lying there unable to move. She moaned in pain as I untangled the mesh. Before I left home to search for Bee, I took the emergency kit with me. Her head need-ed a few stitches and her wing was badly damaged, so I sewed her up best as I could, Papa."

Iota went over to her daughter and inspected the stitch-es on her head and wing. "My my, Zeta, you did such a neat job with these stitches. I didn't know you were able to do this."

Papa Delta went over and placed his arm around his Zeta. "I don't care how you did it, my son, I'm just glad you looked after our little Bee. You're a good sire (male bat) and I'm so proud of you."

Bee gave her brother a hurtful stare, then went to her room. Their home was a comfortable, open concept wood-en cave, situated between two upper rafters on level seven.

Iota was a very perceptive female bat and like most ma-mas she could tell something wasn't adding up. "What's wrong with Bee, Zeta? She looks unhappy with you for some reason. She should be very grateful that you rescued her and fixed her up."

"She's probably just not feeling well, Iota," Delta said, his arm around Zeta. "Once we begin to eat she'll come and join us." Papa hooked a large grub off the table and offered it to his son. "Here you go, Zeta, you can have the honor of the first bite. You've earned it after all."

"It was nothin', Pops," lied Zeta, "I was just lookin' out for my baby sister, that's all."

Iota stared at her son with suspicion. She knew there was more to the story, so she would have to keep an eye on those two.

They celebrated Zeta's bravery over a delicious dinner of maggots and a few exotic bugs they'd found while flying around Potter's Field.

Beta stayed in her room and worked out a plan to see her newfound friends that evening at the Great Rejoicing.

Joseph thought it might be a good idea to get the rake out of the way before someone else got hurt.

CHAPTER 18

THE GIANT AWAKENS

LIFE IS FULL OF OPPORTUNITIES, OF
WHICH MANY ARE DANGEROUS. YET, IF
YOU NEVER TAKE A RISK, YOU WILL NEVER
KNOW THE JOY OF TRULY LIVING A LIFE OF
PURPOSE AND FULFILMENT.

"**I THINK HE'S ALIVE, BUCKS. HE'S STILL BREATHING,**" whispered Troy as he stood on top of me, his sword pointed at my throat. "Hey, wake up! Wake up, giant!"

I'm not sure how long I had been out, but when I came to, everything began to spin. My head pounded and my ears rang like a church bell. I had a large bump beginning to form on my forehead and I moaned in pain.

"What is walking on my chest?" I asked as I slowly lifted my head off the floor. The image was a blur but I'm sure I saw a small mouse peering down at me. He had an old rag tied around his head, which covered one eye. He wore what looked like an old frayed shoelace wrapped around his shoulder. His sword was actually a gold chrome nail and his shield was a brass button attached to his left arm. I chuckled to myself as I noticed the word "Levi" inscribed on the front.

As he came into focus, this strange yet brave little mouse tucked the Levi shield behind his back, placed a hand on his hip and introduced himself.

"Hi, my name is Troy! I don't know who you are, giant, but you'd better leave me and my brothers alone or I'll run you through with my papa's sword!"

I just laid there for a moment not believing my eyes or ears.

I must be dreaming, I thought. Soon I'll wake up and tell my pals at the Salem coffee shop I had this crazy dream where a one-eyed mouse threatened to take my life. Yet, this wasn't even the strangest part of the dream — I could actually understand the little rodent. I blinked my eyes and tried to get up, but as soon as I moved, a searing pain went through my head. "Ahhh," I moaned again, holding on to my aching head.

Troy poked his sword at me. "Quiet down, giant. You'd better stay down or the oats we took will be the least of your problems." This brave little mouse turned to his brothers and motioned for them to attack me. "C'mon, buckos, let's finish him off!"

By now Joab and the rest of Troy's brothers had run back into the tunnel entrance.

"Troy," called Joab, "run towards us as fast as you can before the giant gets up and eats you!"

Troy was distracted for a moment, but he turned back towards me.

"So, what's your name, giant? And why do you want to hurt us?" He continued, "I'm sorry we took your oats but we had no choice. Our clans have run out of food and we need it to keep us alive until spring arrives."

I tried to keep my voice down so that I wouldn't scare them too much.

"This is all so strange for me, little guy. I've never been able to understand a mouse before today and I never thought a mouse would be able to understand me. Are you sure you can understand me?"

Troy squinted his one eye, and smiled. "Of course we can understand you, the question is why? Maybe it has something to do with the bump on your head or maybe it's all part of the Great Creator's wonderful plan. Anyway, now that we have solved that problem, I ask again, what is your name, giant? And can we trust you or not?"

"My name is Mr. Wolfe, little man," I said as quietly as I could. "I'm sorry I was chasing you guys, but, you see, we can't have too many mice running around in a grain elevator. It would be against all health and safety regulations. The Saskatchewan Board of Health would shut us down pronto if they knew we had rodents crawling around the wheat kernels. I promise not to hurt you. Besides, I'm at your mercy and you have me pinned down, remember."

I tried to sit up again and felt the room begin to spin, so I was forced to lay back and stay still. Meanwhile this brave little mouse named Troy marched back and forth across my chest. He stopped, turned back, moved towards my head and stuck the tiny blade next to my throat.

"I want you to promise me that you will not come running after us when we leave with the oats. And," Troy continued, "you must promise that you will not set any more traps in our home or I will run you through with my papa's sword right now. Do you understand me, giant? Do you?"

"Whoa, my little friend," I held my hand up in a gesture of friendship. "What did you say your name was again?"

"Troy, Troy Durum, Mr. Wolfe." The tiny mouse held his head high and continued proudly, "but everyone calls me Mighty Troy of Salem. He pointed to eight terrified mice peering out from the tunnel door, "and these are my 'brave' brothers. Would you like to meet them, Mr. Wolfe?"

Troy kept pointing his sword at my throat so I was compelled to submit.

"Actually, I'd love to meet your brothers, Troy. I won't eat them you know, at least not today."

Shaun stood in the doorway looking at Troy and shook his head back and forth in protest.

"It could be a trick, Troy. Giants are very crafty you know."

Upon hearing their brother's description they all pushed further towards the back of the tunnel, huddling in fear.

Troy continued to beckon them with confidence. "Come on, you guys, it's okay, really. He seems rather harmless and this could be a once-in-a-lifetime opportunity. Just think, you get to meet a real live giant and actually talk to him."

Jacob the Flash was the first one to peek around the corner and without warning dashed across the room and stood next to my head. The speedy mouse slowly brought his paw up and poked my ear.

"Ouch," I protested, "why did you do that?"

Jacob jumped back. "I'm sorry, sir, but I've never seen a real giant up close before and just wanted to know what your ear felt like."

Troy smiled. "C'mon, guys, he actually seems quite harmless."

Shaun slowly made his way out of the tunnel, which seemed to prompt the others to follow.

Soon they all came out and stood around me. I was feeling much better by now, yet knew that if I got up too quickly I might frighten them.

"Would it be all right if I sat up and leaned against the wall, Troy? I'm feeling a little better but I still have trouble focusing."

"I think that would be all right, don't you agree, fellas?" They all nodded in tentative agreement and so I gently placed Troy on the floor and pulled myself up to lean my head against the wall. I noticed they were not ready to trust me as yet and Troy made that fact perfectly clear. "Just make sure you don't try anything stupid, Mr. Wolfe. We are watching you."

The rest of the Durum brothers stood around my feet as I finished propping myself against the wall. "Not to worry, little buck, I'm still feeling kind of dizzy anyway."

Soon, Troy crawled up my leg and back into my open palm. It must have felt warm because that's where he stayed as he introduced his brothers one at a time.

Troy Introduces His Brothers

"These, Mr. Wolfe, are my brothers," announced Troy as he waved his sword in their direction. "Let's begin with Elijah the Risk Taker." He pointed down towards my left suspender where one of the mice was admiring my shiny gold clasp holding up my pants.

The little guy had the bluest eyes and a huge grin that went from ear to ear. As Troy called his name, Elijah looked up with a start, confused as to why everyone was suddenly staring at him. "Elijah is called a 'risk taker' cause Papa said, 'there ain't nothin' that boy is scared of, except maybe flies.' Elijah has always hated flies as long as I have known him."

"Well, they make too much noise, Troy," exclaimed Elijah in defence, "and they always buzz around me when I'm tryin' to eat."

Everyone laughed and the mood seemed to lighten up as Troy continued to tell me about his brother's special gifts.

"Elijah has always been able to stand tall in the face of danger. Hey, Elijah, tell Mr. Wolfe why fear has lost its grip on you."

Elijah looked up at me. "'Cause the Great Creator is my

rock, in whom I find protection. He is my shield, the power that saves me, and my place of safety. He is my refuge, my saviour, the one who saves me from violence."

I was in shock as I watched this tiny little mouse tell me how the power of Logos could make a creature that appears weak become so strong.

Troy jumped off my hand and on to the floor. He stood beside a rather large mouse that was leaning on a wooden staff, supporting an injured left leg.

"This is Shaun," Troy slung his arm casually over his brother's shoulder, "he's like you, Mr. Wolfe, a gentle giant. The first thing Mama noticed was how polite and gentle he was with his siblings. Papa says Shaun is quiet but wise. In fact, he would rather listen than speak, yet when he does have something to say it's always worth the wait.

"The Creator has also blessed Shaun with supernatural strength. You know, I believe He has gifted us all with special powers, Mr. Wolfe and all we have to do is find them." Troy's head turned suddenly to his left. "Samuel! Put those things back in Mr. Wolfe's wallet."

Samuel dropped his head in shame. "I just wanted to check Mr. Wolfe's ID to make sure he is who he claims to be. I also saw something shiny inside and was curious as to what it was, that's all. I wasn't going to steal anything, Troy."

I picked up the shiny coin Samuel had found in my wallet and offered it to him. "That's okay, little guy. Here, do you want to keep it?" The little mouse opened his paw and I placed the dime into it. He was so thrilled, his smile went from one end to the other. Samuel's face was small and made all his other features look much more pronounced.

"Thank you, Mr. Wolfe, sir. It's so beautiful." He carefully placed the coin in the pocket of his trousers, which were always full of strings, candies, keys and other strange things. Sammy thought someday they might be useful for his sleuthing endeavours. He had the brightest green almond shaped eyes, which peered into the soul of anyone looking into them.

"Sorry for Samuel's strange behavior, Mr. Wolfe, this is precisely why Mama called him 'Samuel the Sneak.' He's always been very suspicious about everyone and everything. This trait however made his sleuthing skills highly tuned. He has what many would call, 'spidey' senses. When trying to find out who is lying or who committed a crime Samuel always discovers the truth. Samuel, why don't you tell Mr. Wolfe why you want to become a detective when you grow up?"

Samuel stood up straight and stated, "The Creator loves truth and justice and so do I. My brothers say I'm the only mouse in the world that sees everyone as guilty until proven innocent. I'm not sure about that, however I do believe every society needs law and order."

Troy smiled before he continued, "Being a sneak, is not always a bad thing, Mr. Wolfe. In fact, it can be a great gift if used with the right motives and intentions."

I was distracted by the mouse that stood next to Troy who was constantly moving around.

"What about the tall one with the long legs," I asked, pointing towards the mouse who stood head and shoulders above his brothers. "He seems quite jumpy and ready to go somewhere."

Troy's brothers laughed and exclaimed in unison, "That's Jacob the Flash!"

"Jacob's always been kind of jumpy and he can't stand still," explained Troy who stood beside his brother and looked up—way up. "He may be tall and always on the go but this is one fast buck. Papa calls him 'Speedy Gonzales,' but we just call him 'The Flash' cause he's the fastest mouse in the world. He's also very musical. Around the dinner table Jacob never sits still. He is always humming a tune or drumming his paws on the table. In fact, Mama always says, 'Jake was born with music in his bones and ants in his pants.'"

"So you actually believe the Creator made this mouse fast?" I pointed my finger at Jacob. "Why would He bother gifting a mouse with speed?"

Troy folded his arms. "Well, Jacob, tell this unbeliever what the Creator said when you began to doubt how He could use your special gifts."

"As a matter of fact," began Jacob while jumping up and down with excitement, "Papa told me of a story in the Book of Truth where it pays to be fast. You may even get to see something amazing if you are the first one there. 'Then Peter and the other disciple set out for the tomb. The two were running together, but the other out ran Peter and reached the tomb first. He bent down and looked in at the linen cloths lying there...'"

Troy smiled at his brother with pride. "Jacob, I'm sure Mr. Wolfe would like to hear what you did on the way here. Tell him how many traps you tripped in the tunnel."

"Not sure I could do it again," confessed The Flash,

"but I tripped five traps in a row without losing a hair on my tail. The Great Creator gave me the speed I needed, Mr. Giant, sir."

"I have never heard of a mouse tripping one trap let alone five." I said, quite amazed at the story. "You are a very brave mouse, Jacob, and yes, I'm sure the Creator helped you. I don't see how it would be possible without a miracle no matter how fast you are. Where did you learn to trip traps without getting caught?"

Jacob was honored that the giant would pay him so much attention. "Well, mister, I learned it from Miss Von Trap my teacher at the Royal Academy of Mouse Survival — RAMS. She was the best trap tripper ever — until I came along that is."

"You all go to school?" I was surprised at how civilized they were.

I was still talking to Jacob when I heard something dragging across the floor. To my left I saw a very large, muscular mouse easily lifting the rake I had stepped on and moving it back against the wall. He seemed to carry it with little effort. My mouth opened wide in response to his amazing strength. His brothers just laughed.

Troy casually pointed his finger at the oversized mouse, "That, Mr. Wolfe, is my big brother Joseph the Strong One. He is called that for obvious reasons."

Joseph heard his name. "Hey, why is everyone staring at me? I just thought it might be a good idea to get the rake out of the way before someone else got hurt, that's all."

"How did you get to be so strong, Joe?" I asked.

Joe casually leaned against the handle of the rake and shyly smiled as he peered down at his oversized feet. "Mama told me that when I was born it was obvious I was bigger than the rest of her bucks but she never expected I would be so strong. Socrates the Seer says the Creator gave me His strength to show others His power." Joe continued to speak in a low mumble, "I don't think I'm that special. I just do what I do, that's all."

"You are very special, Joseph," responded Troy. "Remember what else the old Seer told you? He prophesied that someday you would ensure the future of the Durum clan. So, I for one believe you are very special."

"How is it that you all seem to believe in the Great Creator?" I asked Troy. "I didn't think creatures were capable of understanding who He is."

Suddenly, James, who had been quietly listening, piped up. "The Book of Truth teaches, '…the fear of the Lord is the beginning of wisdom, and the knowledge of the Holy One is understanding.' All of the Creator's creatures give glory to their maker when they do what they were made to do, Mr. Wolfe. And yet, not all choose to believe."

Troy began to laugh as he looked at his brother who was sitting in a corner reading his book. "If you haven't already noticed, Mr. Wolfe, James the Wise One is the book worm in our family. Mama says he was born with his nose in a book and his mind full of questions. He spends most of his time under the tutelage of Socrates the Seer and has read the Book of Truth 20 times. For some reason Papa says James is an 'old soul' I don't know why, 'cause he's only a pup."

My attention shifted as I heard an annoying tap, tap, tapping on the wall beside my head. I looked to the right and noticed a husky mouse leaning against the wall. He had a large staff in his hand and was striking it against a large pipe.

Troy noticed my attention had diverted away from James.

"Well, I see that you've discovered my brother Joab the Fighter. He's kind of nervous and suspicious of everyone but loves to fight for what is good and just. Joab has a soft heart for those being mistreated and bullied. He has the ability to see the big picture and figure out the correct battle strategy. He loves to win and usually does, don't you, Abe?"

Joab stood up straight and pointed the staff he was playing with at his brother in protest. "You know I don't like to be called that, Troy," He had squinty close-set eyes, jet-black fur and wore a large chain around his skinny neck.

"Sorry, Joab." Troy turned back to me. "Mr. Wolfe, if you are feeling better I'm afraid my men and I must be going. We truly apologize for taking your oats but our clans are quite desperate. We have run out of food and our families will not survive the winter without it."

I felt the front of my head where the rake had hit me. A large bump had formed and I still felt quite dizzy. "I'll be fine, my little friends. You should leave as soon as you can. Don't worry about the oats." I began to stand using the wall as support and pointed at the oats on their backs. "There's more where that came from. I could even leave some fresh cheese for you someday if you come back to visit. I want you to know I will always be your friend and if you are ever in need of anything just ask."

Judah was off to the side and busy sweeping the rest of the oats that had fallen out of my bag, so I hadn't noticed him until now. He smiled at me and said, "I love cheese!! That would be great, Mr. Wolfe."

Troy and his brothers laughed. "Yep, that's Judah all right. As you may have guessed he loves good food, cleanliness, building and writing music. He writes songs for every major event in his life. He also made our kitchen table and our bunk beds. In fact, when he was only two he built an automatic cheese cutter out of a shaving razor, used Popsicle sticks, rubber bands and a small electric motor he found in the basement. He's quite the inventor you know."

Troy suddenly appeared worried, "I'm sorry, Mr. Wolfe, but we must head out and bring this food to the storage bin. We still have to pick-up our papa and mama at home. Without any more delays it will still take us 20 minutes to get there. We are very grateful for the oats, and it was very nice to meet you, Mr. Giant — I mean, Mr. Wolfe. I'm sure we'll meet again—and sorry about your head."

Troy winked his one eye at me, made an about face and entered the tunnel.

"C'mon, my brave warriors, let's go home." His brothers followed Troy and scurried through the tunnel loaded down with all my oats.

I just sat there in silence thinking to myself. "Did this really happen or am I still unconscious?" I thought about telling the guys at the Hebrew's Coffee Shop in Salem about Troy but then I knew they would never believe me. This would have to be my little secret. I also wondered if I would ever see this special one-eyed mouse again. Little did I know my encounter with Mighty Troy of Salem would be the first of many adventures to come.

CHAPTER 19

SNAP-TRAPPED

REMEMBER PAIN AND SORROW ARE BEST

FRIENDS, BUT THEN SO ARE FREEDOM AND

JOY. THE FIRST TWO ARE BIRTHED FROM

THE FALL AND DEATH; THE LAST TWO ARE

BIRTHED FROM LOVE AND LIFE.

OLIVIA AND FREY TOOK ONE LAST LOOK AT THEIR newfound friend Beta, climbed down the sifter and slipped back under the control room door.

"I can't believe we made friends with an Orange Bat, Olivia!" exclaimed Frey as they made their way towards the large black desk in the corner of the room.

"I know," responded Olivia, "that is so cool. Just wait until we tell our brothers how dangerous our mission op was. They're probably at the storage bin, as we speak, helping Tammy, Ava, and Evalyn set up for the Great Rejoicing."

Frey was concerned. "Well, all I know is that we're late and Mayor Sugar and her husband Spice need time to prepare for the celebration tonight. Let's hurry, Olivia." They scurried up the wall and popped through a hole in the ceiling. As they walked along in the dark tunnel they discussed what they were going to say to Mayor Sugar and began to plan how they would set-up the emergency bin room.

Suddenly there was a loud SNAP!

"AHHHH!" screamed Frey in tremendous pain. Olivia opened her backpack, took out her flashlight and shone it on her sister. Frey was writhing in pain on the wood floor, her tail was caught in a snap trap.

"Oh no! I'm so sorry, Frey! I should have taken the flashlight out and used it sooner. I thought we could see in the dark well enough. How could I have been so stupid?" She started to cry and ran over to where the trap was crushing Frey's tail. Olivia bent down, took hold of the large metal bar and attempted to ease the pressure. She grunted as she pulled harder and harder but it wouldn't budge. "I can't

Frey was writhing in pain on the wood floor, her tail was caught in a snap trap.

move it, Frey, the spring is too strong. What are we going to do?"

By now Frey was in shock. She couldn't stop sobbing and tried to catch her breath.

"I-I, have, have, to think," Frey said in between sobs. "I can get out of this trap. I've-I've done it before and practised it over and over, but never with my tail in a real trap. It hurts more than I thought, Olivia."

Olivia held on to her sister's paw, tears streaming down her face. "I'm so sorry, Frey. Is there anything I can do? Should I go and get Papa? Tell me what to do!"

Frey tried to think through the pain that was now throbbing along her back and up into her spine.

"We need leverage, Olivia, we need lots and lots of leverage."

"What does that mean?" asked Olivia.

Frey's voice betrayed her pain. "It means we-we need s-something long and sturdy to place under the b-bar, and we-we'll need that long piece of rope in your backpack."

Olivia opened her pack, pulled out the rope and looked around for something to use as leverage. "I'll be right back, Frey! I have to look around for something large enough to place under the steel bar."

"I'll be right here when you get back." Frey squeaked out before passing out again.

Olivia switched on her tiny key-chain flashlight and made her way back through the tunnel and into the control room. She knew there must be something she could use as leverage. The room was dark and so she shone her light on the floor but it was clean. As she swept the light around the room, she noticed something on top of the desk in the corner.

"Yes, that's it!" Olivia exclaimed with joy. "A small pencil will be a perfect wedge to lift the bar high enough to free Frey." She scurried down to the floor, up the table leg, onto the desktop and retrieved the leverage she needed. She placed it through one of the loops on the outside of her pack and headed back into the tunnel.

"I found some leverage, Frey!" yelled Olivia as she turned the corner and shone the flashlight in her sister's direction. Frey was still passed out.

Quickly, Olivia placed her knapsack on the floor and retrieved the pencil. She tied the rope to one end, then jammed the tapered end between the bar and the wooden base of the trap. When it was firmly in place she began to pull the rope down with all her might, but it was no use. The spring was too tight. It would take a far greater weight and strength to lift the bar and set her sister free.

Olivia looked at Frey and began to cry. They needed a miracle and fast.

THE RESCUE

KING GOAR AND QUEEN NOAM STOOD UP FROM BE-hind the wedding table and held their cups of sour wine in the air.

"Let us all rise together," announced Goar. "I would like us to honor the marriage bond between my son, Benob, and King Og's lovely daughter, Lilith. May the blessing of Dreck be upon this union and may it bring peace between our two tribes. Benob and Lilith, we pray that you have a mischief (many rats) of pups so that our two kingdoms will continue to flourish."

King Og gazed at the young couple, raised his glass and added, "As the Great Wizard of Salem, I, King Og, charge your offspring to be a scourge of terror to those 'cheese lovers' and may their weak, invisible God be defeated by Lord Dreck once and for all!"

Goar and Og smiled at each other and clinked their glasses as they took a sip.

Benob and Lilith placed their glasses on the table and kissed each other, only as rats do—licking noses.

Both kings finished the last bit of wine from their cups.

"Abigail, Abigail!" bellowed Goar. "Come and fill our cups with more wine."

"The wine is all gone, oh King," replied Abigail with fear, as she ran towards the head table.

"Well, hurry and get some more from my private cellar and take Jonathan with you." Goar raised his brows, stared at them with his red fiery eyes and pointed to the door. "Jon knows where to find the wine. Now go, and don't dilly dally."

SKIPPING ON RAT'S TRAIL

ABIGAIL GRABBED HER BROTHER'S HAND AS THEY disappeared through the doors and down the pipes to level four. They walked together on the Rat's Trail holding hands and talking about how good it felt to escape from the party for a while.

Abigail had found a kindred spirit in her brother Jonathan. He was gentle and kind—a total opposite from his brothers who saw her as more of a slave than a sister. She was too young to remember when she was taken from her family and yet always knew she didn't belong.

"Hey, Johnny, want to skip with me on the path? I love skipping! It makes me happy, like I don't have a care in the world."

Jonathan loved his sister Abi as he liked to call her. She displayed such grace in the midst of her bad situation. He'd never heard her say a bad word to anyone or hold a grudge.

He smiled. "Sure, Abi, I'd love to skip with you but we have to hurry. You know how angry Papa Goar becomes when he has to wait for something."

"Where are we going, Johnny?" Abi was full of questions. "Will the wine be hard to get? Oh, this will be such an adventure. There's no telling what Dreck will have in store for us today. He could be planning an amazing adventure, right, Johnny?"

"Whoa! Slow down, little Princess," responded Jonathan, "I know exactly where we are going and, no, the wine will not be hard to retrieve. We'll find it in a tunnel located just past a large rafter in the middle of the room."

They skipped their way past the rafter and were soon at the entrance to the tunnel. They slowly walked in and stopped to let their eyes adjust to the darkness of the cave. Johnny knew exactly where Papa's wine was. "It's just around the corner Abi." He pointed to a small hole in the wall. "We must be careful, because I remember a mouse trap loaded and ready to go right next to Papa's wine cellar." Turning the corner they were shocked to find someone else in the cave.

Frey noticed Jonathan and Abigail first. She screamed. Olivia was still trying to pull the pencil down to free her sister to no avail and didn't notice the two strangers.

"Olivia," warned Frey, "Run! Don't look back. It's the Rafter Rats!! Above all, you must complete our mission."

"No, I will never leave you," responded Olivia as she withdrew the staff from behind her back. She crouched down in a fighter's stance, her blue eyes blazing like two star sapphires ready to engage the enemy. Back and forth, the staff seemed to move on its own in a graceful deadly dance. Quickly, Olivia moved towards her greatest threat, the larger of the two rats.

Jonathan held up both his hands in surrender. "Wait, we mean you no harm! My sister and I are not friends with King Goar. He is moving the Rafter Rats in the wrong direction and is becoming more dangerous and more powerful by the minute."

"Don't trust him, Olivia! It could be a trick," cried Frey as she groaned in pain.

Jonathan picked up Abigail in his arms and moved closer. "Please just let me explain. This is Abigail. She is not a rat but a mouse like you."

"Don't come any closer, you nasty Rafter Rats," warned Olivia as she thrust her staff in the rat's direction. "She appears to be a mouse but then why is she with you? She's probably your slave and you're using her as bait."

"No, no, you have it all wrong," he explained in a soft

voice. "I am Jonathan, King Goar's youngest son and I do not believe we should be at war with the mouse clans in the Orange Elevator. Princess Abigail has always been like a sister to me. She was taken from her family a number of years ago by King Goar. He wanted her to be his slave, however my Mama, Queen Noam, fell in love with little Abigail. She has been a part of our family ever since. Goar still treats her as a slave but Mama and I take care of her."

"AHHHH!" Frey cried in pain as she tried to move further away from the two unwelcome guests.

Jonathan hadn't noticed the other mouse until now, because he was focused on Olivia, who was still in a battle stance.

NEW FRIENDS

"LET ME DOWN, JOHNNY," WHISPERED ABIGAIL IN his ear.

Jonathan gently placed his sister on the floor and she ran over to the steel bar that was holding Frey's bloody tail in place.

"Look, the poor dear is caught in one of those nasty snap traps. We have to help her Johnny." Abi ran to the mouse who was in obvious pain. "What's your name, honey, and how did you get your tail caught in the giant's trap?"

Frey managed a few words between sobs. "My-my name is Frey. It was dark and I didn't see the trap before it was too late." She continued to cry.

"My dear, Frey," said Abi, trying to comfort her, "you are so blessed the trap did not catch more than your tail. Don't you worry, Johnny will get you out. I will pray Dreck gives you comfort and eases your pain." Abi reached into her pocket and pulled out a small wooden idol made in Dreck's image. She handed it to Frey. "He's powerful and will help you feel better while Johnny tries to lift the bar."

Olivia noticed the idol and turned quickly towards Abigail. "We know you mean well, but we can never pray to your false god Dreck." She placed her paw around her sister. "We worship the Great Creator of all things. He always was and nothing has ever existed before Him. He has commanded us to never worship anything He has made and that includes your god Dreck."

Abigail quickly put the idol back in her pocket not wanting to offend her suspicious friends. "I am so sorry. I didn't mean to offend you. What is your name?"

"Olivia. My name is Olivia from the Durum clan," she said, standing straight and keeping her staff firmly in front of her and aimed at Jonathan.

"I have heard of this God of yours, but Goar says He is weak and has cast His spell of love on you. Papa says your God was killed by the human giants and is no more. Honestly, I don't know what to believe and yet I do know that right now we must get your sister out of this trap before she loses too much blood."

Johnny turned to Olivia, and asked her in a gentle tone, "Let me help your sister? Tell me what you have already tried, maybe I can do something."

"It's okay, Olivia," assured Abi, "Johnny is on your side. I trust him with my life and you have to make a choice to trust him or not. If he wanted to do something to you, he would have done it already. Why don't you ask your God what is true? Maybe He will tell you."

Olivia said a quick prayer after which she still didn't completely trust the Rafter Rat.

"Okay, son of Goar, you can come and help me pull down on this pencil, but you stay away from my sister. Do you understand, rat?"

Jonathan moved slowly towards Olivia with his hands still in the air.

"Okay, just take it easy, young doe." He stared at the stick lodged in place under the steel bar. "The pencil was a good idea for leverage, but what you really need is more weight and I've got lots of that." Johnny was big and strong, yet not overweight. He came close to Olivia and took hold of the rope just above her head.

"Okay," he said looking over at his sister. "Abi, get ready to pull Frey's tail out quickly. We may have only one shot at this so be ready. Pull hard on three. One, two, three— pull!" They both grunted hard and hung in mid-air for a few seconds. The steel bar moved a little, but not enough to free Frey's tail from the trap.

Olivia let go of the rope, bowed her head and sent up a quick prayer to the Creator for wisdom. Suddenly an idea popped into her head. "Hey, Abi, all we need is a bit more weight to lift the bar, what if you came over and the three of us pulled down with all our might. Frey, do you have enough strength to pull your tail out from the bar?"

"I think so," she said, though her voice sounded frail.

Johnny motioned for his sister to join them. "C'mon, little sis, all we need is your added weight to set our new friend free from her bondage."

Abi ran over, smiled at Olivia and grabbed both her paws. "This will work, Olivia, I believe this will work."

Frey twisted herself so she could gently pick up her tail. It hurt so bad.

"Are you ready, young doe?" Jonathan asked Frey.

Frey shut her eyes and braced herself for more pain. "Let's just get this over with."

"Okay, on three," announced Abigail as they counted together. "One, two, three—pull!" The trio pulled down on the rope with all their might and suddenly the bar moved up.

Frey felt the weight lifting off of her tail so she quickly pulled it out before the bar slammed back down. "I'm free!" she yelled, then fell to the floor unconscious. Her tail had been broken and was bleeding.

Olivia ran over to her sister. She took off her backpack and pulled out a bandage Mama had provided in case of emergency. She finished wrapping it around Frey's tail just as she woke up.

"Where am I?" asked Frey, her eyes slowly focusing on her sister's face. "Am I free, Olivia?"

"Yes, you're definitely free, sweetie," acknowledged Olivia, "thanks to our new friends Jonathan and Abigail." She stood and gave Jonathan a hug. "I still can't believe you are Goar's son. And you!" She grabbed hold of Abi's paw, "you're as tough as any rat warrior I've seen."

Jonathan worried that they had been away from the party too long. "I'm sorry we can't stay and assist you with your mission, but we must run before Papa Goar becomes impatient and sends someone to look for us. We were ordered to bring more wine for the wedding feast. My brother Benob married King Og's daughter Lilith tonight." The large rat moved over to the wall and opened a small door. He reached inside and pulled out two bottles of airport wine.

Frey tugged on Olivia's arm. "We have to go as well, Olivia. It is important we complete our mission as soon as possible. Troy may have already arrived with the oats."

Jonathan's ears perked up. "Oats, what oats? Have you managed to find food?"

Olivia punched Frey on the arm, "Frey, no one is supposed to know we have found food, especially the Rafter Rats."

She stared at Jonathan and Abigail with fear. "You can't tell Goar what you have heard. You know what he'll do if he finds out we found oats."

Abi nodded. "Don't worry, Olivia, we won't say anything. Your secret is safe with us—right, Johnny?"

The big rat spoke with authority, "I swear by Lord Dreck not to tell anyone, but you have to be careful not to tell anyone about your find. He has spies everywhere you know. In fact, he might have already heard about it."

Abigail took Frey by the hand. "Hey, we are both heading out of the tunnel anyway, why don't we walk together?"

Frey was thankful for the company as they traveled through the last part of the tunnel. "I'm so glad we met you guys and that we can spend a little more time together."

"Me too," agreed Olivia, "I hope your papa doesn't get too angry that you're late."

Jonathan carefully placed the wine in his backpack. "He'll be fine once he has his wine."

As they reached the end of the tunnel Frey turned to thank her new friends once again. "We will never forget you guys. Maybe someday we will meet again."

"I have a feeling we will, Frey," said Abigail as she skipped behind her brother who was already leaving.

Troy, Judah, and Shaun made the final dash to the pipe entrance. When they arrived, they were totally exhausted.

CHAPTER 20

HEADING HOME

EVERYONE LONGS FOR A PLACE CALLED

HOME. THIS PLACE IS OUR FOUNDATION,

OUR SOLITUDE, OUR FAMILY, OUR BLOOD.

WE ARE LOVED, RESPECTED AND CARED

FOR BEHIND THESE WALLS. HOME TRULY IS

WHERE THE HEART IS.

SHAUN HOBBLED ALONG WITH THE HELP OF HIS BROTH-ers as they moved slowly forward through the tunnel. They squeezed Shaun through the small hole Troy had made on their way to the lunchroom. It took them another five minutes to crawl out the other side.

Troy was the first to exit the tunnel. He peeked out and looked both ways for any signs of danger, then stepped out and hugged the side of the wall.

"It looks good, bucks, come on out." He motioned for his brothers to join him. "Let's rest here a moment before we journey to the gleaning pipe."

"We are late, Troy," Shaun said as he leaned against the wall. "Mama and Papa will be worried by now and our sisters are already preparing for the Great Rejoicing."

"If we change our route," Troy instructed, "we should be through the gleaning pipe and back home in 10 minutes. All we have to do is wind our way through a maze of machines, climb the pipe and we're as good as home. Are you ready?"

Judah placed his hand out in front as his brothers joined the Durum bucks cry: "The Durum bucks are not dissuade, we are stronger together, we're not afraid. We fight for freedom, we fight for love, but look for peace from the Logos above."

Troy suggested another way to get to the pipe. "Bucks, Papa warned us not to run through the middle of a room but to scurry along the walls for safety. I know it will take more time but we must be safe. Do you all agree?"

Samuel put his hand up in protest. "We're very late, Troy. I think we should take the risk and go through the centre of the room. What could go wrong?"

"Papa warned us to stay against the wall, Samuel," Troy answered back. "He has lived his whole life in this elevator and we should trust his judgement."

Jacob the Flash broke in, "Papa doesn't know how fast we can run, Troy and, besides, how hard can it be to move from machine to machine. Look, the pipe is right over there." Jacob pointed to where the entrance was beckoning them to come.

Troy noticed his brothers' heads nodding in agreement. "Okay, let's take a vote," he suggested. "All hands up if you think we should follow Papa's suggestion to stay along the wall." Troy, Shaun, Judah and James voted for Papa's way.

"Okay, those who want to take the shorter but more risky journey to the pipes raise your hands." Of course Elijah, Samuel, Joseph, Joab and Jacob the Flash voted in favor of the more dangerous way through the middle of the room.

Troy was not happy with the decision but honored the free vote. He pulled out nine small whistles Mama had given him to share with his brothers.

"All right, then, Mama told me to give each of you a whistle for safety if the situation warranted. I believe this would be a good time. We'll move out two at a time from machine to machine. Let's pray the Orange Bats are busy elsewhere or we'll be easy targets.

"Shaun, Judah and I will run to the first machine, then as we begin to move to the second one take your partner and run to the first machine. When we move to the third machine the first pair moves to the second one and the next pair moves to the first one, et cetera. This way only one group moves at a time. Now, if anyone sees or hears anything suspicious, blow your whistle — hard."

Samuel waved his paw over his mouth in a fake yawn.

"Are there any questions?" asked Troy.

Samuel raised his hand. "Yeah, can we go yet, Troy? At this rate we'll never get home and besides we won't even need these stupid whistles, the pipe is right there."

Troy shook his head. "Okay, let's roll, bucks." Troy, Shaun and Judah ran as fast as they could to the first machine and stopped. He motioned for Samuel and Joseph to follow just as they headed for the second machine. They had five machines to run past before they made it to the pipe, leading them to freedom and home. The most dangerous run would be from the fifth machine to the pipe. The brothers would be totally exposed for at least 10 feet with nowhere to hide.

Troy, Judah and Shaun made the final dash to the pipe entrance. When they arrived, they were totally exhausted.

So far, everything was going as planned. The rest of the bucks arrived at the pipe without incident. Elijah and Joab, were the only ones left, but they didn't come.

Suddenly, they heard three short whistles echo loudly around the room. Then all was quiet — deathly quiet.

"Hey, is everything okay, you two?" Troy called out to his brothers. "We heard the whistle. Are you safe?"

No response.

Troy knew something had gone wrong. He could feel it. In fact, he could smell it.

"When was the last time any of you saw Elijah and Joab?

Think. It's important."

"I remember seeing them running toward machine number four," answered Samuel, "but I didn't see them after that."

Shaun who had great eyesight squinted at the fifth machine. "I think I see movement at machine number five, Troy."

Troy couldn't see anything but he could sure smell something evil in the room. Troy squinted his eye and could clearly see two shadows huddling close together underneath the fifth machine, but there seemed to be a third shadow with them. It was then he noticed two yellow eyes glowing from within the darkness. A great fear overtook Troy as he began to fully realize what had just happened.

MOMENTS BEFORE

ELIJAH AND JOAB SAW SAMUEL AND JACOB DASH FROM machine four and arrive safely at five. Joab had started to run but noticed Elijah staring into space and hanging on to the leg of machine four as tightly as he could.

"Come on, Elijah!" yelled Joab. "We must hurry!" He grabbed his brother's hand and pulled him free from the leg.

Elijah looked up and blew his whistle. He peered over his brother's shoulder and noticed a large Orange Bat diving down towards them its claws wide open.

CAPTURED BY KAPPA

JOAB TURNED AROUND TO SEE WHAT HAD FRIGHTENED Elijah but it was too late. King Kappa snatched

Joab with his winged claw while Elijah kept blowing his whistle. He helplessly watched his brother dangle from the bat's wing and knew he had to do something quickly or Joab would be gone. He pulled the whistle off his neck and latched the rope around Kappa's legs in mid-air. This lifted him off the ground at first but then he fell back to the floor as the big Orange Bat crashed into machine number five.

Kappa just lay there not moving and so Elijah ran over to free his brother who had gotten up and was coming towards him. They met right in between machine four and five and wrapped their arms around each other.

"Where do you think you're going, you little flea bitten rodents?" snapped Kappa as he lunged towards the unsuspecting mice.

The bat king slowly emerged from the darkness, dragging two very frightened mice who were being held tightly underneath one of his huge leather wings. They were both alive but shaking and wet from the hungry bat's drool.

"My name is Kappa," announced the large bat with a growl. "I am the Great King of the Orange Bats on level seven and I'm about to eat your little friends."

Troy said a quick prayer to the Creator, asking Him for strength and stepped forward to meet King Kappa.

"I tell you what, Kappa. You let my brothers go and I won't hurt you," threatened Troy. Most of Troy's brothers stood strong behind him.

All except Samuel who whispered in Troy's ear, "I don't think you should make him mad right now, Troy. You could be making matters worse."

Kappa's eyes went wide with great surprise as he noticed how tiny Troy turned out to be. A large evil smile stretched across his face as he laughed and taunted.

"Ha, ha, ha, you actually believe you can take these two little morsels from me? Your presence is an insult to my greatness! What is your name, you freak of nature!"

Troy held up his sword in front of him and continued in a clear and calm voice, "My name is Mighty Troy of Salem and I told you to let them go, or my Creator will strike you down." He bravely took another step forward.

Kappa also moved forward. "How have you managed to live as long as you have in your pathetic condition, you one eyed cheese lover." He turned towards Joab, grabbed his tail and held him over his open mouth. "You want them, come and get them, little Troy."

He was just about to drop Joab into his mouth when something very large and furry landed on top of him with a loud thud. The Bat King screeched in pain and let go of Joab, as he lay flattened under a heavy weight. Elijah ran to the safety of his brothers.

Troy took off towards Joab who was lying on the wooden floor. "Take my hand Joab, hurry!" he said, just as a large tail whooshed over their heads. They both scurried back to the pipe and stood with their brothers. As they turned around they noticed an orange tabby cat holding Kappa down with his two paws.

"Did you get him, Willis?" asked Arnie as he came around the corner. Kappa was flapping his wings trying his best to escape but the cat's hold on him was too strong.

"I got my first mouse, Uncle Arnie! He's bigger and stronger than I thought. So, what do I do with him now?"

WILLIS

WILLIS WAS ARNIE'S YOUNG NEPHEW WHO HAD come for his first visit from Cat Hill, a small town of homeless felines located just outside of Salem. It appeared as though he'd never seen a real bat before. Not up close anyway. His father Calvin had sent him to his big brother Arnie for a holiday.

Willis hadn't seen too many mice in his life but was eager to see more. Secretly, he wanted to find some mouse friends he could talk to but when he saw a bat trying to eat the two mice, he knew he had to do something quick. So he pretended to not know what a real mouse looked like.

"Now you've done it, boy!" Arnie was worried. "He's gonna be as mad as a hornet when you let him go."

Willis was all excited. "Oh, I'm not letting go of my first mouse, Uncle Arnie. No sir, he's mine and I'm keepin' him."

"That's not a mouse, Willis!" Arnie exclaimed as he laughed out loud at his confused nephew. "That's a bat! They're on our side! They catch mice like we do. Now let him go before all his friends show up."

Willis pretended to be in shock. He looked down at Kappa who was snarling at the bewildered young cat who began to apologize.

"Wow! You sure had me fooled, Mr. Bat, sir! I'm sorry! I thought for sure you were a mouse 'cause you were crawlin' on the floor and not flying through the air."

"Yeah! So now that you know the truth you can get off of me, you mangy cat. Can't believe you thought I was a cheese lover. I had two of those little rascals in my grasp and was about to eat them when you jumped on me. Now they're gone."

Willis noticed little Troy frantically tossing each backpack into the pipe behind his brothers, most of whom were already in the pipe. Only Joseph and Shaun were still with him.

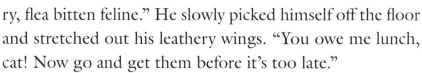

"You mean that little creature over there is a mouse?" Willis let go of Kappa and pointed at Troy.

Kappa was very angry. "Yes, that is a cheese lover, you furry, flea bitten feline." He slowly picked himself off the floor and stretched out his leathery wings. "You owe me lunch, cat! Now go and get them before it's too late."

Troy saw Kappa and Willis poised to attack so he held up Papa's gold sword in defence and waited for the ensuing battle.

Arnie ordered his nephew to attack. "Get him, Willis! This is your opportunity to make things right and to show your papa what kind of mouser you are."

"He's right, Willis," agreed Kappa. "This freak should be an easy test for you. Realistically, he's only half a mouse. Now get him!"

Shaun and his brother Joseph moved in front of Troy as the cat cautiously moved towards them.

The cat cocked his head to one side. "Why do you have only one eye, little mouse?" He sat down, and extended his paw towards Troy. "Hi, my name is, Willis, what's yours?"

Shaun came back out of the pipe and joined his brothers who were between Troy and Willis. "I wouldn't trust him, guys. Cats don't just shake paws and become best friends with mice."

Troy peeked around the side of his Levi shield and said to his brothers. "Sometimes you just have to follow your heart and take a risk." Then with a cautious grin he put out his paw. "Hi, Willis, my name is Troy, Troy Durum. You're not going to eat us, are you?"

Before Willis could answer, Kappa jumped in and moved next to Willis, "Are you kidding me? How can you call yourself a cat? Pounce on those cheese lovers right now, or at least give them to me. I saw them first, remember!"

Uncle Arnie also encouraged his nephew to do the "right" thing. "Willis, what am I supposed to tell your papa? That you made friends with a-a-a mouse, if you can call it that! Now snatch him or I will."

Troy and his brothers became more nervous after hearing their mortal enemies discussing their fate. Troy began to slowly back up towards the pipe opening, pulling his brothers along.

Willis noticed they were leaving. "No wait, Troy! I don't

care what they say, I won't hurt you." He glared at Kappa. "I want you to leave now or else you will be my first catch of the day!"

Kappa bared his teeth at Willis, spit flying from his mouth as he spoke. "Bad decision, little cat! Someday, you will need us and we will not come to your aid. I am King Kappa of the Orange Bats and I will see to it personally that you pay for humiliating me." He looked away from Willis and pointed at old Arnie with his right claw. "Your nephew is out of control, Arnie. He could change the entire balance of nature within the elevator if you don't rein him in. The natural law 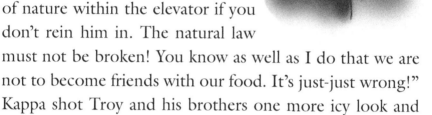 must not be broken! You know as well as I do that we are not to become friends with our food. It's just-just wrong!" Kappa shot Troy and his brothers one more icy look and then awkwardly took flight, disappearing into the darkness.

Arnie lowered his head in shame and motioned for Willis to follow him. "It's time to go, you naughty kitten. You've done enough damage for one night. I won't tell your papa what happened if you come home right now."

Willis knew he had no choice but to obey his Uncle Arnie. "I'll be right there, Uncle." He started to walk away but then turned toward Troy and whispered, "I know your grandpapa. He is a family friend." Willis suddenly changed his tone for the benefit of his uncle, "I'll let you go for now, but you won't be so lucky next time, Troy!" He winked at Troy before catching up to his Uncle Arnie who was already leaving the room.

Troy just stood there for a moment pondering the mysterious words of his new friend. I know your grandfather. He is a family friend. But Papa had told him that grandpapa had died many years ago. Could this cat's statement mean grandpapa was still alive?

"Troy! Let's go!" Shaun suddenly interrupted his thoughts. "Papa will be worried sick if we don't show up soon!"

"I'm coming, I'm coming," answered Troy as he pushed his bag of oats ahead of him and popped into the pipe.

Six of his brothers were waiting at the other end and wondering what was happening to them. They had their bags of oats beside them and were peering down the hole.

Samuel was deeply concerned. "They should have been here by now, bucks."

"Troy! Shaun! Joseph!" yelled Judah. "Are you guys okay? Are you coming?"

As the three brothers crawled through the pipe to freedom Joseph heard his brothers calling. "That sounded like Judah. Judah, is that you? We're coming!"

Judah rose from placing his ear to the hole and hugged Samuel in relief. "They're okay, Samuel."

A few minutes later, Shaun popped out of the hole pushing his bag of oats ahead of him. Troy and Joe followed close behind. They embraced each other as they remembered how close they were to losing Joab and Elijah.

Troy relayed the story of the encounter with King Kappa and Arnie and Willis. "It was sure funny to see good old Arnie. He was so embarrassed that his nephew couldn't tell the difference between a mouse and a bat." Troy laughed.

"But then something strange happened. Willis figured out his mistake. He let Kappa go and came towards me. I was ready for him with Papa's sword but then instead of pouncing on me he sat down and asked me why I had only one eye."

"What did you tell him, Troy," asked Joab.

"Well," explained Troy, "I didn't get a chance to answer because his Uncle Arnie told him if he wasn't going to eat me, then they had better get going. But that's when things got really strange. Willis leaned over, and whispered in my ear something about being friends with my grandpapa."

"But we have never even met our grandpapa," Samuel said. "We were told he died long before we were born."

"I know, right?" answered Troy with a puzzled look. "We'll have to ask Papa about that when we get home. Speaking of which, let's go, bucks. The Oats Mission has been accomplished!"

As they hung tightly to the bottom of the beam, a squadron of flies began to swarm Chuba.

CHAPTER 21

THE DANGER TEST

WARNINGS ARE ONLY BENEFICIAL TO

THOSE THAT HEED THEM BECAUSE MOST

DANGERS THAT ARE SEEN CAN BE AVOIDED.

THE UNSEEN TRIALS ARE NOT FOR THE

FAINT OF HEART AND YET, CAN BE USED

TO STRENGTHEN ONE'S RESOLVE.

As Jonathan and Abigail made their way back to the wedding feast, Frey and Olivia rested for a few minutes outside the tunnel entrance. They opened their backpacks and took out some water and a piece of cheese before heading to the mayor's house. Olivia pulled out Mama's map, which had directions to the Kamet and Bulgur clans.

"It says once we are through the tunnel we should turn right and cross a rafter," said Olivia. "Once we cross the other side, the map has an X over top of a red door."

Frey held on to her tail so it wouldn't drag on the floor. It was quite swollen and still very painful, but she tried to ignore it. She rose up on her tiptoes, peered at the map over Olivia's shoulder and pointed out some words that were written in big bold letters. "Look, Olivia, what is a Danger Test?"

Olivia picked up the map to take a closer look. "Mama says we should follow the wisdom of the danger test. It has saved her life on many occasions." She began to read it out loud:

The Danger Test
Beware the rats and their cunning ways. They may
try to catch you and end your days. Do the danger
test as oft as you can. Lift your head to the sky to smell
rat or man. If a rat is near, your tail will tingle. If a
giant is near your forehead will wrinkle. Heed the call
of a positive test, aborting the mission may be the best!

Frey's tail began to tingle a bit.

"Olivia, do you feel that? Does your tail tingle?"

Olivia was feeling a bit uneasy herself but encouraged Frey. "We're probably still sensing Jonathan's presence. I don't think we need to worry about it, sis, besides the Rafter Rats only hunt at night. We'll be fine." The two young does held paws and slowly walked around the corner towards the large beam.

THE RAFTER CROSSING

UNDERNEATH THE RAFTER, FOUR RED EYES GLOWED in the darkness, patiently waiting for the two unsuspecting mice. King Goar's grandsons, Rodney and Chuba, were on their way home after the humiliating battle with Troy and his brothers when they heard the mice. Drool dribbled down the sides of their mouths at the anticipation of an easy meal.

"I'm awful hungry, Rodney, can we eat them now?"

Rodney placed his paw over Chuba's mouth. "Quiet down, will ya? We must be patient and wait until they are halfway across the rafter, then you come up from behind them and I'll come up in front. They'll be trapped and then we can eat them Chuba."

As they hung tightly to the bottom of the beam, a squadron of flies began to swarm Chuba. He tried to swat them away with his paw and almost slipped off the beam.

"Get 'em them off of me! Get 'em off of me!" Chuba whined as quietly as possible.

Rodney stretched out his arm and placed his paw to Chuba's lips. "SHHH!"

"Well, you know how I hate flies, Rodney," Chuba complained as he shook his head. He tried shooing them away with little success. "They're freakin' me out."

Unknown to the rats, the flies were not ordinary elevator insects and they did not randomly swarm Chuba. The flies had noticed Olivia and Frey in trouble and tried to help them, so they attacked Chuba knowing he hated them. The fly squadron were legends in the Orange Elevator, but very few had ever seen them. They were known as Buzz, Ace, Bell and the twins, Robin and Sparrow. When they noticed their fear tactics hadn't worked they flew away and watched the drama unfold from the wall.

The girls arrived at the front of the rafter and stopped.

"Did you hear that, Olivia?" Frey was quite jumpy and her voice, shaky. "It sounded like a low raspy voice and I think my tail is tingling again."

"I don't feel anything, Frey," answered Olivia. "You're just spooked because of Mama's warning. Like I said, the rats don't come out until most of us are in bed. Let's go."

Olivia took a few steps on to the rafter and looked back at Frey with a reassuring smile. "See, there's nothing to worry about and my tail feels fine. Come grab hold of my hand."

Frey reached out and grabbed her sister's paw as they began crossing the beam. Just past the halfway mark Olivia's tail began to tingle—a lot, but she wasn't about to let her sister know that now, so she did the next best thing—panic.

"Run, Frey, run!" screamed Olivia, but it was too late.

Chuba climbed out from under the rafter and jumped in front of Olivia. The girls quickly turned around and started going back but Rodney blocked their exit. He stood on the beam with an evil smile on his face.

"Looky at what we have here, Chuba. A couple of sweet little cheese lovers to brighten our day."

"They look real tasty, Rodney. Can we eat them yet?" asked Chuba as he stepped slowly towards Olivia.

"Don't you come one step closer, you, you big bully," cried Olivia with tears in her eyes. "If you even touch us, my brothers will come and hunt you down."

Rodney's ears suddenly perked up. "Are you talking about that freak Troy and his little minions downstairs? We killed them, didn't we, Chuba?"

"Well, actually, we didn't kill them, Rodney," squeaked Chuba as he licked his lips. "But we sure taught them a lesson they'll never forget. I think they ran home with their tails between their legs, ha, ha, ha."

"You're lying!" Frey slowly walked backwards away from Chuba. "They're just bluffing, Olivia! Troy and our brothers probably humiliated them somehow. If these dirty rats had actually won the fight they would have at least taken one of them captive."

"Let's just get this over with, Rodney!" Chuba said as he lunged towards Frey, and Rodney closed in on Olivia.

The girls were trapped with no way out, so Olivia began to pray. "Oh, Great Creator, please help my sister and I in our time of need." Before she could finish she heard the sound of flapping leather wings. There was a swoosh and a scream as Chuba suddenly disappeared from the top of the rafter. This stopped Rodney as he helplessly watched his brother being carried in the air by a bright Orange Bat. Instinctively, Rodney turned around and ran to the other side of the rafter and out of sight.

Olivia moved to the opposite end of the beam and joined her sister just in time to see their new friend Beta land safely on the ledge. The girls stood at the end of the rafter, their arms wrapped around each other and shaking with fear.

"Whew! You are an answer to our prayers, Beta!" Olivia said.

The young bat folded her wings and just grinned. "I was worried about you and told my parents I wanted to make sure that I could still fly with my injured wing. Seeing I was in the area, I wanted to make sure you two made it to the storage bin in one piece."

Frey glanced over at their new friend. "What did you do to Chuba?"

"Well," explained Beta, "I came around the corner and noticed that both of you were trapped by those pesky Rafter Rats, so I honed in on the large one and grabbed him with my talons. I carried him to the bottom of the floor. He won't be bothering you for awhile, I suspect."

Frey came over and hugged Beta. "I'm so glad we became friends. I think those stinky rats meant business you know. They really wanted to eat us. I hope Troy and our brothers are okay."

"They were so lying," exclaimed Olivia, "I could see it in their eyes."

Beta was concerned for her new friends. "You're both

very lucky to be alive. It's almost as though someone is looking after you."

Olivia winked at her sister. "More than you know, my little bat friend, more than you know."

Beta turned her head from side to side, bent her knees and motioned to her back. "Hop on, ladies. Those rats may be back soon with more of their friends and the sooner you're at the storage bins the safer you'll be."

Frey began to climb on the back of her new friend but Olivia grabbed her paw.

"Frey, no, we haven't completed our mission yet. We must tell Mayor Sugar and her husband Spice about the delivery of the oats and invite their Clans to the Great Rejoicing tonight."

"Well, what are we waiting for, does? Let's go and give them the good news," exclaimed the Orange Bat.

"Beta, I'm so sorry but have you looked at yourself in the mirror lately? You're an Orange Bat, if we bring you into the village, just the very sight of you would cause a major panic."

Beta lowered her head sadly. "You're right, Olivia, I'll wait for you to come back, then take you guys to the bins, if you want. Once I know you are safe I'll go home and rest."

The sisters gave their friend another hug before they headed for the door.

"We won't be long, Beta. We'll be back before you know it and I can't wait to have a ride on your back."

Olivia wanted to find a way for Beta to come to the celebration. "Why don't you come later tonight and watch the party from one of the rafters or meet us behind one of the bins?"

Beta thought to herself for a moment. "Well, I could wait till my family leaves on their nightly hunt, then sneak out and watch the party from a distance. Anyway, you'd better go before my brother sees you. He doesn't like the fact that cheese lovers saved me."

"OK. See you later," Olivia said, as she and Frey continued across the beam.

The girls found the red door leading to the Bulgur and Kamet clans and disappeared.

Beta called after them. "Hurry back, my little friends!"

ZETA RETURNS

AS IF ON CUE, THERE WAS A FLAP OF WINGS AS ZETA landed in front of her with a loud thump.

"Hey, Beta, where have you been? You should be resting. Mama is worried sick. You told them you were going to test your wing and be right back—by the way, who was that you were talking to just now?"

Beta attempted to hide the guilty look on her face. "It was no one, Zeta."

Her brother didn't buy it. "I saw a blur by that wall right over there." He pointed close to where her new friends had slipped behind the red door. "I clearly heard you say something like, "'Hurry back, friends.'" He scowled. "You're a lying rat, Beta! I know who you were talking to. Just wait until Mama and Papa find out."

"Okay, okay," sobbed Beta, knowing she had to tell the truth. "They're my friends now, Zeta, and I don't want you to kill them."

"I wouldn't kill them but if Mama and Papa knew that you were still hanging out with Gemma and Pi, just after they told you not to, you'd be hanging upside down on the top of the roof, alone, for a month. You know those girls are rebellious and will get you into trouble someday."

Beta chuckled inside when she realized her brother had no idea she had met the mice once again.

"Please don't tell Mama and Papa, I promise not to see them anymore and I will owe you, big time."

"Okay, little Bee," promised Zeta as he rolled his eyes, "I won't say anything, but you do owe me big time. Now, let's get home before our parents send someone to look for me too."

Their leathery wings snapped together as they both lifted off the ledge and headed for home on level seven, but not before Beta looked over her shoulder towards the door where her two friends had disappeared. When they returned she knew they would wonder where she had gone.

RED CIRCLE

FREY SHONE HER FLASHLIGHT TOWARDS THE END OF the hallway, the light reflecting off of a bright red wall.

"It's a dead end, Olivia." They both ran down the hall and stopped in front of the wall blocking their way forward. "Are you sure Mama didn't make a mistake and want us to go the other way?"

Olivia took another look at the map and shook her head. "I don't think so, Frey. Mama would have been very careful about these things."

Frey went over to the wall and felt around it. "Maybe there'll be a secret panel leading to Mayor Sugar's house and…."

Olivia was still gazing intently at the map. "There's nothing here indicating a red door, but I wonder what this red circle means." She looked up for a response from her sister who had disappeared. "Frey, Frey, where are you?" Olivia walked over to where she had been moments before. Suddenly, she felt herself flying down a large slide. She squealed at the top of her lungs.

Meanwhile, Frey popped out of the hole and landed hard on a bright red floor. Olivia landed on top of her with a thud a moment later.

The does slowly stood and gazed in wonder at the red room surrounding them.

"Wow! It's like we're inside a bright red cherry," exclaimed Frey while spinning around in circles with her arms stretched out.

Olivia, being the more practical of the two, tapped her sister on the shoulder in mid-spin. "What do we do now?"

Frey didn't answer. She just looked up, her eyes transfixed on two soldiers in red uniforms, standing behind her sister's back.

"What are you looking at?" inquired Olivia as she turned to see what Frey was so interested in. She was surprised to see the soldier's spear pointing at her nose. She grabbed onto her sister and closed her eyes in fear.

"Get up! Now, both of you!" commanded one of the guards. "How did you two get in here, anyway?"

MAYOR SUGAR

Mayor Sugar and her husband Spice were HAVing tea on the front terrace when the intruder alarm rang.

"Oh Heavens darlin!" the mayor exclaimed as she jumped from her chair, "It could be those nasty Rafta Rats?"

Sugar's fur was pure white and her eyes were bright red. Her mama called her Sugar because of her enormous sweet tooth. Besides her red nose and small ears she had a perpetual smile on her face. She wore a stylish red monocle on a gold chain, which stood out against her long white fur.

Her husband Spice was born in the back room of the Salem Bakery. His family fled to the elevator after being chased by the owner's cat but Spice was left behind. Papa went back to look for his pup and found him hiding inside a large bag of cinnamon. They brought him home and noticed he smelled like the wonderful spice he was found in.

Spice rose from the table. "Sit down my sweet thing. We could have dangerous intruders. Maybe I should go and check?"

"No Sa, don't worry your head, my brave buck," responded Mayor Sugar. "Jack and Adam will take care of whateva managed to crawl through our secret doa."

Spice casually turned to his wife. "You are probably right, my little love bug." He picked up a shiny gold bell and rang it a few times. "On the otha hand we might have some unexpected guests who may want some of our fine southern hospitality. I'll have the servants bring us two more teas and some more cheese.

THE RED SOLDIERS

Olivia and Frey slowly rose from the floor, holding onto one another.

Olivia couldn't stop crying, so Frey began to speak in a soft non-threatening voice, "We are so sorry to barge in like this, sir. My sister and I were trapped in a long hallway looking for a door that Mama told us would lead to the Bulgur and Kamet clans' village. We were sent on a mission to deliver an urgent message to Mayor Sugar. I went to the end of the hall and began feeling along the side, when suddenly my feet fell out from under me and I ended up in this lovely room."

By now Olivia was frantic. "I just followed my sister! Please don't hurt us! We mean you no harm!"

The two soldiers placed their staffs behind their backs and began to laugh.

"You should have seen the look on your face," chuckled the small guard. "It was priceless. I'm Colonel Jack and this is Sergeant Adam. Actually, you both fell through the Mayor's secret hallway installed last year. It was created as an emergency escape route from the Rafter Rats. When you both came to the end of the hall it must have triggered the escape hatch. We thought you might be Rafter Rats."

"You are both just plain mean!" shouted Olivia as she wiped the tears from her eyes and whacked Jack and Adam with her backpack. "You scared us half to death."

Adam took Frey's hand. "C'mon, you two, we'll take you to see Mayor Sugar. She's having tea on the front terrace and may even have some cheese for both of you. Do you like cheese, Frey and Olivia? I do. Both of you must be awfully hungry by now."

With Adam still chattering non-stop, they made their way towards the terrace.

TEA TIME

THE TWO SOLDIERS MARCHED TO THE FRONT TER-RACE with the young does in tow. They tapped their lances on the floor in unison as Sergeant Adam announced the guests' arrival.

"Introducing Lady Olivia and her delightful sister Lady Frey from the Durum Clan on level three."

Mayor Sugar looked up with surprise and patted the two chairs on either side of her. "Come, come sit here, my two lovelies. You must be famished and desperate for some tea by now."

"Why, thank you m'lady." Olivia sat down and motioned for Frey to join her.

Spice waved her paw signalling the servants to pour the does some tea and place a yummy plate of cheese and biscuits in front of them.

Sugar faced the young sisters. "So tell me ladies, how are your papa and mama these days? Are they still so much in love with each otha?"

Both sisters giggled. "Yes, ma'am, they still embarrass us every morning with their long kisses and hugs."

Mayor Sugar laughed. "Have your parents ever shared how they met? They were so romantic. It was during the 1CW or the First Clan Wars. Your papa Jesse was a real looka—and your mama Evette—my, my, she was quite the catch. I still rememba their wedding day. They were as happy as two peas in a pod."

Spice interrupted his wife. "My sweet, I'm sure the does did not come all this way to hear you chatterin about their mama and papa's romance."

Sugar's nose turned red with embarrassment "I'm so sorry, my dears, why have you sweet young things graced our presence on this fine afta noon?"

Frey was excited to share. "We have great news, m'lady." She popped another piece of cheese in her mouth and remembered it was proper to hold up her pinkie as she took a sip of hot tea.

The Mayor moved in closer. "Well, then get on with it, lovelies, I cannot wait another moment."

Olivia placed her tea on the table and finished chewing her last piece of biscuit. "Yes, we do have great news. Papa has sent our brothers on a mission to retrieve a large bag of oats from the giant's cupboard today. If all goes well they should be home as we speak and on their way to the storage bins with Mama and Papa. We were to inform your clans to meet in the emergency bin room tonight at seven o'clock. We will be dividing the oats equally among the clans and afterwards have a Great Rejoicing."

Spice arose from his chair and began to dance around the room. "Well, well, I do declare! Sugar and I do love a good party that's for sure!"

Mayor Sugar sat there with her mouth open. "How in heaven's name did you all manage to discover oats at this time of year?"

Frey interrupted, "Do you remember hearing about my little brother Troy?"

Spice stopped dancing for a moment. "Do you mean that poor blind little buck who was born with other terrible disabilities?"

Olivia answered, "He's not blind, Master Spice. He still has one good eye and the Creator has blessed him with a supernatural nose to sniff out danger from a great distance. He has also been blessed with sensitive ears that are able to hear a Rafter Rat breathing in the next room."

Mayor Sugar was full of compassion. "Oh, my, your poor mama would have to work day and night to take care of a disabled pup, I mean, on top of the other 13 healthy kin to look after."

Frey continued to defend her brother. "Papa says the Creator's strength can be seen clearer through those that are weak. He has blessed Troy with the strength and courage of ten bucks. Our brother is exceptional, Mayor Sugar. When he was born Papa told us the Old Seer that lives near Potter's barn was visited by a large Watcher. He was told to come to our house and anoint Troy with oil. That night the Creator told Socrates that our little brother would one day become King of the Orange Elevator and unite the mouse clans."

Tears began to gather in Spices eyes. "Child, I find it extraordinary that your brother Troy would be anointed to become a future king. Why would the Creator of all things endow a seemingly insignificant rodent with special powas to compensate for his obvious short comings?"

"The Creator cares about all His creatures, Master Spice," Olivia answered proudly. "They give Him glory when they do what they were created to do. The Book of Truth tells us to 'ask the animals, and they will teach you, or the birds in the sky, and they will tell you; or speak to the earth, it will teach you, or let the fish in the sea inform you. Which of all these does not know that the hand of the Lord has done this? In His hand is the life of every creature and the breath of all mankind.'"

Mayor Sugar shook her head in amazement at Olivia's words.

"I find it amazing that the Great Creator would choose a little ol' mouse with major disabilities to lead his creatures. He must have somethin mighty special planned for that young buck to bestow upon him such a high honor."

Frey just listened to the mayor as she munched on her biscuit smothered with orange marmalade.

Mayor Sugar suddenly stood. "My lovelies, we must hurry and get you on your way to the storage bins so you can prepare for the clans' arrival tonight. Troy and his brothers could already be there and I have to prepare for the Great Rejoicing."

She called for Sergeant Adam and Colonel Jack to escort Olivia and Frey back to a secret elevator. When the door opened they were next to the entrance where they had told Beta to wait. The does peeked out of the elevator and looked both ways before stepping out. Beta was nowhere to be seen, thank goodness. No telling how the two guards would have reacted to their new friend.

"It was very nice to meet you both," Frey said to Jack and Adam as she waved goodbye. It was quite obvious to Olivia that Frey had a crush on Jack and decided to do some matchmaking.

"Will you both be coming to the party, tonight?" Olivia asked as she winked at her sister who blushed with embarrassment. "I'll make sure Frey saves you a dance if you come to the Great Rejoicing tonight, Jack."

Frey slapped her sister on the nose. "Stop that, Olivia, you're embarrassing the young bucks."

Adam pushed the button to close the door and smiled. "We'll see you soon, does. Make sure you head to the bins as quickly as you can. It is not safe at this time of night. The Orange Bats will begin their evening hunt soon."

Frey and Olivia placed their paws over their mouths to hide their smiles. They were thinking the same thing: What would the guards think if they knew Beta the bat was their friend?

Since Beta was nowhere in sight, the does made their way through tunnels, scurried around a few machines and stood in front of the doorway to the storage bin room. They stood there for a moment and stared at the door before entering.

"I sure hope our sisters made it here okay," Olivia said.

Frey smiled. "There's only one way to find out, little sister." Then she scurried under the door.

"Hey, wait for me!" Olivia followed Frey to their final destination. Standing on the other side of the door they were relieved to find Tammy, Ava and Evalyn setting tables and lighting wall torches. Frey closed her eyes and thanked the Creator for His protection.

At the same time Olivia whispered, "Good News Op completed."

It became very noisy for a moment and then as they passed he saw two giants sitting inside a fast moving machine.

CHAPTER 22

THE SHADOW

SHADOWS ARE MERE REFLECTIONS

OF REALITY AND YET THEY GENERATE

SO MUCH FEAR. IF LIGHT CREATES THE

SHADOW, WE SHOULD FEAR WHAT IT MAY

EXPOSE. SIN FEARS THE LIGHT AND HIDES IN

THE SHADOWS OF UNREALITY.

THE DURUM BROTHERS GRABBED THEIR KNAPSACKS full of oats and headed toward the long hallway leading to the gleaning room and home sweet home. Jacob the Flash was so overjoyed that he took off at full speed.

"Papa and Mama will be so excited to see us, Troy," he cheered as he blew past him.

Troy was distracted by his nose telling him something was not right and so he put up his hand.

"Stop, Jacob!" He pulled the gold sword from behind his back and held the Levi shield in front of him watching for danger.

Jacob knew Troy's nose and ears were never wrong, so he stopped, turned around and went back to where Troy was standing.

He leaned close to his brother and whispered, "Do you hear a giant breathing? Do you smell a Rafter Rat's breath? Are Rodney and Chuba following us?"

"We're so close to home, Troy," Joab interjected. "Maybe we should make a run for it."

Troy was standing perfectly still with his head cocked to one side, still listening intently with his super sensitive ears.

"I heard something move towards the other end of the hall, but it doesn't sound like a rat's tail dragging on the floor and it doesn't sound like a bat's wings either. A giant's breath would be unmistakable. No, I hear a light

tap, tapping sound that I haven't heard before and smell something familiar and yet foreign." They all stood in silence and watched their brother who was unmoving for what seemed like forever.

Finally, Judah broke the silence. "Well, if it's not a rat or a bat then what could it be, Troy? Maybe it's Papa coming to look for us."

"Maybe it's old Arnie who couldn't hurt a fly, anyway," Shaun suggested.

"Or maybe you're just paranoid, Troy," Samuel added, as he turned towards his brothers for support. "Let's go home and leave Troy to his imagination. We have these oats to deliver and they're getting heavier by the minute."

Suddenly, Troy put down his sword and smiled. "You know, you could be right, guys. Maybe all this excitement we've been having has made me a little edgy. I don't hear the tapping anymore but I have noticed a strange light coming from the outer wall." Troy pointed to his right. "Why don't you bucks take the oats home and I'll catch up with you after I check this thing out."

"You've always liked shiny things, Troy," exclaimed James. "I'll take the bucks the rest of the way and we'll meet you there in a few minutes. Samuel stop!" commanded James. He was already heading down the hall towards home. "Samuel, you stay here with Troy. He shouldn't be left alone."

"What? Why me?" Samuel protested. "I want to go home. Why do I have to stay with Troy?"

"Because," answered James, "you need to spend more time with your brother and learn to appreciate his talents and his special gifts, that's why. Besides, we can't leave him alone, Papa said."

"Thanks, James," responded Troy, "but make sure all of you follow the wall the rest of the way home, safety first. Samuel and I will be right behind you."

"Okay, Troy," replied James, "but don't take too long. Papa and Mama will want to know that you are all right."

Troy watched as his brothers followed James down the dark hallway and out of sight. He turned back to Samuel. "Hey, Sam, do you want to come along and check out the light source?"

"No thanks, Troy," Samuel answered quickly. "I'll just stay here and wait for you to come back. I'm not interested in lights. I just want to go home." He promptly leaned against the wall, sat down and crossed his arms in frustration.

Troy smiled. "Well, if you don't want to experience something new then suit yourself." He promptly turned and headed towards the light, which shone through a hole in the wall at the opposite end of the hallway. As he got closer his nose picked up that same strange and yet familiar scent and he heard a slight movement. Troy stopped for a moment to listen but then continued forward until he reached the end of the hall. The light seemed to shine right out of the wall, so he reached out and touched it with his paw. Then he inched closer until his eye could peer through the hole.

"Wow!" is all he could say before he fell to the floor on his back. He lay there for a moment to process what he had witnessed. Everything he'd seen was so white and clean. There was a big white ball in the middle of a dark sky. "I have to see more." He scrambled to his feet to take another look.

Troy was surprised to see the ground sparkle like diamonds and the wind blowing the diamonds up into the air. He saw the sky dancing with colours of green, red and yellow. They moved as one in a complicated and yet perfectly choreographed pattern. Troy had never seen anything quite like it. As he continued to watch the light show in the heavens he noticed some tracks in the snow below. There were more lights and they were coming closer and closer to the elevator. It became very noisy for a moment and then as they passed he saw two giants sitting inside a fast moving machine. Suddenly, his thoughts were interrupted by a voice that whispered next to his ear.

"Troy, Troy, you like the outside world? Would you like to see more?"

He turned around quickly to see who it was, but all he saw was darkness. He adjusted the rag over his eye.

"Who's there? Who's there? Show yourself, or are you a coward who prefers to hide in the shadows?" A figure emerged out from behind a large beam near the wall where he was standing. Troy raised his sword and readied his shield, preparing for action.

"You have nothing to fear, my buck," said the voice in a soft and gentle tone. "I have been watching you for quite some time, Troy, and I must say you have grown into an amazing young buck. You seem to have found favour in the eyes of our Great Creator."

The shadow's voice was old and a bit raspy, but it held an air of authority.

"Who are you, Shadow Man? And how do you know my

name?" Troy still held up his Levi shield and gold sword in defiance. "Show yourself quickly before I run you through with my papa's sword of justice."

The Shadow Man chuckled and stepped forward into the light where Troy could see him.

"That's a very large shiny sword for such a small mouse, don't you think? How is it that you can carry it so well? It's like a feather in your paws, isn't it? I also noticed your Levi shield, young buck, but I promise you, your weapons will not be necessary. I'm afraid these days I'm quite harmless.

"I have come to you today because I have something very important to tell you, Troy. You see, I'm your grand-papa. I have been searching for an opportunity to talk to you for some time now, however, it has proven quite difficult."

Troy was shocked. Standing before him was an old grey mouse with a long white beard, which hung down to his waist. His eyes were bright green and he wore a black hood-ed overcoat.

"What do you mean, you're my grandpapa?" Troy asked, very confused. "My papa told me he died many years ago and so you cannot be him."

The Shadow Man responded, almost with delight. "So I keep hearing that I am dead and yet here I am."

"If you truly are my grandpapa," Troy accused, "what is your name and why have you been gone from our family for all these years?"

The old mouse looked down in shame. "Well, what I have to say will be difficult for you to accept, my young buck. My name is Methuselah and I am your papa's papa. A long time before you were born, my friend Alex and I were on our way home after working all day up in the storage bins on level four. We turned the corner and were preparing to crawl into the pipe, which led to our homes on level three, when we noticed some boards missing along the outside wall. Just like you, my curiosity got the better of me and without thinking I ran over to the gaping hole and peered outside. It was so beautiful, Troy. I had never seen anything like it before.

"My friend Alex warned me to step away from the hole, but it was too late. I must have slipped on one of the fallen boards and fell through the opening three floors onto the grass below. All I remember is when I woke up it was dark and very cold. My head hurt something awful and I had a large bump on my temple.

"Apparently, Alex had gone to the hole where I had fallen down and when he couldn't see any sign of movement, he ran to tell your Grandmama Edna. She called the elders and asked them to go outside the elevator and look for me. In fact she begged them to, but they refused. They told her if I was outside they could not search for me because the law is the law even if it is broken by accident. The Elders

knew if I managed to survive the fall and the natural predators, I would be back the following day. Well, I never made
it back until two years later.

"After I awoke from the fall, I tried to find my way back
inside but was caught by a large cat named Jeffrey. He carried me in his mouth to his home, which I later found out
was a strange place called, Cat Hill, a city of stray cats and
castaways of the giants. The cat placed me in a small room
inside his home with the intent of serving me for the next
day's family dinner.

"I paced around the room desperately trying to find a
way of escape, but it was hopeless. Later that evening, Jeffrey's two young nephews Willis and Chester visited his
family. His older brother Calvin (Arnie's brother) had sent
his two children to borrow some dried fish. I heard Jeffrey
telling his nephews about catching me outside the Orange
Elevator and that I was going to become their meal tomorrow. What I didn't know was that secretly Calvin's family
was mouse friendly. They had reformed and did not believe
it was right to eat mice anymore.

"So, Willis came up with a plan to rescue me. While his
brother Chester distracted Uncle Jeffrey, Willis snuck into
the room where I was being held, placed me inside the bag
with the fish, and brought me back to his home.

PRINCE TOGA

"WE HAD A GREAT TIME TOGETHER, TELLING STO-
ries and playing games. After a few days, Willis
and his papa secretly led me out of Cat City. We walked in
the country for two days until we came to a place called

the Dragon Forest. There were large trees and rocks everywhere surrounding a large dugout of water. I had never seen anything so wondrous. They brought me to the entrance of a dark cave and told me to wait next to a large waterfall while they went inside.

"Soon, I heard a loud roar and fire came out of the opening of the cave. I closed my eyes, not wanting to see what would come out of the darkness. It became very quiet, so eventually I opened my eyes and saw a large dragon standing before me. The beast had shimmering green/black armor covering his head. He had bright yellow eyes and his chest was a blue plate of steel. He had four silvery wings and a long dark red tail that came to a point. I drew my gold sword of justice, held it up towards the dragon and commanded. 'Stop right there, devil, or I will drop you where you stand.'

"The dragon turned his head to one side and smiled at me, showing off his sharp front teeth. His wings softly fluttered together creating a beautiful sound like angels singing in harmony. Suddenly, a voice came out of the darkness of the cave, 'Methuselah, put down your sword. He will not hurt you. He is our friend.'"

"Calvin came out of the darkness and stood next to the dragon, 'This is Prince Toga, our family friend and my fellow warrior. He is the great commander of the dragon army and son of Roag, King of the Dragon Forest. They have all agreed to keep you safe, Methuselah. Toga said he'll take you wherever you want to go.'

"I thanked my newfound friends, said goodbye and followed Toga into the cave to meet his family.

"As time passed I learned to fly on Toga's back. He took me many places and we had amazing adventures together. One day, I told him it was time for me to go home to the Orange Elevator in Salem. As I was about to leave, the Prince presented me with what he called, 'The Brass Levi Shield.'

"Toga shared the story of how he found it. He was flying over Potter's field one day when he saw something shiny in the black dirt. He knew it was something important, so he brought it to his family's cave in the Dragon Forest. Eventually, I passed it down to your Papa Jesse and he used it in the Battle of the Clan Wars."

Methuselah pointed to the Brass Levi Shield fastened around Troy's arm. "I see that my son Jesse has passed it on to you, Troy. What an honour. I'm sure it has already served you well. Did you notice the Hebrew word I placed on the inside of the shield?" he said as he pointed to a strange inscription carved close to the handle.

"Yes," exclaimed Troy, "I've always wondered what it meant."

"Well," continued Methuselah, "It says, 'It is Finished,' and refers to the words the Logos said before He died for our rebellion. He took our sins upon Himself and knew that when He died the penalty would be paid in full. It is finished."

Grandpapa placed his paws inside of Troy's, looking intently into his one eye. "Troy, I have always known the Creator chose you to be a leader, my grandson. You will be king over all the mouse clans and I want you to experience the world outside the elevator. It will give you a much broader understanding of the Creator's world. It is vast outside the elevator my precious grandson. Someday when you are ready, I would like to take you with me so I can show you the wonders of the Creator's world."

Troy interrupted in protest. "Grandpapa, don't you know the law must not be broken. It is strictly forbidden for anyone to venture outside the Orange Elevator. I could never go with you. Which begs the question, why were you allowed back into the elevator? The law states that no one is to ever leave the Orange Elevator or they will be banished to the dungeons."

Methuselah now spoke in hushed tones. "Well, my little buck, when I first arrived home my family and all my friends had a Great Rejoicing. I began to share my stories about the outside world. I told them there were many opportunities outside to gather food for the winter. I even found friendly cats outside the Orange Elevator and there are creatures we have never seen like dragons in the nearby forest. As I continued to share my adventures with others the elders grew more and more worried. They soon arrived at my house and claimed my stories were placing the clans in grave danger. The elders accused me of breaking the sacred Law of Isolation.

"A secret trial followed and I was banished to the dungeons. Sadly, over time, most of the clans forgot I was even down there. The Elders didn't forget. They came down to see me one day and I hid from them. When they arrived and noticed I was not in my cell, they decided to tell everyone I had perished.

"At night, I still make my way outside the Orange Elevator and meet the many friends I have made on the outside. I only wish I had someone to share the adventures I continue to have."

Before Troy could respond to Grandpapa's amazing story, Samuel appeared around the corner of the wall. "Who are you talking to, Troy?"

Troy quickly glanced where Methuselah had been standing, but he'd disappeared.

"Ah — no one, Samuel," Troy lied. "I was admiring the amazing coloured lights that are dancing outside. You should see them."

Samuel turned around and walked back down the hall. "Let's go home Troy, it's been a long day and I'm tired."

"All right, all right I'm coming," responded Troy. He ran towards his brother but not before taking a quick glance over his shoulder to see if his grandpapa was still there, but he was gone. Samuel waited for him and they walked home arm and arm.

Before they reached the door, Papa and Mama saw their bucks coming and ran out to meet them. Mama wrapped her arms around Samuel and wouldn't let go. Papa just stood there and looked at Troy from head to toe, as though he couldn't believe it was really his special little buck.

"We were so worried for you all," said Mama as she let go of Samuel and took Troy's face in her hands and showered him with kisses. All of Troy's brothers came out to join in the celebration and were happy to see Troy and Samuel safe and sound.

Shaun was curious as to what Troy had heard down the hall. "Was there anything to be concerned about back there, brother?"

Troy attempted to be as vague as possible. "I can tell you

it was not what I expected, but I'll let you know about that later."

Papa folded his arms and declared proudly, "Through your bravery and sacrificial love for others you have saved thousands of lives today. Because of you, the clans in the Orange Elevator will not starve this winter. Let us bow our heads and thank our Creator for protecting you on this mission and let us ask Him to protect your sisters as they complete their mission to inform the clans and prepare for the Great Rejoicing tonight."

*Suddenly, out of nowhere the famous elevator Fly Squadron
circled around the two rats.*

CHAPTER 23

BEING PREPARED

ONE CANNOT BE PREPARED FOR EVERY

EVENTUALITY, UNLESS ONE COMMANDS

THE EBB AND FLOW OF THE UNIVERSE.

ONE CAN ALWAYS LEARN TO ADAPT TO

CHANGE AND ACCEPT THE OUTCOME AS

FOREORDAINED.

Olivia and Frey leaned against the doorway of the bin room and watched their sisters frantically running about preparing for the Great Rejoicing.

"This will be the celebration of the year!" squealed Tammy, jumping up and down with excitement. "There will be food, dancing, singing and time for catching up with the latest gossip. I wonder if Rodger Spelt will come? If he does I think I'm going to tell him how I feel."

Evalyn was lighting the torches with the fire sticks and came over to where Tammy was gazing up with dreamy eyes. "It's so obvious he's sweet on you, Tammy. I've seen him sneak a peek during our self-defence class."

"C'mon, you two romantic rodents, get back to work already," chided Ava as she made her way to the cupboards and pulled out the jars that would soon be filled with oats. "Olivia and Frey will be here any moment. I wonder what's taking them so long? They should have been here already."

Suddenly a voice called out from the bin room door. "We thought if we waited long enough you would have everything prepared by now."

Olivia and Frey ran over to their sisters. They all squealed as they embraced one another and cried for joy. Tammy was so overwhelmed she kept thumping her left foot on the floor. They gathered in a circle, clasped their paws together and recited the Durum girls motto: "The Durum girls are not dissuade, we are stronger together we're not afraid. We fight for freedom, we fight for love, but look for peace from the Creator above. Durum girls rule!"

WATCHING

AS THE DURUM SISTERS CELEBRATED THEIR REUNION
and completion of their mission, no one noticed the
four red eyes peering at them from behind one of the storage bin doors.

"When can we eat them, Rodney?" asked Chuba. He
and his brother peeked through the iron mesh of the storage bin. "I'm hungry again."

"Not yet, my little brother, not yet," Rodney looked
over at Chuba who still looked a bit dazed from the fall.
"You don't look so good, buddy, come and lie down for a
while." Rodney placed his brother's right front leg around
his shoulder and carried him to the far corner of the empty
storage bin. He gently laid him down on his back and went
back to watch the cheese lovers prepare for the party.

"I feel terrible, Rodney," said Chuba in a weak voice.

"I know you're in pain. You're going to be okay, Chuba.
Rest here a while."

Chuba was nursing four holes in his side after being
picked up by Beta's sharp claws and had a bum leg from
being dropped ten feet to the elevator floor.

After that traitor of an Orange Bat had come to rescue
those two little cheese lovers, Rodney had slipped away
and scurried downstairs to see if he could help his brother
Chuba. He found him lying on the cold floor totally unconscious. As he stayed with his brother stroking his head,
he'd overheard Beta talking about the meeting of the clans
at the storage bin. He thought it would be a swell place to
hide Chuba until he woke up, then they could have an easy
lunch before heading home.

Rodney slowly turned to Chuba. "Be patient, my little brother, be patient. Soon they will come with all the oats and this is where they will put them. We will let Grandpapa Goar know where their food is being stored. We'll be heroes! Our names will be forever etched on the walls of our ancestors. I can see it now, Rafter Rats for generations to come will call their little ones Rodney and Chuba!"

"Yah," cooed Chuba, "Grandpapa Goar will be so proud of us."

Rodney took one last look at the cheese lovers working feverishly in the centre of the room and went to care for his brother who had fallen fast asleep.

THE DURUM SISTERS PREPARE

"I CAN'T BELIEVE YOU GUYS MADE IT!" EVALYN KEPT saying with tears of joy.

"We were so worried you were captured by the Orange Bats or the Rafter Rats ate you or worse, that King Goar took you to level five and made you his slaves," Ava rambled.

"We were just fine, does," Frey responded. "The Great Creator was watching over us but we have some amazing adventures to share with you."

"So do we!" blurted Evalyn. "Ava was almost eaten by Arnie the patrol cat!"

"Sorry, does," Olivia interjected, "I'm sure we would love to hear each other's adventures but we only have a short while until the Great Rejoicing begins. I say we wait until we are back home and can share them with Mama over a cup of tea and oatmeal cookies. For now, it is important we are ready to distribute oats to the mayors and their clans."

Tammy picked up a broom and began to sweep the floors while talking to Olivia. "So all the clans have been informed of the Great Rejoicing. This is going to be sooo much fun! I, for one, can hardly wait to start dancing. Maybe Rodger will come, sweep me off my feet and ask me to marry him. He is soooo cute."

"What do you think Papa would say about that?" asked Ava with a bit of sarcasm.

"We all know the answer to that," responded Olivia as they all laughed.

Evalyn turned to Frey who was busy placing more decorative napkins on the tables. "So, was Mayor Sugar excited that we found food for the clans?"

"I don't know who was more excited, Mayor Sugar or her husband Spice," answered Frey. "When they heard the good news, Spice began to dance and sing for joy."

Olivia was so pleased at how everything was turning out. "Just think about it, does, we have accomplished our dangerous Good News Op. Our papa and mama will be so proud of us."

As Frey completed preparing the tables for their guests, the rest of her sisters went about their own various tasks, cleaning the jars, setting tables and hanging up party streamers.

RODNEY AND CHUBA ESCAPE

As THE LITTLE MICE SCURRIED ABOUT IN THEIR party-planning mode, Rodney peered through the door of bin number one planning their escape. Hearing a large amount of oats would be arriving tonight, he planned for them to sneak out undetected and inform their grand-papa Goar of the good news.

Chuba woke up and noticed his brother spying on the Durum sisters. "Let's go now, Rodney, they're probably too busy to notice us leaving," exclaimed Chuba as he hobbled towards the door. "Besides, my stomach is growling and there'll be lots of food waiting for us at uncle Benob's wedding party. Are you sure we couldn't just grab one little cheese lover as a snack before we go home?"

"How can you think about food at a time like this, Chuba?" chided Rodney as he looked disapprovingly at his brother's rather large waistline. "Focus, bro, focus! We have a mission to complete and timing is everything. We'll leave when I say it's time to leave and not a moment sooner. Besides you can't move very fast right now, anyway, you're injured, remember? So, we wait until all those girlie cheese lovers are on the other side of the room before we make our move."

Chuba placed his elbow on his brother's shoulder. "Okay, Rodney, I guess you're right as usual, but can you promise that we'll eat right after we tell Grandpapa Goar about the oats?"

Rodney ignored his brother and kept staring straight ahead through the crack in the door. After a short while, he placed his arm around Chuba's large waist.

"Okay, the coast is clear. As soon as I open the bin door

we make a run for the exit." He looked at his brother. "You sure you can keep up with me?"

"I don't know, Rodney." Chuba lowered his head. "My leg hurts an awful lot, and my side's still bleeding."

Rodney knew the girlie cheese lovers would catch Chuba before they were even halfway across the room. "Okay, change of plans. When they aren't looking, we sneak out real slow, stay along the walls until we get to the exit and slip underneath the door. The plan is foolproof."

Chuba was only thinking about his immediate need for food. "I still think we should wait until one of them comes real close and then eat 'em."

There were times when his older brother couldn't stand it when Chuba's brain was in his stomach.

"I know it's hard for you to focus when you are hungry, Chuba, but you must learn to use your brain like me. First, there are five of them and two of us. Actually one of us, you're not able to fight right now. Second, as yet, they don't know that we know they have found food. With that information our grandpapa can surprise them and steal the oats from right under their cheesy little noses."

"Wow! I wish I was smart like you, Rodney," praised Chuba, "that's a great plan."

"Of course it is, little brother. It's my plan, isn't it?" Rodney held his head high then slowly opened the door. He had forgotten one thing. The door to bin number one was old and rusty. As he pushed it open, the hinge squeaked, the sound echoing throughout the room.

The sound immediately alerted the five does. They turned around, saw the rats and squealed, running in all directions except Tammy, who was standing right behind bin number one. As soon as she heard the door open she stayed very still so as not to draw attention to herself.

Rodney and Chuba stood there for a moment in shock and unable to move.

"Rafter Rats!!" yelled Tammy from behind them as she jumped up and down not knowing in which direction she should run.

The rats turned around and looked at the jumpy cheese lover who was blocking their escape. Chuba lunged forward trying his best to grab the bouncing little rodent. Then, when it seemed like he had her in his grasp she disappeared into thin air.

"Where did she go, Rodney?" asked Chuba.

By this time, the girls were over their initial shock and grabbed torches off of the walls and ran towards Rodney and Chuba. The rats didn't even notice the does coming. They were too busy trying to figure out where the jumpy cheese lover had disappeared to.

Olivia came up behind Rodney and struck him over the head with the burning torch. He fell to the floor in pain.

"Look out, Chuba, they have fire sticks."

Chuba was still searching for Tammy but turned around just in time to see Evalyn swinging two torches of fire at his face. He turned around to escape but Ava took an arrow from her quiver, placed it carefully in her bow and fired. The arrow pinned Chuba's sweater to the wall. Evalyn moved in close and held the torches in front of his face.

Chuba was afraid of fire. He had burned his foot as a pup looking for food in Salem's garbage dump. Someone had carelessly thrown away burning charcoal and he stepped on it.

"No, no!" yelled Chuba! "Get the fire away from me."

"Well, well," responded Frey who had slipped unnoticed beside Chuba, "you had better leave now or things are going to get really ugly in the next few minutes."

Still pinned to the wall, Chuba was shaking and holding his hands up in fear.

Rodney quickly recovered from the knock on the head and grabbed Olivia's arm before she could take another swipe at him. He pulled her towards him, grabbed a knife from inside his coat and held it to Olivia's throat.

"You girlie cheese lovers had better move away from Chuba now or this is the last time you will see your sister alive."

Seeing Olivia in grave danger, the sisters backed away from Chuba. He quickly removed the arrow that was holding him to the wall and slid into his brother's side.

Rodney had an evil grin on his face and spit when he talked. "Put down those fire sticks right now or my brother and I will take your little precious to our Papa, Prince Lami, and he will make her his personal slave."

The does threw down their torches and stepped back from the two very angry Rafter Rats.

"Okay, we did what you asked. Now let Olivia go," demanded Frey.

Rodney looked over at Chuba while continuing to move back towards the exit still dragging Olivia in front of him. "What do you think, little brother, should we keep this little precious morsel as a snack for later or should we hand her over to Papa as his servant?"

"No, you promised to let her go if we put our torches down," pleaded Ava who began to cry.

Tammy was angry. "You will let my sister go now because I have just asked our Great Creator to deal with you."

Chuba laughed. "I'm not afraid of your little god. What can he do to me?" He turned to Rodney. "Let's eat her now and get home. She'll just slow us down anyway."

"Or we could always sacrifice her on the altar of Dreck. It would please King Og, as Grand Wizard of Salem," replied Rodney, holding the knife closer to Olivia's throat.

Suddenly, out of nowhere the famous elevator Fly Squadron circled around the two rats. Their leader Buzz landed on Rodney's nose while Ace, Bell, Sparrow and Robin flew around Chuba's head.

Buzzz.

"Oh, no, they're back! I hate those flies! They're attacking me on purpose! Let's get out of here, Rodney!" Chuba ran towards the door desperately swatting at the precision flyers.

"Where are you going, Chuba?" asked Rodney, who was still holding on to Olivia and trying to blow Buzz off of his nose. "They are just flies. They can't hurt you. Now get back here!"

Chuba ignored his brother and continued shaking his head and waving his arms as he scurried under the door with the flies in hot pursuit. Rodney was now alone, but he still held on to his prey who was struggling to get free.

Buzz held on to the rat's nose but soon chose to try something new —crawl inside the rat's nostril and distract him. Yet, as soon as he entered the hole, he knew he'd made a mistake.

Rodney stopped moving for a moment as he felt a tickle in his nose. Suddenly he let out a big sneeze. Buzz shot out like a cannon and smacked against the wall. He slowly slid down the wall and fell onto the floor covered in slime. The fly's squadron leader lay on his back buzzing his wings, trying to right himself but the liquid was too sticky. He finally flipped over, cleaned his wings and flew right back at the rat's face.

Rodney ignored Buzz, for the most part, but still held on to Olivia. Just as he was about to crawl under the door, Ava shot an arrow and struck him in the leg. Rodney lay beside the exit still holding onto his captive. The rat began to slip under the door but, before he could, Tammy appeared behind him. She snatched Olivia from Rodney's arms just before he arrived on the other side empty handed.

He hobbled along slowly until he caught up to Chuba, who was still being dive-bombed by the squadron of brave flies.

"What happened to you, Rodney?" asked Chuba as he swatted at the flies and noticed something protruding from his brother's leg. "You're bleeding."

"Ya think?" answered Rodney. "You're such a genius, Chuba. Be quiet and keep walking."

"Sure thing, Rodney, don't you worry," consoled Chuba, "those girlie cheese lovers will wish they had never laid eyes on us after Grandpapa Goar declares war."

Chuba smiled as he placed his arm around Rodney's waist for support as they headed for the Rat's Trail. "Those mice will all cry for mercy once Papa Lami and Uncle Saph get through with them. "

The two young Rafter Rats held each other as they slowly hobbled their way towards home. Rodney and Chuba moved in total silence both thinking of only one thing— telling King Goar about the large stash of oats just waiting to be stolen.

RELIEVED

OLIVIA GRABBED ON TO TAMMY WITH BOTH ARMS and wouldn't let go.

"You saved me, Tammy, you saved me!" cried Olivia.

Ava, Frey and Evalyn joined Tammy as they all jumped up and down with great joy.

Ava suddenly stopped and exclaimed, "Don't you does see what happened? The Great Creator answered my prayer! He sent our friends, 'The Squadron,' to distract those nasty rats until Tammy could use her special gift and save Olivia."

"Yeah," agreed Evalyn, "but did you see Ava's arrow land a perfect shot from clear across the room? She hit the rat in the leg without hitting Olivia."

The girls laughed and agreed that they had just witnessed a miracle.

CHAPTER 24

SON OF GOAR

HATRED WILL SUCK LIFE FROM THE

SOUL UNTIL IT IS COMPLETELY VOID

OF FRIENDSHIP. REVENGE FOLLOWS

CLOSE BEHIND, AND WILL DESTROY ANY

OPPORTUNITY OF FORGIVENESS. LOVE IS

THE ONLY CURE FOR THE DISEASE OF

CONTEMPT.

FTER PAPA PRAYED FOR A SAFE TRIP TO THE STOR-
age bins, Mama gathered what she needed for the
Great Rejoicing.

Troy and his brothers strapped on their burlap bags filled
to the brim with oats as they began their short journey to
the storage bins on level four.

For the most part they traveled single file, hugging the
wall for safety; however, there were moments when they
were able to walk together in a larger group. During these
times, Troy and his brothers shared their many adventures
with Mama and Papa. They told them about their fight
with the Rafter Rats, Rodney and Chuba and how Troy
stood up to them with no fear. Joab shared how he and
Elijah were almost eaten by Kappa, king of the Orange Bats
and how old Arnie's nephew Willis saved them in the nick
of time.

"We actually believe that Willis is a friend of mice," declared Elijah.

"What?" Papa stopped walking and turned around.
"Cats are never friends with mice. You should know that
from your training at RAMS. A rat's red eyes never change
colour and a cat will always be a killer." Papa resumed walking.

"But it's true, Papa!" Joab cried. "Before Willis left he
went close to Troy and whispered, 'I knew your grandpa.
He was a family friend.'"

"Well, I never!" gasped Mama. "I have never heard of a
cat befriending a mouse and I don't ever recall Grandpapa
telling us about that event, do you, Jesse?"

Papa scratched his head. "Grandpapa had many adventures, that's for sure, but I don't remember him telling us a story about having a friendship with a cat. Yet, if that is what Willis told Troy, it might be true."

Before Troy could respond Jacob the Flash turned to his mama and shared the story of his daring run through five traps.

"I'm so proud of you, Jacob," Mama responded, as tears flowed down her cheeks. "Were you frightened, my dear?"

"Yes, I was at first, Mama," answered Jacob with a smile, "but when Troy prayed for my successful run, I had a strange calm come over me and I knew I could not fail. You and Papa were right; the Creator was looking after us all the way."

"Jesse and I prayed for you bucks the whole time you were gone," stated Mama as she put her arms around Jacob and Shaun and kissed their cheeks.

"You really met a real giant, I don't believe it," Papa muttered in awe. "I would love to have been there just to see our little Troy climb on top of the fallen giant, holding Grandpapa's sword to his throat and telling him to stand down." Jesse turned and faced his sons. "I just want to say how proud I am of you bucks and how well you worked together to fulfill your mission. You supported each other in times of need and risked your own lives for the sake of the clans."

As Papa finished talking they arrived in front of the opening to the heating duct. "Bucks, I want you to go through the duct one by one, placing your bags of precious oats ahead of you. When you arrive on level four wait for your mama and papa. We are not as fast as we used to be, but

"Your sisters will be worried something has happened to us, so we are going to take a short cut through the Rat's Trail."

we'll follow close behind you. Your sisters will be worried something has happened to us, so we are going to take a short cut through the Rat's Trail."

"But, Papa," protested Troy, "venturing through the Rafter Rat's trail could be very dangerous at this time of night."

"I agree with Troy, Papa" defended Samuel. "What if we run into King Goar and his hunters? We would be no match for them. Why don't we just play it safe and take the long way around?"

Everyone murmured in agreement until Mama interrupted, "Now, bucks, quiet down, quiet down and listen to your Papa. I'm sure he has a very good reason to take the shortcut. You know that he would never recklessly endanger our lives." She turned towards Jesse and kissed him on the cheek.

Jesse smiled at his lovely bride. "That's right, my sweet little cheese puff, I happen to know that Goar and the whole Rafter Rat clan are celebrating the wedding between his son Benob and King Og's daughter Lilith as we speak. They'll be gorging themselves all night at the reception. You know how Rats love their garbage food. Thus, the Rat trail should be safe and besides, taking that route will save us a lot of time."

"Okay, Pop! I'm good with that," agreed Troy who turned towards the duct opening, placed his bag of oats inside and crawled after it. The rest of his brothers followed him and popped in one by one. Soon, Mama and Papa crawled in and slowly made their way to the top.

The journey through the galvanized pipe was slow as

they pushed their bags of oats in front of them inch by inch. Troy was the first to make it through. He climbed out and placed his bag along the side of the wall, then went back to the entrance to help his brothers. They climbed out one by one and handed him their bags, which he placed alongside his own. Shaun the Gentle Giant was the last brother to come out of the pipe because of his injured leg. They all moved over to the wall, sat down next to their bags of oats and waited for their Mama and Papa to catch up.

"Here we are," Mama said with a sigh as she placed her basket of party treats on the rim of the pipe and slowly crawled out with the help of Samuel and Jacob. She peered down the duct and yelled, "Are you coming, you old buck? If you don't hurry, the rat's wedding party will be over before we can even begin ours."

Papa's voice echoed through the ducting, "Don't rush me, Sweet-Pea, you know I have a bad hip courtesy of Lord Kappa and can't move as fast as I used to. If you recall, I did save you from certain death."

"That was a long time ago, my hero," Mama laughed, as she pulled her husband out of the hole. "Now, let's go dancing."

Jesse took his wife's hand in his and announced, "It's time to go, my young bucks, just follow close behind and we'll be on the Rat's Trail in a few minutes."

Troy and his brothers gathered their backpacks filled with oats as they followed behind their parents. Troy came alongside his Papa and told him about his surprise meeting with Methuselah. "Papa, why didn't you tell us that our grandpapa was still alive?"

"Are you sure the old buck you talked to was Methuselah, Troy?" asked Jesse. "The clan elders told us that they found him dead in his cell."

A tear formed in Troy's eye. "The old buck I met in the shadows told me that he was my grandpapa. Why didn't you ever tell us that our grandpapa was the famous 'Methuselah'—the crazy mouse who broke the sacred Law of Isolation?"

Jesse turned his head to look at Evette for support. She gazed back at him with sad eyes. "You might as well tell the bucks the whole truth darlin'. It seems like the cat is out of the bag anyway."

Jesse spoke with tears in his eyes. "We're sorry we didn't reveal your grandpapa's true identity, Troy. You see, when he came back to the elevator after being missing for two years, we were just so happy that he was home we didn't think about the fact that he had broken the law. As Grandpapa shared his adventures outside the elevator with more and more people they became curious. Papa Durum couldn't help himself, he kept telling everyone about the adventures he had and that being outside the elevator was an adventure.

"The elders asked Methuselah to stop sharing his stories, but he wouldn't, so they had a trial. Even though he didn't leave the elevator on purpose, the clan elders didn't see it that way and sentenced him to the dungeons for life. We never heard from him again until the elders told us he was dead. You say he talked to you? That would be amazing if it were true, son."

"Grandpapa told me the whole story," Troy continued

as they walked. "He even told me how he escaped from the dungeons. When the elders came to check on him he hid in the janitor's room until they left. He said they must have thought he escaped and left the elevator. To save face they told everyone he died. Grandpapa even said he had been watching all these years in secret and that he was very proud of me."

"That's amazing, my precious buck," responded Jesse. "I can't believe that my Papa is alive and well. Evette, did you hear that? Papa Durum is truly alive! This day keeps getting better and better."

Troy changed the subject as he noticed they were approaching the Rat's Trail. "Papa, is that the forbidden road you were searching for?" The well-worn path was a secret passage in between two large rooms and was off limits to the mouse clans.

Jesse knew it would cut their journey in half and that actually the chance of meeting a rat would be slim to none.

PRINCE SAPH

"I CAN'T BELIEVE I'M MISSING THE PARTY." SAPH SPIT out a small piece of chicken bone as he entered a section of the Rat's Trail. He had quickly grabbed a large rotten piece of chicken off the groom's head table before reluctantly leaving on his quest.

King Goar, his father, had sent him to find out why his two nephews, Rodney and Chuba had not reported back. They were sent on a mission to find out if there was any wheat left over in the grain pit located in the basement of the Orange Elevator. The Rafter Rat clans were also running out of food because the garbage dump outside of Salem was frozen solid.

"Why am I always the one that has to do Papa's dirty work," complained Saph, as he kicked the bone to the side of the trail. "Why couldn't Lami go and look for his own little brats? He is their papa after all." The Prince knew he had no choice but to obey Goar. The king's words echoed painfully in his mind. "Lami is busy in the kitchen so you have to get out there and look for them, you good for nothing misfit."

No one could ever say no to Papa, even his children—especially his children. When he spoke, everyone was expected to obey and they did so out of fear or duty. In the beginning some challenged his word, in the end, though, they always obeyed.

Saph was still grumbling to himself when he heard a noise coming from the far end of the trail just around the corner from where he was. He stopped and listened. Yes, there it was again—the sound of tiny little feet marching in unison, strange, but unmistakable.

"Cheese lovers," he muttered. His mouth began to water and drool slid down the side of his sticky, matted fur. Saph ran to the opposite side of the trail and hid against the wall just before the turn. With an evil grin, he waited for his meal to fall into his lap. "Come to papa, my little tasties."

THE FIGHT

JOSEPH MARCHED ALONG THE RAT'S TRAIL BEHIND his brothers.

"This is so much fun. I feel like a real soldier who has been called to fight a noble war in a far off land."

"Shh, keep it down, Joe," warned Troy as he cocked his head to one side and stopped to listen. "I think I heard something."

Samuel looked over at his Mama and then at Troy. "Not again, Troy. Mama, he always does this. He stops our forward progress because he 'hears something.' Everything's a danger to him." He stuck his tongue out at Troy. "I think he just wants attention."

Mama placed her paw around her son. "Now, Samuel, I thought you were getting along better with Troy. He's just trying to keep us safe. You know he can hear and smell things long before anyone else can. We should trust him."

Troy didn't say anything at first but his super sensitive nose had caught something very familiar.... Something, like....

"A rafter rat!!" he yelled at the top of his lungs. "Run for your lives!" Troy turned around, his sword drawn and his shield placed in front of him. What he saw was his worst nightmare. A large Rafter Rat was holding his Mama by his one arm and a medieval mace club in the other. He had an evil crooked smile on his face and meant business.

His brothers saw the terrifying sight and scurried to safety behind their Papa as they were taught to do.

"Let go of my Mama, you nasty old rat!" demanded Troy as he began to advance closer to the oversized rodent.

"Ha, ha, ha, what are you going to do you pathetic little pip-squeak, poke me with that tiny toothpick of yours? You look about as harmful as a flea on the tip of my tail. I will gladly eat your Mama and you in the name of Dreck the Great Rat god of Salem."

Troy smiled at Saph with a quiet confidence. "My Creator is the maker of all things and Dreck is no match for Him!" The little mouse moved closer with the gold sword of justice pointed straight ahead. "Yahweh will grant me the strength to strike you down with one blow if He so chooses. Now, for the last time, let my Mama go!"

Papa told the rest of his sons to hide inside one of the holes in the wall. Then he went to stand beside Troy who had never seen his Papa so angry and scared at the same time.

"Troy, give me the gold sword," Jesse demanded as he opened his hand and stared at Saph, not letting him out of his sight.

The Prince was a giant rat as were his two brothers Benob and Lami. He had muscles bulging from every part of his matted fur. He had a large mole on the side of his nose and one of his eyes was larger than the other and tilted to the left. His mouth was crooked, which made his tongue hang out to one side and drool constantly. His weapon of choice was a large wooden mace club, which looked as terrifying as it was deadly.

"Papa, I've got this!" cried Troy. "He has my Mama and is mocking Yahweh. Our Creator has already delivered me from a human giant, from the jaws of a cat, two Rafter Rats and Kappa, king of the Orange Bats and He will surely deliver me from this rat and his dead, stone god Dreck."

Saph became so angry that he threw Evette to the side and lunged towards Troy with his mace.

"You will not live long enough to say good-bye to your Mama, you defective piece of trap bait. You had better run now because the Creator you worship will not save you, he is invisible and does not exist."

Jesse saw the rat coming towards his son and did what any Papa would do—protect his pup. He ran forward and met Saph head on, cutting him off at the legs.

The rat got up and lunged at Troy once more. The small mouse dodged the hulk who stumbled and ran head first into the wall. Saph groaned, shook his head back and forth, and snapped his neck towards Troy. "First, I'll finish off your papa, then I'm coming for you, little flea!"

Troy ran in front of his papa with the gold sword pointing at the large rat who was advancing closer and closer.

Suddenly, Evette jumped on top of him, taking him completely by surprise, and wildly pounded her fists on his head. The prince shook her off and she landed right beside the hole in the wall where her sons were hiding. They saw their Mama lying unconscious and that did it. They all came running towards Saph with abandon.

"We're coming, Troy," cried Shaun as he ran over and began striking the rat on the legs with his staff. Meanwhile, his brothers swarmed Saph, biting him wherever they could find skin. He flailed his mace back and forth trying to swat at them.

Troy saw an opening and the sword of justice moved in perfect rhythm, back and forth. He swung it towards his foe but the prince laughed and dodged it with ease.

Saph stood to attack the cheese lover but the gold sword caught his tail and sliced it open. The rat screamed in pain as he grabbed his tail and limped off, disappearing out of sight.

Mama woke up and went over to where Papa Jesse was lying. "Wake up, Jesse, wake up. You will not die on me today! The Great Creator has saved us!"

Slowly Papa moved his head, looked into his wife's eyes

and smiled, "Have I died and gone to heaven? I think I see an angel."

Evette laughed and kissed Jesse's nose. "No, silly, it's just me. You're still here and your children are safe and sound. After you were struck by the rat, I jumped on top of him and when he threw me off, your mighty bucks came to the rescue. Troy struck his tail with the sword of justice and the son of Goar ran off in pain."

Jesse slowly got up and the Durum family gathered around for a group hug as they bowed their heads and gave thanks to the Great Creator for saving their family from the giant rat.

THE SCROLL

TROY AND HIS BROTHERS ENTERED THE HOLE TO retrieve their backpacks but when Samuel went for his, he noticed something strange. Behind the pack was a brown parchment tucked in the corner. He picked it up and brought it outside to show his brothers.

"Hey, guys, look what I found in the hole that we were hiding in."

Jesse walked up next to Samuel. "May I take a look, Sam?"

Samuel handed the scroll to his Papa as everyone crowded around to take a closer look. "It sure looks old. I wonder who left it here?"

Jesse slowly unrolled the piece of parchment and a gold key dropped to the floor.

Troy picked it up and examined it closely. "I wonder what this opens, Papa?"

Joab grabbed the key from Troy. "Maybe it opens a large chest filled with gold, jewels or lots of cheese!"

Papa placed the scroll on the floor so that everyone could study its contents. "Look, it's a map which seems to lead underneath the Orange Elevator. And there is a picture of a large black tree with a key at the base."

Evette noticed some strange words written at the bottom left hand corner of the scroll.

"What do you make of this, Jesse?" she asked, pointing to the artistically written cursive.

ולשכיי סהמ רתויו וסני סיבר,
סירבוג סיקידצה רצואה תא אוצמל
תיחצנ הבהל קיילדי חתתפמה יכ
.הנעטה סע דדומתי בלה רוהטו
.ויהי הרשע דוע ,סיזמרה תא ארק
.ץעל תחתמ ואצמת הנושארה

Jesse put his reading glasses on and took a closer look. "I have seen this language before but I can't place it. Troy, you studied ancient languages at school, do you recognize this?"

Troy picked up the map and brought it close to his eye. "Well, it looks a lot like ancient Hebrew, Papa. Trouble is, I don't know how to read Hebrew."

"Who do you think can read ancient Hebrew, Troy?" asked Papa.

Troy suddenly lifted his head with excitement. "I know who can read this language. My grandpapa Methuselah! We just have to find him. When he met me today he translated the meaning of the Hebrew words on the inside of my shield." He turned over the shield and showed everyone a leather pouch beside the handle. Methuselah had carved the strange words that looked very similar to the ones on the scroll.

"Well, what does it say son?"

Troy responded with pride. "It says, 'It Is Finished' זה רמגנ. Grandpapa told me these were the last words the Logos said on the cross before He died. He was telling everyone that His work to save the world was complete."

"Those are great words, little buck," Mama replied, "we must all remember them. The pouch behind your shield will make a great hiding spot for the map until you can show them to Grandpapa Methuselah."

Jesse gazed at his wife with pride. "That is a great idea, my lady." He reached over Troy's shoulder and carefully placed the scroll into the shield's pouch. "There, that should keep it safe. Now, let's get to the Great Rejoicing. We have much to be thankful for."

CHAPTER 25

THE ARRIVAL

TO FINALLY ARRIVE AT A DESTINATION

CAN BE A COMFORT OR WORRY.

IT ALL DEPENDS ON WHO INVITED YOU

AND IF YOU'RE WELCOME OR NOT.

The door to the emergency bin room burst open as the leaders streamed in with their families.

THE DURUM DOES WERE BUSY COMPLETING THE FInal preparations for tonight's great rejoicing.

Ava smoothed a wrinkle out of one of the tablecloths and gazed around the room. "It looks amazing, ladies. I think we did a fabulous job. In fact, Papa and Mama will be so proud of us when they see all the work we've done."

BULGUR AND KAMET CLANS

THE DOOR TO THE EMERGENCY BIN ROOM BURST open as the leaders representing the Bulgur and Kamet clans streamed in with their families. They took their seats at the tables and waited patiently for the Honourable Sugar and her husband Spice to arrive.

The mayor's guards Jack and Adam marched into the room and snapped to attention.

Frey's heart began to pound when she saw Jack and Adam in their perfectly pressed red tunics and glistening black boots. She cupped her paw up to Olivia's ear.

"Isn't Jack the most handsome buck you've ever seen?" She glanced his way and gave him a cryptic wink.

Jack smiled and gave her a nod. Frey melted, blushed and quickly looked down at the floor.

Adam and Jack lifted their trumpets and blew them loud and hard, then announced, "Introducing the Honorable Mayor Sugar and her husband Spice of the Kamet and Bulgur clans." Everyone stood up and cheered as the mayor and her husband entered from under the door arm and arm.

Sugar swept into the room wearing a laser red cape and white pearls. Her husband Spice followed proudly behind sporting a formal black tux with long tails.

The mayor gazed around the room. "Where are my two sweeties, Olivia and Frey?"

The does ran forward to greet their guests and curtsied one after the other.

"We are so glad you have come, Mayor Sugar," Olivia said, "and pleased to see you as well, Mr. Spice."

Frey stepped close and kissed each of them on both cheeks.

"Olivia and I had a wonderful time at your home, Mr. Mayor. Thank you so much for your hospitality. The marmalade and biscuits were to die for."

Sugar smiled. "I'm so glad you liked them, dear. You are both so delightful." She looked around the room with an approving eye. "Well, well, I do declare!" whooped Sugar in her best southern accent. "I have nevah, evah seen such colorful party decorations in all mah life. You have done wonders to this room, my dears. It looks absolutely festive."

Spice placed his paw on Olivia's shoulder. "Sugar and I are indebted to you and your family for your bravery and generosity, young does." He looked at the empty jars. "By the way, where are your parents and your brothers? Were they not supposed to be here with the oats by now? I hope nothing has happened to them."

"Don't worry, Mayor Sugar. They'll be here," answered Olivia with as much confidence as she could muster. "We're expecting them at any moment. Troy and my brothers know how important the oats are to all the clans. Besides, our Creator will see to it their mission is accomplished." She pointed to the table and continued. "We have some cheese snacks that you can try while you're waiting for the rest of our family to arrive."

Sugar smiled, took Spice's hand and headed for the goodies. "That sounds just lovely dears. You know how I love appies." She turned to her husband, "Let's go and get some food, Mr. Kamet, I'm famished."

Jake and Adam moved forward and pulled out two chairs so they could sit down.

Frey ran up beside Jack, took his hand, and batted her eyes at him. "I'm so glad you could make it to the party, Jack. Will you be able to free yourself for a few moments to dance with one of the prettiest does in Salem?"

Jack turned all shades of red.

GRAHAM AND SPELT CLANS

NO SOONER HAD THE BULGUR AND KAMET OFFICIALS sat down than they heard a noise from behind the front door. One by one the Graham and Spelt band members marched in under the door, trumpets blaring, drums banging. Young bucks and does were singing songs of joy to their Creator for providing food near the end of winter. Mayor Smore and his lovely wife Ginger brought up the rear dressed in their best party clothes.

Ginger noticed Evalyn, Tammy, and Ava coming towards them and held out her hands. "Well, well, you lovely ladies have outdone yourselves and are a tribute to the Durum clan. Has the hero of the party arrived yet, my lovely does?"

Ava hid her private fears and smiled politely at Ginger and Mayor Smore. "Troy is small, your Honour, but he has a strong will and was anointed by Socrates, Seer of Salem. I have no doubt he and his brothers will be here with the oats as promised."

Her two sisters nodded in agreement as the rest of the Graham and Spelt clans came in and took seats around the well decorated tables.

THE FLY SQUADRON

THERE WAS A BUZZ OF EXCITEMENT IN THE ROOM. Some of the younger does danced, while the older folks sat around the tables eating snacks and catching up on juicy gossip. In many ways the Great Rejoicing had already begun.

While everyone eagerly anticipated the arrival of the oats, members of the fly squadron clung firmly to the wall in a perfect row. They carefully watched for opportunities to obtain some crumbs of their own. The two males, Buzz and Ace, were laughing at their latest battle with the Rafter Rats and their successful diversion to save the three young does from certain death.

Ace leaned towards his brother and fluttered his wings. "Can you believe how terrified Chuba was of a bunch of tiny flies, Buzz?"

Buzz moved his head down and cleaned himself with his front leg. "Well, maybe the rat was thinking we were bumblebees and that we'd sting him to death." They both buzzed their wings loudly as they laughed, picturing themselves stinging Rafter Rats on their derrières.

At the same time, the twins, Sparrow and Robin, were discussing Mayor Sugar's laser red cape and shiny pearl necklace.

"Did you see the size of those pearls around Mayor Sugar's neck, Robin?" asked Sparrow with a hint of jealousy in her voice. "I can't imagine how much they must have cost. And that red cape, it's way too formal for an event like this, don't you agree, Robin?"

Robin agreed with a nod of her head and a short buzz of her wings. "I know, right? What a waste. All that money spent on those pearls and that shiny red cape could have been used on food for her pups."

Sparrow suddenly turned her head completely around to see if Bell was listening to their conversation but she was not there. "Where did Bell go?"

"I don't know," answered Sparrow, "she was here a few minutes ago." They both turned towards Buzz and Ace who were still laughing and buzzing about their encounters with Rodney and Chuba.

"Hey, you two maggots"—Robin had no problem interrupting her brothers—"do you know where Bell disappeared to?"

Buzz stopped laughing and pointed with his tiny leg. "I saw her fly underneath that table over there to look for cheese crumbs. You know how she dies for cheese and crackers."

Bell finished eating the small bit of cheese that fell from Mayor Sugar's plate and then noticed a few cracker crumbs on the floor where some pups were sitting. She buzzed over and picked up enough to share with her friends, who were still stuck to the wall. She had trouble taking off with her load so she moved her wings faster and eventually landed next to Buzz.

"Look what I found!" she exclaimed. "I knew there would be something to eat down there. Mice are messy eaters."

Sparrow moved close to her friend Bell. "Did you bring

enough to share with your friends, or is this all for you?"

Bell carefully took one crumb at a time from underneath her wings and handed some to her friends. "You don't think I'd forget you guys, do you? I mean, someone has to think about supper around here."

Buzz was starving and nearly swallowed his piece whole. After his tongue licked up the leftovers he cleaned his face and looked up at the front door.

"I wonder what's keeping Troy and his brothers. I hope they didn't get caught by that big ol' giant. They must complete their mission or the mouse clans will not survive winter."

TROY AND HIS BROTHERS ARRIVE

BUZZ WAS STILL SPEAKING WHEN SUDDENLY A GOLD sword and shield slid under the doorway with a loud clang, followed by nine large knapsacks filled with oats. All the chatter in the storage room went quiet as Troy crawled under the door. He stood up and brushed himself off without noticing every eye was on him—and the nine bags of precious oats. He picked up his gold sword and Levi shield and slowly raised his head. The whole room erupted in one cheer.

Mama and Papa entered the room just as the crowd began to shout, "King Troy, King Troy, King Troy!"

His eight brothers came up beside him and joined in the chant. Troy's five sisters ran from where they were sitting and showered their brothers with hugs and kisses.

Olivia stared at her brothers and then focused on all the bags filled to the brim with oats.

"Troy, you did it! You actually took the giant's oats from

his cupboard. Your O-Plan worked!"

Tammy just stood in front of Troy as her eyes filled with tears of joy. "I was so worried. I prayed for you every minute we were apart. You are my best friend, and I'm so glad you're home, Troy." She stood there trying her best to be calm, but then she was like a geyser exploding from the ground. She began bouncing for joy on both feet and then jumped six feet in the air. When Tammy finally settled down, her left foot kept vibrating and her cloaking gift kept turning on and off.

Troy stood there with his arms crossed and a big grin on his face. "I'm so glad to see you haven't changed a bit, Tammy. In fact, if I could see you, I'd give you a big hug."

The two mayors made their way over to shake the paws of each Durum buck.

"We are so proud of you, my warriors," stated Mayor Sugar, beaming with pride.

Spice ran over to Jesse and put his arm around him as though they were long lost friends. "Well, well, well, did you evah think your children would end up the heroes of all the clans one day, son?"

At the same time, Ginger approached Evette and gave her a hug and then a kiss on both cheeks.

"Your lovely does were so brave, my dear. They risked their lives just to tell us about the oats and the Great Rejoicing tonight. They are all as cute as pie. They must have had some good training at the Royal Academy of Mouse Survival."

Evette glanced over at her does with pride. "Yes, they were at the top of their class, Mayor Smore. And the Great Creator was looking after them and my young bucks. He knew the importance of their missions and that's why they couldn't fail."

The whole place was filled with joy as Troy's sisters picked up the nine knapsacks and began to pour the precious oats into each jar.

When they were finished, Troy picked up his gold sword and Levi shield, climbed onto one of the tables and held his hand up for everyone to quiet down. The place became so

quiet he could actually hear one of the elevator flies, scratching its ears.

Troy tucked his sword into the shoelace behind his back. He bent down and took hold of a large container filled with delicious oats. He held it up above his head.

"Clans of the orange elevator, on behalf of my whole family and for the glory of our Great Creator, it is my honour to present to you— the oats from the giant's cupboard!"

Everyone cheered and chanted his name, "Troy, Troy, Troy!"

The crowd slowly quieted down again so that the new hero could continue to speak. "It is my pleasure to announce that my brothers and I met the great giant named Mr. Wolfe. He actually caught us stealing his food, but during the battle he had the misfortune of knocking himself out by stepping on a garden tool. When he woke up I was standing on top of his chest, so I pointed my sword at his throat and said, 'My name is Troy! I don't know who you are, Giant, but you'd better leave my brothers alone or I'll run you through with my Papa's sword!'" Everyone gasped as Troy continued. "Then Mr. Wolfe looked at me and began to speak. The strangest thing was that we could both understand each other. It was a miracle. I think the Creator wanted us to meet and this was all a part of His glorious plan."

"But how did you get the oats, Troy?" asked Mayor Sugar. The crowd became very still, waiting for Troy to answer.

Goar, feeling quite pleased with himself, motioned his 12 mouse slaves to bring the golden litter to his side.

CHAPTER 26

PRINCE SAPH'S EVIL PLOT

THE SNAKE SITS AT THE TABLE AND

PLOTS YOUR DESTRUCTION AS HE SERVES

YOU DESSERT AND WHISPERS SWEET

WORDS INTO YOUR ITCHING EARS.

SAPH SAT DOWN AGAINST THE WALL AND MUMBLED TO himself as he tore a piece of cloth he found and wrapped it around his bloody tail. His leg hurt and his nose was quite tender.

"I swear by the name of Dreck, those little cheese lovers are going to pay for humiliating me," declared the prince while smashing his fist on the wooden floor. He raised his head, as he continued down the empty Rat's Trail. "Where are those two overgrown knuckle-heads anyway? They can never do anything right." He slowly stood up and limped down the trail. Saph hadn't gone more than a few yards when he heard Rodney's annoying nasal voice. He was criticizing his brother as usual.

"Why are you so scared of flies, Chuba? We would have been able to capture those pathetic girlie cheese lovers, if you hadn't panicked."

Chuba ducked his head down in shame but then quickly perked up with a positive thought. "At least we can tell Grandpapa Goar that we found enough oats to keep our tribes well fed until spring."

"Yeah," added Rodney with an evil grin, "and all we have to do is to interrupt their little celebration and steal the oats. I don't know about you, Chuba, but I would love to wipe the smile off that one-eyed freak."

Chuba laughed. "Ha, ha, then they'd all starve this winter and we'd be rid of them once and for all."

The two brothers turned the corner and bumped into their uncle Saph, his hands on his hips and his red eyes glowing with anger.

"Where have you been, you little worms?" He picked

up Rodney by the throat. "King Goar has been waiting for you all day. You were to be back hours ago."

"Chuba slowed us down," Rodney squeaked out as he pointed at Chuba. "He was caught by an Orange Bat and dropped two stories onto the floor. We had to wait until he recovered and then we were attacked by five well-armed cheese lovers."

"Cheese lovers? You were attacked and beaten by cheese lovers?" Saph was about to mock them even further but he too was attacked and beaten by those flea-bitten rodents.

Chuba reached up, tapped Saph's back and smiled. "Uncle Saph, we have some good news."

The giant rat looked down at Chuba and dropped his brother to the floor. Rodney clutched his throat gasping for air.

"That's Prince Saph to you little ingrates! Well, speak up, what is it?"

"We-we didn't find any wheat under the loading bins, Uncle... I mean, Prince Saph, sir," Chuba continued nervously, "but we did find out the cheese lovers have oats... lots and lots of delicious oats. Troy and his brothers stole a large bag from the giant's storage room. We saw them preparing for a celebration tonight in the bin room"—Chuba turned to his brother for support—"didn't we, Rodney?"

Rodney shook his head up and down while rubbing his neck as Chuba continued.

"The cheese lovers will all be there by now and are waiting for Troy and his brothers to return with the oats. We heard them say they were going to distribute the food among all the clans tonight."

A smile spread across Saph's crooked mouth. "Ha, ha, ha, well, well, well, the freak and his little minions have been busy, have they? C'mon, you two losers, I must inform the King of my brilliant plan."

The three rodents slowly hobbled down the Rat's Trail and made their way to Benob and Lilith's wedding banquet to inform the king.

"Are we gonna steal the oats from those cheese lovers tonight, Prince Saph? Huh? Are we?" Rodney asked.

Saph just stared straight ahead holding his bleeding tail and scheming of ways he could make Troy pay.

"Once I give King Goar the good news," Saph said in a low voice through his gritted crooked teeth, "I'll suggest he send me with 100 of his best warriors to their celebration. I'll steal the cheese lovers' oats and then take their precious little Troy and make him my personal slave. That will teach them to mess with Prince Saph and the Rafter Rats of Salem."

The trio made their way back to the wedding celebration as fast as they could without another word.

When they arrived on level five the wedding banquet was in full swing. King Goar was dancing with his wife Noam, as the musicians played a lilting tune on the pipes.

King Og and his wife Jair were gorging themselves on a large turkey drumstick.

Prince Benob and his new bride Lilith were at the Temple of Dreck asking him to bless their marriage.

Abigail, Goar's adopted daughter was faithfully serving the guests when she noticed the prince come into the room with an evil grin. She knew right then her adopted brother was up to no good.

Rodney and Chuba spotted Papa Lami coming out of the kitchen with more food.

"Papa, Papa, we're back," Chuba announced as they both ran to his side.

"We found some more food," said Rodney as he looked up and smiled at his Papa, "and all we have to do is steal it from a bunch of unsuspecting cheese lovers, tonight."

Lami noticed Chuba was limping and his side was bleeding.

"You look like you were in a fight and lost badly. What happened, Chuba? Have those bullies from school been after you again?"

Rodney thought it would be better if he explained how it happened. "Actually, it was an Orange Bat, Papa. It came out of nowhere and attacked Chuba while we were crossing a rafter on level four."

"An Orange Bat!" shrieked Lami. "We have a peace pact with them. Did you do something stupid to provoke it? I know you, Rodney. You can't keep your mouth shut and I told you to look after your little brother, didn't I?"

Rodney looked down. "I tried but it took us by surprise.

We trapped a couple of cheese lovers and were about to capture them when the bat swooped down, grabbed Chuba and dropped him to the floor."

Lami looked at his son with suspicion. "Why would a bat protect a cheese lover, Rodney? Something doesn't add up son. By the way, did you find any oats in the loading bin?"

Chuba suddenly wasn't feeling well but wanted his Papa's approval. "The loading bin on level one was totally empty, but we discovered the cheese lovers have a whole bag of oats they stole from the giant's cupboard." As soon as he finished talking he fell on the floor unconscious.

Lami was now worried for his son. "Rodney, take Chuba to your Mama, she'll take care of his wounds. I must tell the king the good news."

But Saph had gone straight to the King when he arrived and interrupted their dance. Goar seemed upset at first but then as his son told him the good news his eyes grew bigger with every word. When Saph had finished he knelt on one knee.

Goar let go of his wife Noam and bellowed, with spit flying from his mouth, "Stop the music! Stop the music, I say!" The room went deathly silent and the great Goar began to speak.

"Listen-up! Listen up, you Rats of Goar and Rats of Og, Prince Saph has discovered a large stash of food just waiting for us to take!" At first the wedding guests gasped, then cheered. Goar paused for effect and then continued. "The mouse clans are in a room on level four as I speak celebrating a large discovery of oats. They are about to distribute the find at this very moment and I say we go down there right now and take what belongs to us." The rats cheered, whistled and stomped their feet with unbridled joy.

Saph stood up and stuttered nervously, "Oh, great Goar, I-I, your humble servant and son, have-have a plan that will guarantee total success."

"Well, then speak up, son, and quit mumbling," Goar demanded, slightly irritated.

Some of the guests snickered and Saph lowered his eyes in shame. Then as he thought about Troy, his feeling of defeat was soon replaced by anger and revenge. He had a score to settle with the Durum family and didn't want to blow this opportunity.

He looked at his papa with determination. "My King, I would humbly propose choosing 100 of our best warriors and take back what is rightfully ours. I say we march down to level four, enter the room from on top of the rafters and surround them. Then we take their one-eyed hero they call 'Mighty Troy of Salem' captive. He's a tiny freak of a cheese lover who they credit with stealing a large bag of oats from the giant's cupboard.

"They also worship this pathetic invisible god they call the Great Creator. We could show them their god is no match for all the powerful Dreck. I believe if we take Troy captive we could ensure they will not fight back." Saph knelt at his father's feet. "And I humbly ask the King if I could take Troy as my personal slave."

Goar's mouth stretched into an evil grin from one ear to the other. He stroked his long beard as he looked at Saph and then waved a paw upwards.

"Arise, Prince Saph. That's the first good idea you have

had since you were born, my son. Maybe there is hope for you yet. Okay, Saph, this is your chance to prove yourself and don't screw up. I'll allow you to choose 100 of my best warriors, however, you must take Prince Lami with you. He will make sure you succeed. And regarding this Mighty Troy character, I would like to have him as my personal slave. He may be a good companion for Abigail. She gets lonely for her own kind. But first I will need to break his spirit."

He turned to King Og. "Sir, I would be honoured if you would accompany me and my litter to the battle field. We will follow Saph and Lami and see this historic event unfold before our very eyes. What do you say?"

Og seemed excited at the prospect of witnessing a good ol' fight, even if it was a bit lopsided. "It would be my pleasure to go with you, King Goar," he said as he bent down and kissed his wife Jair. "This will give our wives a chance to get to know one another better and I would like to see this little warrior mouse they call 'Mighty Troy' for myself—he sounds intriguing."

Goar, feeling quite pleased with himself, motioned his 12 mouse slaves to bring the golden litter to his side. The guards whipped the cheese lover slaves as they struggled to carry the litter.

"Come quickly, you lazy vermin! We don't have all day!"

The slaves ran as fast as they could and then set down the heavy golden crate. Goar motioned for Og to climb aboard, then followed him and sat on the opposite side so they could talk. Goar moved his paw forward, the guards yelled at the slaves and they picked up the litter.

Og smiled. "This is going to be so much fun."

Saph and Lami gathered their weapons and motioned for Goar's 100 warriors to fall into line as they marched towards the hole in the floor, which would take them down to level four.

At the Great Rejoicing, Troy stood on the table to tell the story of how he and his brothers managed to retrieve the precious oats.

CHAPTER 27

THE GREAT REJOICING

SOMEDAY, THERE WILL BE A "GREAT REJOICING!" THERE WILL BE NO MORE HUNGER AND NO MORE THIRST, NO MORE TEARS AND NO MORE SORROW, NO MORE SICKNESS AND NO MORE DYING. WE WILL LIVE FOREVER. LOVE WILL TRIUMPH OVER HATE AND LIGHT OVER DARKNESS.

AT THE GREAT REJOICING, TROY STOOD ON THE TABLE to tell the story of how he and his brothers managed to retrieve the precious oats.

"First of all, Mayor Sugar, it was not easy, but our family had a plan. We mapped out the details for our mission and then another plan for my brave sisters. My brothers and I were to move out in the early hours and crawl down the pipes until we reached level one. Then we were to make our way through the ancient tunnel of our ancestors, leading to the giant's cupboard. Thirdly, we were to bring down the large bag of oats on the shelf, fill our backpacks and head for home."

"Did you have any trouble, Troy?" the mayor asked.

"Actually, there were many surprises and obstacles on both our missions. Yet I know that anything worth doing will always have mountains to climb and rivers to cross. Missions never go as planned, however, the Great Creator provides wisdom and strength to complete them."

The adult mice shook their heads in amazement, as Troy described his adventures.

"Wow, Troy," said Mayor Sugar "I think I speak for all the clans here when I say thank you to you and your brothers and sisters for all you sacrificed on our behalf."

"You're very welcome, Mam." Troy humbly nodded.

The young pups had shuffled closer to the table where Troy was standing and stared up at him with eyes of wonder.

"How big was the giant, Troy? Was he gonna to eat you? Did you see any Orange Bats? Do they have red eyes? Was old Arnie mean?"

Troy looked at each of the eager pups, smiled and continued the story. "After we bumped into old Arnie, we slid down the tunnel and fought off two Rafter Rats. Jacob actually tripped five traps in a row near the entrance to the tunnel."

A small pup called Joey looked up at his new hero Jacob and asked him many questions. Troy noticed he spoke with a cute lisp. "I'm really, really fast you know. Someday, I'll trip five traps just like you."

Jacob went over and lifted little Joey onto his shoulders, "I bet when you're my age you'll be able to trip six in a row."

The little guy giggled, and looked back up at Troy. "So did you see the giant, Troy? Did you run him through with your sword of justice? Can I see it? My papa told me it's very heavy to everyone else, but in your hands it's as light as a feather."

Troy was not used to all this attention and felt a bit awkward. He jumped down from the table, pulled the sword from behind his back and placed the handle in Joey's outstretched paws.

"Be very careful with this weapon, little buck, it's not a toy."

Joey grabbed it with both paws but the weight pulled him to the floor.

Troy bent down and easily picked up the sword, which began to glow as he placed it behind his back.

The little pups were awestruck as Troy hopped back up on to the table and continued telling the story of his adventure with the giant of the Orange Elevator.

"I climbed onto his chest, pointed the gold sword at his throat and said, 'Don't move, giant, or I'll run you through with my Papa's sword!'"

"You should have run for the tunnel and never looked back, Troy," Mama said. "You could have made the giants very mad, motivating them to get rid of us."

Troy smiled. "Actually Mama it turned out okay. The giant's name is Lyle Wolfe and he seems quite friendly. He even said we could keep the oats and if we needed any more to let him know. The Great Creator did amazing things today."

"When the giant let you go, I heard you had some trouble coming home, Troy," Papa said.

"Actually, Papa, we were the ones who let the giant go. We thanked him for the food and made our way back through the tunnel. Arriving safely on the other side my brothers were divided on which route to take to the pipe. Some wanted to take the faster more dangerous route and others the safer but longer path. In the end, the majority chose to take the faster route through the machines."

Papa frowned and shook a paw. "Troy, I gave you clear instructions not to take unnecessary risks. You were told to always choose the safest routes."

"I know, Papa, and I said that at the time, but we had a vote and most said they wanted to take the faster route. It turned out alright in the end. Eventually we did make it safely to the pipe."

"I know you did, little buck, but I placed you in charge. Your mission was not a democracy. Part of being a great leader is to make difficult choices even when it's not popular. So, what happened next?"

"I realize that things could have gone very badly, Papa," admitted Troy. "Two by two we arrived safely at the entrance to the pipe. The only ones who hadn't arrived were Elijah and Joab. Soon it became clear that Kappa had taken them captive. The Bat King was about to eat them when, out of nowhere, a small cat named Willis pounced on him. This made Kappa drop Elijah and Joab and they were able to escape. It was a very close call."

Joey's ears perked up when he heard there was a cat involved in the story. He knew they were dangerous but that's what made them exciting.

"Wow, you saw a real kitty cat? Was he friendly? Did he have fuzzy fur?"

Troy nodded. "His fur did look very soft and as it turns out he was friendly. Willis eventually let Kappa go and he flew off into the darkness of the rafters. This strange little cat came close to me and said he knew my grandpapa and was a friend of the family. Before I could ask Willis more questions his uncle forced him to leave. I got the impression Arnie didn't like the fact that Willis was talking to a cheese lover."

"Troy, I heard on the way to the storage bin you ran into another Rafter Rat. Is that true? Was it Rodney or Chuba?" Olivia asked.

"It was a very large rat by the name of Saph," answered Troy, "I think he's one of King Goar's sons. Why do you ask, Olivia? Did you guys run into him as well?"

Olivia laughed. "No, no, we didn't have the pleasure of meeting Saph, however we did have a major run-in with those nasty rats, Rodney and Chuba, twice. They even told us they beat you up and left you for dead."

Troy looked surprised and began to laugh. "You met

those two little pests, twice? The truth is we were the ones who chased them into the darkness."

"So what happened with Goar's son Saph?" urged Frey. "Are you all okay? I hear that he's a giant rat with the strength of ten warriors."

"Well, yes, we did run into him and he is large for a rat, but, as you know, the bigger they are the harder they fall. The Great Creator was truly with us. Saph actually attempted to take Mama, but during the battle to free her I managed to slice his tail with the sword of justice. I'm afraid he left quite angry, ashamed and in great pain."

As the clans listened to Troy's miraculous accounts and his brothers, they cheered and jumped for joy. Never had they heard such bravery and miraculous feats of courage.

Troy was sure to let everyone know it was only because of the Creator that they were able to retrieve the oats.

"Enough talking! Let's begin the Great Rejoicing." Troy jumped down from the table and the band from the Bulgur and Kamet clans began to play popular mouse tunes. Everyone gathered around and danced for joy.

Jesse and Evette held each other's hands as they walked over to the centre of the room and began to jump to the joyful music.

Olivia turned to Frey and whispered in her ear. "Why don't you ask Jack to dance? You know you want to." They both giggled, drawing Jack's attention.

He turned towards Frey and extended his hand. "May I have the pleasure of this dance, Frey?"

Frey's cheeks turned all shades of red. "I thought you'd never ask."

BETA JOINS THE PARTY

HIGH ABOVE THE RAFTERS OF THE STORAGE BIN ROOM and deep in the shadows, Beta smiled as she hung upside down watching her new friends Frey and Olivia.

"Oh, I wish I could be there with you," she whispered to herself. "I have never been to a Great Rejoicing before." Beta pulled herself right side up and was preparing to fly home when she noticed a dark corner of the room, which gave her an idea. "I could hide behind that large conveyor belt," she thought aloud, "and maybe get Olivia or Frey's attention, then they would know that I did come to their party after all." She dove down as quickly as she could, ducked behind the machine and waited for an opportunity.

Olivia watched Frey and Jack for a while and then called the rest of her sisters over. They held hands in a circle and danced for joy before the Creator. They sang songs of praise thanking Him for accomplishing their mission and for blessing them with so much food. The group began to grow as more and more mice from every clan joined the circle. They danced around the room three times before Olivia heard Beta's chirp.

Their eyes connected for just a second as Olivia circled past Beta's hiding place one more time. "Pssst, Pssst!"

Olivia slipped out of the crowd and moved toward the sound. Could it be? Was that Beta she'd caught a glimpse of a moment ago? No, it couldn't be. Suddenly a clawed wing came out from behind a machine and pulled her into the shadows. Olivia tried to scream but Beta placed a wing tightly over her mouth.

"Olivia, don't be afraid. It's me, Beta." She dropped her wing from Olivia's mouth and smiled at her little friend. "I told you I would come to your rejoicing."

"It's really you!" Olivia tucked herself inside Beta's wing. She couldn't believe her eyes. "I'm so glad you came, but how are you feeling? You must be careful. You can't be seen by anyone. Does Zeta know you are here?"

"I'm a bit sore but feeling much better, Olivia." Beta then shook her head. "As far as my brother is concerned, I would never tell him I'm with you. He hates the fact that we are friends."

Olivia giggled. "Well, I'm so happy we met you and thanks for coming. I'd go and get Frey, but she's busy dancing with Jack. She thinks he's the love of her life, ha, ha, ha."

Beta peered around the corner and spotted Frey in Jack's paws enjoying a slow dance. "Aww, that's so sweet." The bat looked back to her new friend. "I wish I could stay, Olivia, but I had better go now before Zeta finds out I'm gone." The small Orange Bat wrapped her wings around her friend, then took off and disappeared into the darkness.

KAPPA JOINS ZETA

HIGH ON A RAFTER ABOVE THE STORAGE BIN ROOM Zeta's bright yellow eyes squinted as he watched his sister hug the cheese lover.

"What are you up to, little Bee? This is an unholy friendship that has to end." Just then he looked up and noticed King Kappa soaring above his perch, so he called him over with a high whistle.

The King looked around for a moment and honed in on where the sound had come from and soon locked eyes with Zeta. Kappa was larger than most bats and when he stared into one's eyes his gaze seemed to pierce the soul. Even his friends never really knew if he was actually on their side or just using them for his benefit.

"This had better be good, Zeta," Kappa said, saliva dripping from his chin. "I was closing in on a juicy, fat fly until you disturbed me and now I'm getting very hungry." His head pushed up against Zeta's in a gesture of dominance.

This close up, Zeta could see that Kappa's fangs were stained with the blood of his latest prey. Zeta looked down in respect and fear, now regretting that he called the king to inform him of what now seemed to be a trivial matter.

"Well, what is so important that you would take your king away from his hunting and gathering hour? Shouldn't you be hunting at this time, Zeta?"

"Yes, my lord," responded Zeta, his eyes and head still lowered in respect. "My great King, I have bad news about Beta. She has come in contact with some female cheese lovers and I fear it has become an unholy relationship. It is shamefully unnatural and must be stopped before it spreads! I thought you would like to be aware of this."

Kappa snorted and spat in Zeta's face. "You disturbed me for this? Why tell me, why not your parents? Are you sure? This does not sound like Beta. I personally taught her to hunt the cheese lovers without mercy. Did it ever occur to you that she might be using the bat's famous luring tactic to bait her prey? She might be biding her time and building trust in order to have her fill later."

Zeta now felt foolish and tried to explain. "But, sir, I thought it was forbidden for the Orange Bats to have a relationship with their prey."

Kappa's eyes glowed. "Baiting a cheese lover under false pretences is not having a real relationship, you fool. It is a tactical hunting method. How did you even graduate from hunting school, you little maggot?"

Zeta suddenly thought of some new information the King might be interested in. "My King, I did notice the female cheese lovers have a brother named Troy and he seems quite popular among the clans. They even call him a king."

At the mention of the name "Troy" Kappa's ears perked up and his nose began to twitch nervously as he recalled his humiliating scrap with Willis the cat. Oh, how he hated that cat, but not as much as he hated the name "Troy."

There was something about that little cheese lover that made his eyes burn with anger. This one-eyed freak seemed to have an air of authority and superiority about him. Nothing would please him, the King of the Orange Bats, more than to wipe the smile off Troy's face.

Kappa's demeanor suddenly changed as he placed his wing around Zeta and a sinister grin spread across his pushed-in face. "Did you say Beta is friends with the sisters of that freak Troy"?

"Yes, my King," agreed Zeta, feeling more confident. "Their names are Olivia and Frey and they claim to have saved Beta's life at one point."

"Never mind the girls, Zeta, although we may be able to use them to get to the freak." Kappa began to stroke Zeta's head with his claw in a fake nurturing manner. "I want to know everything you know about this one-eyed rodent Troy."

"Well, my King, I have been watching them closely tonight and Troy seems to have found a large amount of fresh oats. They have come to the storage bin to celebrate and distribute the find among the clans." Zeta stopped for a moment to see if he was still holding Kappa's interest.

"Well, go on, go on, my brave Zeta, and tell me more." The king kept stroking Zeta's orange fur and began to drool even more at the thought of revenge.

"They call him Mighty Troy of Salem, my King. I don't know why." Zeta now wanted to tell him everything. "As you pointed out, he only has one eye and I agree, he looks more like a freak than a king."

Kappa cocked his head to one side. "They used the word 'mighty', did they? What an interesting adjective to use for a tiny mouse with so many disabilities. I wonder what makes him so special?"

Zeta lifted his head with excitement as he recalled something else. "I heard they worship a strange god they call "the Great Creator". They seem to love Him very much and say He has blessed this Troy with extraordinary powers."

"Then I would like to know more about this god of theirs and the powers he bestows," stated Kappa. If I could have those powers for myself, nothing would stop me. I could be the King of the World! He turned back to Zeta. "Do you know the source of the powers bestowed upon Troy?"

Zeta sat up and felt a bit nervous at his lack of information so he took a stab at what Kappa might want to hear. "Not exactly, sir. I heard Troy felled the giant with his extraordinary strength. They say he actually climbed on top of his large chest, held his golden sword to the giant's throat and threatened to kill him."

The king was quite pleased with this story. "Is there anything else you noticed while watching Troy this evening, Zeta?"

"Yes, sir. When the clans called Troy a king, his gold sword began to glow brightly and hummed as though it was alive with power."

"Wait, the sword glowed and hummed?!" Kappa's evil grin spread even wider, as his gaze locked with Zeta's. "I must get a hold of that sword. That must be the source of his power."

"And, there's one other thing, sir," Zeta continued. "The Rafter Rats are also out of food and they want to steal the oats from the cheese lovers."

"Hmm."

Before Kappa could decide what to do with that last

bit of news about the rats, his highly tuned sonar picked up some movement coming from the pipes on level five.

"What is that noise?" asked Kappa. "It sounds like—like—" He turned his head to one side and listened more intently. Then a grin slowly began to form on his flat, wrinkled face. "The Rafter Rats are marching to war! They're coming for the oats the cheese lovers have found. I can use this battle to my advantage and besides, this will be so much fun to watch." The two Orange Bats hung upside down and made themselves comfortable as they waited for the ensuing battle to begin.

The rat warriors held their swords high in a silent cheer and waited for their orders.

CHAPTER 28

THE COMING STORM

PEACE AND SAFETY. TWO ELUSIVE

WORDS, ESPECIALLY IN A WORLD FILLED

WITH WAR AND RUMORS OF WAR. A DEEP

AND LASTING PEACE CAN ONLY BE FOUND

IN THE HEART OF THOSE THAT HAVE BEEN

CHANGED BY THE ONE WHO IS LOVE.

METHUSELAH RETURNS

TROY LEANED AGAINST ONE OF THE STORAGE BINS and watched the ongoing celebration. He'd dreamt of a time when all the creatures in the Orange Elevator would be at peace. He desperately wanted to begin a new kind of revolution—a revolution of love. His chest burned and his heart began to pound in anticipation as he thought about this new mission.

Troy was pleased the clans were finally unified because of the success of the Oats Mission and had some peace knowing everyone would not go without food this winter. Yet, he couldn't shake this unsettled feeling that something wasn't quite right. Something lurked in the shadows. He didn't know what exactly, but he knew it wasn't happy.

As he watched the clans dance around in circles, Troy remembered all the unbelievable adventures his family had had that day. He and his brothers had actually met and spoken with a real giant. He had met his grandpapa Methuselah whom everyone had thought was dead but was very much alive.

A tap on his shoulder and a whispered voice saying, "Troy. Troy," startled him out of his thoughts. Instinctively, he raised his Levi shield in front of him and thrust his sword at the intruder lurking in the shadows.

"Put that thing down before you hurt someone, young buck," scolded Methuselah with a chuckle as he slowly peered into the light.

"Grandpapa! You came!" Troy lowered his sword and wrapped his arms around the old mouse. Maybe it was Grandpapa he had sensed watching him, though the sense of impending dread lingered. "I'm so glad you made it to the Great Rejoicing! You must come and see Mama and Papa! They will be so pleased to see you."

Methuselah held his paw up in protest. "Now hold on, young buck. I'm not sure the clans are ready for me to rise from the dead just yet and quite frankly neither am I."

Troy lowered the Levi shield and placed his sword behind his back. "Well, maybe the elders are ready to drop the charges against you and we can be a family again."

"Maybe someday, son, maybe someday." Methuselah slowly turned to leave. He wasn't as hopeful as his grandson. The Elders who had placed him in the cell many years ago were still alive and none of them were as forgetful as he wished they were.

"Wait, Grandpapa, wait! You can't leave yet." Troy grabbed hold of Selah's arm. "You must see what we have found first." He placed his shield down on its face and reached into the hidden pouch beside the handle. He carefully removed the delicate parchment and unrolled it on the wooden floor. "Samuel found this map in a hole next to the Rat's Trail." Troy knelt beside the map and looked up at his grandpapa with pride. "Is it a treasure map?"

BELL'S MISSION

BUZZ AND ACE OF THE FLY SQUADRON WERE SITTING on the wall right next to where Troy and his grandpapa were talking. Bell, Sparrow and Robin were busy gathering crumbs off the floor and soon returned to share with the guys.

Bell flew in with food in her mouth and landed beside

Buzz. "I found some delicious oats, want some?"

Her two sisters followed close behind and Sparrow was excited to share their find. "We have cheese and cracker crumbs." She just couldn't contain herself and buzzed round and round her brother Ace. "Isn't this the best party ever, you guys?"

The squadron was busy enjoying their food when suddenly the wall began to shake. "Did you feel that?" Asked Buzz as he turned his head around 360 degrees to get a complete view.

Ace nervously rubbed her legs together. "Yeah, the wall keeps pulsing in a perfect rhythm, should I go and check it out?"

"No," replied Buzz, "Bell should go, she's faster and her eyes are much better in the dark."

Bell dipped her head and washed her face before taking off in a flash to check out the strange pulse. She flew under the door, rounded the corner and hovered in midair. Bell couldn't believe what she saw. The Rafter Rats were marching out of the pipe. First Prince Saph then 100 well-armed warriors.

Goar and Og came out a short while later laughing and talking about a coming battle with the cheese lovers. The 12 mouse slaves slowly placed the golden litter on the floor and sat down to rest.

"Who told you to sit down!" bellowed Goar. The young slaves jumped to their feet and stood at attention. Goar climbed out of the box, held out his hand and assisted his guest who clumsily stepped out and stood by his side. Both kings crossed their arms and puffed their chests out looking as regal as possible. Goar turned to his sons. "Saph, Lami! Get these warriors to stand at attention!"

When they were lined up nice and straight, the princes stood in front scowling. Lami glanced at his papa then pointed to the ceiling. "I suggest we climb up the walls, in through that hole and then stealthily climb onto the rafters. We could have 25 warriors stationed on all four corners of the room in under five minutes, sir. I brought four ropes to drop our warriors to the floor below. Before the cheese lovers even know what's happening they'll be surrounded. When we have them captured we'll open the door and let you and King Og inside."

"It's a good plan, Lami," Prince Saph interjected, "but only because it was mine first. This sneak attack will be like taking cheese from a mouse pup and at the end of the day Troy will be mine."

The warriors laughed.

"SHHHH!" Goar held up his long claws. "Pipe down, you idiots, before we lose our element of surprise." He rolled his eyes, looked at King Og and then the ceiling. "By the name of Dreck, why did I keep having more pups? Noam warned me that if we had another litter they might not turn out so good."

Prince Saph looked down, obviously hurt by his papa's remarks. He wanted nothing more than to make his papa proud and yet he always seemed to fall short of his expectations.

Prince Lami smirked, knowing that he was Papa's favourite and obviously next in line to the throne, and oh did he look forward to being in charge.

The king leaned over and said in a low voice that no one could hear, "Show no mercy to those cheese lovers if they resist. Do you hear me? No mercy!" Goar raised his hands in the air and blessed his sons. "Now go, and may Lord Dreck grant you victory." The rat warriors held their swords high in a silent cheer and waited for their orders.

Upon hearing King Goar's command, Saph and Lami divided the company into quarters. They gave each captain a rope and ordered them to begin climbing the wall and into the hole of the storage bin room.

KAPPA ENJOYS THE VIEW

MEANWHILE, HIGH ABOVE THE RATS, KING KAPPA and Zeta were hanging upside down, eagerly watching the drama unfold.

"Well, well, well," jeered Kappa, "it appears Mighty Troy will not be mighty much longer, eh? We'll just wait until the chaos begins, swoop down and the gold sword will be mine."

Zeta turned towards his king and smiled. "While you're stealing the sword, o king, I will capture Olivia and Frey and end this unholy friendship they have with my sister once and for all."

Kappa squinted his eyes as he watched the rats scurry through the hole in the ceiling. "Just to think, I almost missed the showdown of the year." Kappa tilted his head towards Zeta, smiled to show-off his fangs and wrapped his leathery wings around him. "Just be patient, my little worm, just be patient."

BELL RETURNS

BELL HAD HEARD ENOUGH AND HEADED BACK TO-wards the emergency storage room. "Somehow, I have to let the mice know they are in grave danger." She crawled under the door and flew back to where the rest of her squad was patiently waiting.

By now the Great Rejoicing was in full swing and everyone was making a joyful noise. There was singing and dancing and talking and eating. The mouse clans were totally oblivious to what was about to happen.

Bell stood in front of her fellow fliers. Ace, Sparrow and Robin were buzzing with anticipation.

"We have to tell Troy the clans are in big trouble. There are one hundred Rat warriors poised to attack them from high above the rafters. They've already made their way into the room and are going to descend on four ropes at any moment. I also heard them saying they are going to steal the oats from the mice and capture Troy as their slave. What are we going to do, Ace? The mice don't even know we exist and they need to be warned."

Buzz scratched his head and cleaned his face a few times. "I have an idea. Troy has amazing hearing abilities. In fact, I'm surprised he hasn't heard the rats approaching as yet. Anyway, I could fly into to his ear and warn him."

Bell laughed. "Flying into Troy's ear will only annoy him and he will flick you out. I think we should try something more subtle."

"Wait a minute, Bell, it just might work." Buzz turned his head towards Ace and smiled. "Make sure when you hover around Troy's head, you don't land in his ear. Keep yelling 'danger' as loudly as you can. Troy will understand. Now go quickly, there is no time to waste."

Buzz took off, his wings humming in perfect rhythm. He headed straight to where Troy was kneeling on the floor with his grandpapa studying the strange map.

INTERPRETING THE SACRED SCROLL

TROY PATIENTLY WAITED FOR METHUSELAH TO SAY something about the strange parchment.

The old buck had never seen anything quite like it, yet he did recognize the words written on the side. They were inscribed in ancient Hebrew.

"What does it say, Grandpapa?" Troy could hardly contain his excitement.

"Where did you say you got this, little buck?" Methuselah was amazed. "I have heard stories of a Sacred Scroll and of the wonders it contains, but I just thought they were mere legends. This is not the Sacred Scroll, but it could lead us to it."

"Wonders? What wonders?"

He was so excited he didn't hear Buzz yelling, "Look up, Troy! Danger, danger!" in his ear.

Troy swatted the fly away with his paw.

"Is the Sacred Scroll important to our clans, Grandpapa?"

"More than you'll ever know, more than you'll ever know." The old buck told Troy about the secrets of the scroll and how they were passed down through many generations as far back as the beginning of creation. "My Grandpapa Jared told me about a sacred scroll written just after the Great Creator made mammals to roam the earth.

Our Holy Book tells us where we came from and that the 'giants' or humans would be our caretakers. In fact, Troy, the giants were the ones who gave us our name 'mice.'" Methuselah closed his eyes as he quoted the words from memory:

Now out of the ground the Lord God had formed every beast of the field and every bird of the heavens and brought them to the man to see what he would call them and whatever the man called every living creature, that was its name.

"The legend tells us that the Sacred Scroll holds a secret of eternal value and a key to peace."

Troy pointed at the Hebrew words on the bottom corner of the map. "So what do these strange words say, Grandpapa? Do they tell us the way to the treasure?"

"I'll tell you in just a moment, little buck." Methuselah was silent for a while as he tried to interpret the strange words:

ולשכיי מההמ רתויו וסני םיבר

םירבוג םיקידצה רצואה תא אוצמל

"I think the first line says, 'Many ... will try and... more will fail...' And the second line, 'To find... the treasure... the righteous... prevail.' Troy, so far I believe the riddle is revealing that only someone who is the chosen one will be able to discover the treasure. I was there when Socrates prophesied that you are the righteous branch, Troy. There is no doubt that your next mission is to find the Sacred Scroll, which will hold the key to peace between all the creatures in the orange elevator."

"Why would the One who made all things choose me for this new mission, Grandpapa?" Troy's voice was shaky. "I have so many disabilities. There are so many others who would be better qualified than me, don't you think?"

Methuselah looked into his little grandson's eye. "My dear, sweet Troy"—he placed his paw on Troy's head—"the Creator doesn't look at His creatures as the world does. He looks at what they can do through Him, not at what they cannot do. The Book of Truth tells us through Him all things are possible. Mighty Troy, this is your destiny, all you have to do is follow Him and He will guide your way and light your path."

Troy was wild with excitement at the thought of a new adventure. "Tell me the rest of the riddle, Grandpapa. This discovery is so exciting, don't you think?"

Methuselah smiled and looked back at the parchment. "Okay, okay, my eager one. Let me see what it says." The old man squinted his eyes to decipher the final Hebrew words:

תיחצנ הבהל קילדי חתפמה יכ
.הנעטה םע דדומתי בלה רוהטו
.ויהי הרשע דוע ,םיזמרה תא ארק
.ץעל תחתמ ואצמת הנושארה

For the key shall light an eternal flame and the pure of heart will stake the claim. Read the clues, ten more will be. The first ye shall find beneath the tree.

"That is so cool! What does it mean, Grandpapa?" Troy was trying his best to listen to the old buck but a pesky little fly kept buzzing around his ear and so he tried to flick it away. "Are there 10 riddles before we find the treasure? I have so many questions."

Selah placed his paw on his head and began to think.

"Yes, Troy, I believe this parchment is not the Sacred Scroll but only one of 10 riddles pointing to it. I believe the Sacred Scroll itself will hold the key to peace in the elevator and throughout all of Salem."

Buzz kept yelling over and over in Troy's ear. "Danger, danger."

The old buck was closely examining the Hebrew script written on the parchment and was very interested in the reference to the black tree. He knew something about it looked familiar but he just couldn't put his finger on it.

Finally, Troy heard a distant voice in his head, "Danger, Troy! There is danger on the rafters!"

He swiftly pulled the gold sword from behind his back and placed the Levi shield in front of him in a battle stance. He glanced up into the rafters, but he was too late.

Methuselah rose from the floor to share the secret of the Black Tree, but was interrupted by a loud booming voice high in the rafters. He turned to warn Troy but he was already in a battle stance. He quickly rolled up the precious parchment and threw it to Troy who immediately tucked it into the back of his shield.

Methuselah drew a staff from his back and stood beside his grandson. It would soon be time to fight evil and the old buck was ready. He was always ready.

Troy slowly got up, held on to the chains and quietly followed after his captor.

CHAPTER 29

CAPTURE OF TROY

POWER AND CONTROL BREEDS ONLY

FEARFUL FOLLOWERS OF HATE. JUSTICE

AND FREEDOM BREEDS RIGHTEOUS

FOLLOWERS OF LOVE AND BREAKS THE

CHAIN OF SIN.

THE RAFTER RATS ATTACK

"**T**ROY OF SALEM!" ROARED PRINCE SAPH AS HE stood on top of the rafter, pointing his bony finger at the little cheese lover. "King Goar has sent us for you and your prized oats! The time has come to pay for what you have done to the family of Goar. We are here to take the oats you stole from the giant's cupboard, they belong to us."

Troy turned to his Grandpapa Methuselah who was in battle mode next to him. "Run, Grandpapa. Quick, hide yourself in the storage bin."

"No, Troy, I'm not leaving you. Durum's never run from a good fight." Methuselah stood firm, swinging his staff back and forth in a secret pattern of the Watchers. He smiled at Troy. "I may be old, but I can still hold my own in a battle with the Rats of Goar."

"You are surrounded," Prince Saph ranted. "There is no escape and you are no match for Goar's mightiest warriors."

Troy moved to the centre of the room, holding tightly to his Levi shield. His gold sword hummed and glowed as though eager for the fight.

The clans ran frantically in every direction trying to hide. Pups were searching for their parents, the clan guards and soldiers were searching for the weapons they had put aside during the dance.

Rafter Rats were quickly scaling down the ropes from every corner and had begun to herd the terrified cheese lovers into the centre of the room where Troy was now standing.

Lami and Saph towered over Troy with an evil grin and

stared at the mouse clans.

"Give us the oats," Prince Lami growled, "and Lord Dreck will have mercy on your souls. Sacrifice Troy and the Rats of Goar will leave you in peace."

Prince Saph moved forward and slammed his face into Troy's forehead. He stared into the cheese lover's eye, which was wide with righteous anger.

"Remember me, you pathetic excuse of a mouse?" Saph's tongue flapped back and forth as he reached for his tail and pointed to a deep wound that was still bleeding. "You'll pay for this, freak. You and your useless little god will not be able to stop us now."

Lami nodded. "You and your sisters will now atone for humiliating and assaulting my sons Rodney and Chuba. For these crimes you shall be sentenced to the cages of Goar and serve our king and our god the rest of your miserable days."

Methuselah came out of the dark, went to the center of the room and stepped in front of Troy. "Never, you pagan idol worshipping rats!" He swung his staff with lightning speed, striking Lami's leg sending him crumpling to the floor in pain.

Saph countered with a swing of his mace at Methuselah. Selah quickly ducked and jumped, easily avoiding Saph's every chop and thrust.

Jesse joined in the fight standing beside his newly found papa.

"Need some help, Old Buck?" He dodged to one side avoiding a jab from Saph's medieval club. "It's about time you showed up. We thought you were dead."

"You know I couldn't see you, son, the clans banished me from any contact with my family." The old buck flipped in the air and struck Saph's nose. "As it was, I had to watch you from a distance but I've always loved you, my precious buck."

Prince Lami had had enough and roared out orders to the rest of the warriors. "Attack, Rats of Goar! No mercy!"

Troy began to swing his golden sword with ease. It seemed to have a power of its own and hummed with anticipation. In two seconds he had taken out five rat warriors and was now fighting Lami.

Meanwhile, Elijah the Risk Taker held onto one of the ropes and swung in a circle, knocking down five rats as if they were bowling pins.

Joseph the Strong One had a Rafter Rat under each arm. "Do you give up, you dirty rats?" He said while squeezing them as hard as he could.

Samuel the Sneak crept up behind one of the warriors who had grabbed a young pup and tapped him on the shoulder.

"Hey you, pick on someone your own size." When the

surprised rat turned around Samuel knocked him down with his staff and took the pup back to his mama.

James the Wise One swiftly led Mama Evette into a storage bin where many families had already hid.

Joab the Fighter had one staff in each hand and was striking down rat after rat with surgical precision. As they saw him approaching they ran in fear.

"Where are you going so fast?" Joab shouted after them. "Are you shy? I just want to get to know you better."

Judah the Builder dove under one of the tables he had built, and pulled off one of the legs. He used it to strike down as many rats as he could, all the while singing songs he had written.

Jesse had left Saph and was now battling one of the rat commanders.

Evette watched her buck from the safety of the steel storage bins. "Don't you die on me, Jesse Durum."

Saph attacked Troy from behind and was soon joined by his brother Lami. "You need to give up now, while you have the chance, you one-eyed freak." Saph struck the side of Troy's Levi shield with his large mace.

"So where is your silent god now, Troy?" Lami taunted. "Is He sleeping? Has He forgotten you?"

Troy swung his golden sword with lightning speed hitting the side of Lami's armour and pushing him back. Saph responded by whipping his weapon around trying to catch Troy off guard.

Methuselah saw Troy was in danger and swung his staff around to easily deflect the mace to one side.

"Thanks, Grandpapa, I didn't see that one coming."

"My pleasure, young buck. It sure is good to fight a righteous battle alongside my family." He dodged another swipe from Lami's sword.

Meanwhile, Shaun the Gentle Giant was grabbing the tails of as many rats as he could.

"Come here, you little vermin!" he yelled, tossing them into the walls, head first.

DURUM GIRLS FIGHT BACK

AS SOON AS THE FIGHTING BEGAN, THE DURUM GIRLS set a number of battle plans they learned at RAMS into motion.

Ava quickly moved toward the steel bins, climbed to the top of the platform and readied her bow for action. She knelt on one knee, strapped on her quiver and began to fire one arrow after another, easily hitting ten rat warriors as they climbed down the ropes.

Meanwhile, as Frey stood on one of the tables she noticed a large rat grab Olivia who had just finished discussing battle strategies with Tammy.

"Don't you touch my sister," challenged Frey as she flew across the long row of tables, landing multiple handsprings and slamming into the surprised rat. He promptly let Olivia go and fell to the floor unconscious.

Olivia high-fived Frey. "Thanks, sis, you saved my life."

Frey helped Olivia up who immediately engaged with multiple rat warriors. Olivia's staff was a blur as it connected with one rat after another.

Frey used her martial arts skills to throw a couple of rats on the floor without breaking a sweat.

Tammy had the best superpower of all when it came to surprising the enemy, especially the Rafter Rats, because they were very curious creatures. She would become invisible, walk up to a rat warrior and steal the sword right out of his hands. The rat's eyes grew big when he saw his sword moving in mid-air and then fly straight towards him swinging and slashing. They would turn around in fear and run for the door bumping into others along the way. "It's a ghost! It's a ghost! This place is haunted!"

Troy and Methuselah were still fending off the two sons of Goar. They were exhausted except for Troy who seemed to gain strength with every swing of his golden sword.

Saph could barely hold on to his large mace and his armour was feeling heavier and heavier. He knew he couldn't carry on much longer.

"Lami, you've got to do something," Saph panted.

Prince Lami was also having trouble with the old buck and couldn't seem to get the upper hand but he had an idea.

"Okay, Saph, follow my lead. " He used all his remaining energy to slash his way towards Methuselah. He reached forward, grabbed Methuselah's arm and twisted it behind his back. "On your knees, ancient one." Lami forced him down to his knees. The Prince held his sword under Methuselah's neck, looked over at Troy. "Put down your sword, you one-eyed cheese lover, or I will put an end to the oldest member of your family tree."

Troy turned around and noticed Grandpapa on his knees, his head hung low in defeat. There was fear in his eyes and yet he shook his head.

"Don't do it, my son. Just keep fighting, don't worry about me," he pleaded.

But Troy looked into Lami's cold eyes and knew he meant business.

"Okay, okay!" he surrendered. "I'll put down the sword, just don't hurt my grandpapa." He dropped his Levi shield and slowly put down the golden sword. As soon as the powerful weapon left Troy's hands it stopped glowing.

Saph bent down and tried to pick it up. "It's stuck to the floor, Lami. I can't lift it." He said with surprise.

Lami pushed his brother to the side. "Then you watch them while I give it a try, you weakling." The prince smiled as he reached down expecting to easily raise it off the floor, but it wouldn't budge. "What's wrong with this stupid thing?" He glanced over at Troy, "Hey, did you jinx this sword?"

Troy stared at Lami in silence.

"Just leave it, Lami," Saph said. "It's no good to them now anyway, besides we have his precious grandpapa."

Prince Lami frowned at Troy and then laughed. "Who's going to save you now, cheese lover? Why has your power suddenly vanished? Why don't you beg your pathetic, invisible god to save you?"

Troy said a quick prayer to His Creator. He opened his eye and stared at Lami for a moment before lunging towards his throat. Lami ducked to one side and grabbed Troy's scarf.

"Where do you think you're going, you little cheese puff." He wrapped his arms tightly around the helpless mouse.

Lami's eyes looked dead as he pointed his sword at Troy and shook with anger. "Tell your warriors to stop fighting now and tell them to step away from the oats. The food belongs to the Rafter Rats of Goar. If you refuse to give them up, I have orders to take all of you into captivity."

Troy gazed around the room at his brave young warriors, both bucks and does still fighting gallantly without reservation. He knew it was over.

"Mouse clans of Salem" — Troy's voice shook — "You must stop fighting! Step aside from the oats and give them what they want. The Creator will find another way to feed us. He will not leave nor forsake us. We are not alone."

Bit by bit, they all stopped fighting, mouse weapons clattered to the floor and the room fell silent. Saph and Lami lifted their heads in victory. Saph had a crooked grin on his face and his tongue hung lower than usual, drool dripping on the floor.

There was a moment of complete silence before the door flung open and King Goar and King Og marched in each holding a piece of chicken in one hand and a glass of wine in the other. As many kings do, they had watched the battle from the upper rafters. Waddling over to a table, they placed their food and drinks down.

Goar bowed deeply and slowly clapped his hands together.

"Well done, well done, sons of Goar! See what we can actually do together when we put our minds to it. That wasn't so hard now, was it?"

King Og raised his glass in the air as if giving a toast. "I must admit, Goar, this has been very entertaining? I honestly didn't think I would enjoy coming to this wedding party of yours. I guess there's hope for you yet, my friend. Lord Dreck will be very proud of you. As Grand Wizard,

I will put a good word in to the council for your promotion as Priest of the Orange Elevator."

Goar stood proud as a peacock. "Why thank you, good sir, I would be honoured to let my name stand. Now, what do you say we bring those oats to where they belong—to the Rat's Kingdom on level five and to the Kingdom of Og in Potters barn!"

KAPPA MAKES HIS MOVE

KING KAPPA AND ZETA WERE STILL PERCHED UP ON rafter six; their eyes open wide with excitement at what was unfolding before them. He could see no one could pick up the sword, but he thought they were just too weak.

"Now is my chance to possess the golden sword," exclaimed King Kappa. "I will use the distraction of the Rat Kings to my advantage. The power of Troy will be mine and I will rule the Orange Elevator and all of Salem." He smiled at Zeta then spread his wings, readied his talons, and swooped down towards the sword, which was lying on the floor.

He dived in fast dodging the mice and rat warriors in his path and landed with precision on the sword. He tried to lift it but it wouldn't budge. It seemed to be glued to the floor. Kappa tried again, and again but it still wouldn't move. Suddenly, he felt something hit him hard on the head.

Tammy had seen the large bat grab for Troy's sword. She jumped in the air as high as she could and pounced on top of King Kappa.

"That sword does not belong to you, Mr. Bat," she scolded as she stomped down on his head one more time.

Kappa shook Tammy off and gave her an evil scowl. "I will not forget you, little doe. You will be my very next target." He left the sword on the floor and fled for the safety of the rafters high on level seven. Kappa went home dejected that he couldn't have the sword and embarrassed by his humiliating encounter with a little mouse once again.

Zeta steadied himself on the rafter and watched as the king failed to seize Troy's Golden Sword. He felt bad for Kappa and wished he could have helped him but he had his own score to settle.

I must have a good plan, Zeta thought. I will bide my time and wait until Olivia and Frey are alone, and then I will have my revenge.

ABDUCTING TROY

THE RAT KINGS GOAR AND OG MADE THEIR WAY towards Troy who was being held tightly by Saph. Methuselah was struggling to get free but the more he moved the harder Lami pressed the sword to his neck.

"Well, well, well, what do we have here?" Goar eyed Troy and then turned to look at King Og. They laughed hysterically and tapped their glasses of wine together.

"So, this is who they are calling, 'Mighty Troy of Salem,'" stated Og, as he pointed the chicken bone in his hand at little Troy. "You are much smaller than I expected and actually quite pathetic looking, even for a cheese lover."

Troy held his head high and stared at King Goar. "I pray that my Creator will forgive you for what you are about to do. If you continue with your plan to steal our oats, you will surely suffer His wrath. The Book of Truth says, 'Deceit is in the hearts of those who devise evil, but the counsellors of peace have joy. No harm befalls the righteous, but the wicked are filled with trouble.'"

"Ha, ha, you pray for me?" Goar's red eyes glowed with anger. "I will suffer His wrath? Have you looked around you, Troy? Do you see who has the sword at the throat of your people? Where is your weak god now? If He is real, why doesn't He strike me down where I stand?"

Methuselah interrupted. "The Creator gives all His creatures opportunity to change their ways, Goar. There is forgiveness and redemption even for you if you are willing to humble yourself."

Og turned to Goar. "I know this old buck." He looked at Methuselah and smiled as he recalled where they had met before. "So we meet again, Selah. I heard you were eaten by a cat, but it seems you have as many lives as they do. And I see you are still trying to convert the rats of Salem to worship your weak invisible god."

Goar looked puzzled. "I thought you told me you threw this troublemaker in prison for preaching to your subjects, Og? What happened?"

"I placed him in the deepest, darkest hole I could find under the barn," Og exclaimed in a cold voice. "I even chained Him up. Yet, two days later the guards told me the door suddenly flew open and the chains of the prisoner dropped to the ground. They said it was a miracle. I think his buddies helped him escape somehow."

Goar stood beside his enemy. "Well, Methuselah's god will not be able to help his grandson today." He grabbed Troy's arm and placed a chain around his neck and arms. He gave the chain a yank and Troy fell down. "I can assure you, Troy, these chains will not miraculously fall off while I'm in charge." As though on cue, all the Rafter Rats roared with laughter.

Troy slowly got up, held on to the chains and quietly followed after his captor. He gazed over his shoulder and took one more look at his Papa Jesse who was being detained by two guards.

Jesse winked at his precious pup and gave him a wide grin. "Be strong and courageous, Mighty Troy! Remember you were anointed by Socrates and the Great Creator to lead the Clans." Then he turned to Goar who was now walking towards the litter. "Goar, you hurt my little buck and I will hunt you down if it's the last thing I do! He is only a small mouse that was trying to find enough food for the remainder of the winter. Righteousness will prevail."

"He is not righteous! He stole the oats from the giant's cupboard and then stole them from me!" countered Goar looking back at Troy's Papa with disgust. "Everyone knows that I own everything in the Orange Elevator. It all belongs to me! And don't you forget it, son of Selah." He turned away and gave Troy an extra tug on the chain. "Therefore, I declare 'Mighty Troy' is now my property because of your sin of unbelief in the great Lord Dreck. For this insolence, He will languish in the cages of Goar and serve me and our true god until the end of his days."

Og followed Goar to the litter as the Rafter King gave instructions to one of his sons. "Lami," Goar instructed as he followed Og to the litter. "I want you to stay behind and make sure you take all the oats from the cheese lovers. Have the warriors empty every jar and every knapsack, don't leave behind a single kernel of those precious oats."

Goar opened one of the bags, placed his paw inside and grabbed a bunch of golden oats to share with Og. He went over to his friend and dropped some kernels into his paw. They both began to stuff their faces as soon as they were settled in their cushioned seats. Then, with his mouth still filled with food, Goar pointed forward and ordered the mouse slaves to take them to the rafters on level five. Little Troy was chained to the back of the gold litter and stumbled along as the slaves moved forward. Saph followed behind Troy, pushing him to go faster.

"Move it along, mini-mouse, you belong to the family of Goar now!"

Troy glanced over his shoulder at his family and friends and encouraged them.

"Be strong in the Lord and in His mighty power. Put on the full armor of the Great Creator, so that you can make your stand against the devil's schemes."

As he disappeared from sight the clans heard Saph and the Kings roar with laughter.

Troy's sisters began to cry and his brothers struggled to get loose from their captors to no avail.

"Do not lose hope in the Logos my little buck," Mama cried out. "He goes before you as your protector, Troy! He has promised to set the righteous captives free. He has a plan and will rescue you at the appointed time. And always remember we love you, Mighty Troy of Salem."

THE END

THE STORY CONTINUES

THANK YOU FOR READING "MIGHTY TROY OF SALEM: The Oats Mission". It is difficult to believe how a dream about a small mouse with disabilities could become a full novel. So, now my grandkids have demanded the story continues.

You will not want to miss book two, "Mighty Troy of Salem: The Sacred Scroll" coming soon. Find out what happens to Troy in the cages of Goar and search for ten clues to find the treasure. All your favorite "cheese loving" characters will be back along with new friends and foes. If you would like Troy to send you a free copy of Chapter 1, Book Two, you can email him at mighty-troy22@gmail.com.

Conrad L. Neudorf, Author

Made in the USA
Las Vegas, NV
29 January 2023

66441004R00203